SERIOUS LIVING

Also by Tom Lorenz

Guys Like Us

Tom Lorenz

SERIOUS LIVING

VIKING

VIKING
Published by the Penguin Group
Viking Penguin Inc., 40 West 23rd Street,
New York, New York 10010, U.S.A.
Penguin Books Ltd, 27 Wrights Lane,
London W8 5TZ, England
Penguin Books Australia Ltd, Ringwood,
Victoria, Australia
Penguin Books Canada Ltd, 2801 John Street,
Markham, Ontario, Canada L3R 1B4
Penguin Books (N.Z.) Ltd, 182–190 Wairau Road,
Auckland 10, New Zealand

Penguin Books Ltd, Registered Offices:
Harmondsworth, Middlesex, England

First published in 1988 by Viking Penguin Inc.
Published simultaneously in Canada

Library of Congress Cataloging in Publication Data
Lorenz, Tom.
  Serious living.
  I. Title.
PS3562.0753S46   1988   813'.54   87-40319
ISBN 0-670-81060-6

Printed in the United States of America by
Arcata Graphics, Fairfield, Pennsylvania
Set in the United States of America by
NK Graphics, Keene, N.H.
Designed by Quinten Welch

For Sue, Katie, and Gina

SERIOUS
LIVING

1

On his way to the VFW lodge, where he went every Thursday night to drink and play cards and discuss the sorry state of civilization with other old soldiers, Big Joe Kohler stopped by his grocery store to pick up a roll of antacid tablets and discovered he was being robbed. Big Joe spotted the stranger as soon as he rounded the corner, his heavy galoshes squeaking on the cold, ice-slick walk, and he immediately ducked out of view, taking cover in front of the big Coca-Cola sign in the window.

The guy was standing behind the open register, no doubt having rifled it, beating on it with the palms of his hands. He was short and slightly built, with a pair of sleek dark glasses wrapped around his skull and curly black hair. Abominable music was blaring from the portable transistor radio Big Joe kept on a shelf behind the counter; he could hear it from where he crouched. That was a new one on him; Big Joe had dealt with thieves before, but never one who'd provided a soundtrack.

Suddenly the thief did something so astonishing that Big Joe almost smacked his head against the thick plate-glass window in surprise: he put one hand on the counter and vaulted over onto the other side and began dancing through the otherwise deserted store. That's when Big Joe realized he was dealing with a madman. He watched as the mop-headed thug huckle-bucked up and down the aisles of dusty canned goods—Big Joe's aisles, and the aisles that had belonged to his father, Big Hans, before him—jerking his head and moving his arms and legs like a chicken, now profaning the refrigerated cabinet that housed Big Joe's cheeses and sandwich meats, now moving on to the bins of vegetables and whirling around to mock him with a zucchini in his hand.

Where the hell was Ritchie?—that's what Big Joe wanted to know. His son was supposed to be in charge, guarding the register and watching over things, but there was no sign of the little idiot. Big Joe clenched his teeth. The kid had probably sneaked away with Margie Glotz again, or maybe he was out back, by the dumpster, feeding New York strips to that stinking pack of strays he'd befriended, leaving his post so that anyone and his brother could waltz in and rob the place blind.

Then, abruptly, Big Joe had another thought: What if this deranged hoodlum had done something to his boy? What if, even as Big Joe crouched there on the frozen pavement and the madman danced up and down the aisles, his boy lay bleeding on the floor behind the register or was stuffed, bound and gagged, in a corner of the freezer, wedged in between the Popsicles and the ranks of Swanson heat-and-serve TV meals?

There was one thing Big Joe did know for certain—he wasn't about to wait around to find out. He crouched down a little lower and hulked closer to the door; then, when the thief turned his back to boogie toward the cookie rack, Big Joe sprang up out of a three-point stance and burst into the store. He charged past the Manhandler soups and pear halves in heavy syrup, maintaining that same low center of gravity he'd employed to pulverize enemy linebackers in his glory days, and nailed the punk with a picture-perfect cross-body block, sending him sprawling head first into the Little Debbies.

Big Joe wasn't sure what happened next. All he remembered was sitting on the wise guy, both hands wrapped around his throat, when suddenly he heard a familiar voice bleating in his ears.

"What are you, fucking crazy?"

As soon as he heard this, Big Joe relaxed his hands and blinked his eyes back into focus. In the struggle, the madman's dark glasses had flown off his head. The curly black mass of a wig lay on the floor beside them. It took Big Joe another few seconds to realize what it was, exactly, that was happening here. This was not the throat of some half-deranged drug addict he had his hands wrapped around—far the hell from it: he was choking his own son.

A little while later, Big Joe found himself sitting alone at a table in the corner of the lodge, squeezed in between a rolled-up American flag on a pole and a big picture of the President. In the middle of the hall, at one of the large banquet tables, Louie the mailman and Frankie the cop and some of the other vets were playing gin rummy and periodically monitoring the basketball game on the color TV mounted on a stand high up on the wall. Ordinarily, Big Joe would've joined them over there and taken a couple of bucks off Louie—who couldn't play gin rummy for shit—but he didn't feel like playing gin rummy just then. He was too depressed to play gin rummy. On the table, right under his nose, lay his pack of Chesterfield kings, two small glasses, a pitcher of ice water, and a bottle of Early Times he'd gone behind the bar and helped himself to the minute he'd walked through the door.

He didn't feel like talking either. As soon as he lumbered in, still flushed and obviously upset and heading straight for the whiskey, Louie the mailman had come up and asked what was eating him and Big Joe had just waved him away. How could he talk about something like this? How could he explain that, moments before, with his bare hands, he had nearly strangled his own son? How could he explain the wig and the dark glasses and the crazy dancing when the little idiot couldn't even explain it himself?

"Why?"—that's all Big Joe had wanted to know after they had both calmed down and stopped shouting at each other. Ritchie was bent over behind the counter rubbing his throat, while Big Joe stood on the other side of the counter staring at the wig. He bent down and picked it up and held it close to his face; it looked like something a voodoo man might wear to put a hex on his enemy. "Why would you wear a thing like this?"

His son took a big gulp of soda and shrugged and said it was just something to do. That was it. No remorse, no apology, not even an attempt to explain what had possessed him to wear false hair during business hours and dance like a witch doctor through the store. *Just something to do.* After one quick glance Big Joe could've easily indicated any number of things there were to do—the store was a mess—but he decided not to bother. What was the point?

Big Joe was on his third or fourth whiskey now—he'd lost track—

and the hooch was fueling the fire in his ventricles with every gulp
he took. Additionally, he was well into his second pack of Chesters
and could feel it in his lungs. At his last checkup the doctor had
said he was in pretty good health for a man his age, but Big Joe
didn't believe this for a minute. He had aches, pains. His back was
frozen stiff each morning, his belly burned at night, and every time
the weather changed he could feel the fronts collide inside his
swollen football joints.

Lately he'd developed this interest in the obituaries; he liked to
read them on the john each afternoon to see if anybody he knew
had dropped dead the previous day. It seemed that, lately, people
his age were dropping like flies. The water, industrial pollutants,
the pressures of everyday life—Big Joe wasn't sure what it was, but
it was clear to him that more and more people of his generation
were dropping over. He kept warning Ritchie that he better be ready
to take command—he himself could go any day now. He had a
steady throbbing pressure in his temples, as well as too much Polish
ham built up around his heart.

Laughter suddenly erupted at the banquet table. Big Joe recognized Frankie's mulelike bray. Glancing over, he saw Louie the
mailman smack his palm on the table and hurl down a fistful
of ragtag cards. Big Joe poured himself another whiskey and began thinking about his own bonehead plays. Sure, he'd made his
share of them. After all, Milly had died when Ritchie was just
a baby, and, although Hilda had been a big help, Big Joe was
the dad in the picture—essentially he'd had to raise his boys alone.

He supposed he'd made a mistake pushing Joe Junior so hard in
sports like he had. Still, it was a natural temptation given that Big
Joe himself had been a gridiron star, a one-man gang in high school.
He might even have become a Bear. It was true, goddamnit. He
had the clippings to prove it. They were tucked away in an old
scrapbook he kept up in the attic, along with his letter sweater and
his trophies and that moldy bladder ball from the city championship
game. The thing about the scrapbook was, it was only half full;
there was plenty of space for great stuff to come later, only whatever
was supposed to happen never did. Korea broke out and he went
into the service and that was the end of his pigskin days. When he
finally came home, his legs were gone. Asian detail had ruined his

wheels. He had to forget all about being a Monster of the Midway and go to work with Big Hans in the store.

The truth was, he had always hoped Joey would fill that scrapbook. He'd looked at Junior and seen another ball-carrier, a Kohler who would lug the mail all the way to the NFL. Big Joe had sent him to Holy Redeemer, a big Catholic boys' school that was famous for its sports teams. The Fighting Saints were the scourge of Chicago. The football team was composed of tough North Side Slavs and Polacks who kicked the hell out of everybody, especially their own subs. Every day, Joey used to crawl home from practice with a bloody nose and cleat marks all over his body; they looked like measles, or a new type of plague.

"I can't do it anymore," he'd whine.

"Quit talking like that," Big Joe would warn him. "Suck it up. Hang tough. A Kohler never quits."

Big Joe had to give Joe Junior credit: he hadn't quit. He'd hung in there and toughed it out, winning his letters and getting good grades. He wasn't a football player, he was a scholar. Eventually he earned a sheepskin from Notre Dame. Big Joe had had to go into hock up to his eyeballs to finance the deal, but it had been well worth it: now Junior had a good job in the loan department of one of Chicago's larger financial institutions, a nice wife, a split-level home in the suburbs. He was thinking of going to law school at night. He was moving up in the world and Big Joe was bragging him all over the neighborhood. It was as though Junior had finally hit the game-winning homer, or stopped the end sweep at the goal line. He'd made first string. Who knew?—he might fill that scrapbook yet.

With Ritchie, it was a different story entirely. Right from the start Big Joe could see that the kid wasn't going to be a scholar *or* an athlete, and so instead Big Joe tried to instill in him the value of a hard-earned dollar and an honest day's work: when Ritchie was about fourteen Big Joe bought him a sturdy new bike with a wire basket mounted on the handlebars, and put him to work in the store, delivering groceries.

"Just a second," Ritchie had shot back. "This is America. I'm still a child. You can't force a child to work in this country—there's statutes that prohibit stuff like that."

Big Joe gnashed his jaws. He never liked it when the kid used the Bill of Rights against him; it was like getting slapped in the face with the Flag.

"Go ahead and exploit me if you want to," Ritchie had continued, "but you'll be in utter disregard of the law."

"What the hell are you talking about?" Big Joe said. He went on to explain that he had a very good reason for wanting Ritchie to work in the store: he wanted him to familiarize himself with all aspects of the grocery business because one day the store would be his. The way Big Joe saw it, he would pass the store down to Ritchie just as his own father, Big Hans, had passed it down to him.

"Why me?" Ritchie had said. "I don't want it."

It was only logical, Big Joe reasoned. Joe Junior had the brains and would one day make something of himself. He would become a lawyer or a politician, maybe President. He wouldn't need a grocery store. That left Ritchie.

"You're my legacy," Big Joe had added, hoping his son would be suitably impressed by the lofty sound of that word.

Instead, Ritchie had squinched up his face, as though Big Joe were passing down some hereditary defect, or a communicable disease. "I still don't want it. Why would I want to get stuck with some dinky little grocery store? I plan to travel—and live by my wits."

"What wits?"

"Okay," Ritchie had said. "Go ahead and leave me the store, but you'll be sorry. I'll make some changes."

"What kind of changes?"

"Something modern. Fried chicken, maybe. A car wash. A taco stand. Maybe a car wash *and* a taco stand."

Big Joe lifted his eyebrows at that. "If you do, you'll be the sorry one. I'll come back and haunt you. I'll get you from the grave."

"Hah," Ritchie had said. "Fat chance."

Big Joe went ahead with the idea anyway and put Ritchie to work in the store, but he immediately regretted it. Within days, his son had easily established himself as the worst, least dependable delivery boy Big Joe had ever had. Not only was he rude to Big Joe's regular customers, most of whom were elderly and looked forward to chatting awhile with a courteous young man who would spend a few moments with them and listen to their stories over a glass of lemonade, but he spent half his time hanging around the park with his good-for-nothing friends, smoking cigarettes and gambling with Big Joe's money. Big Joe wasn't stupid. The park was right across the street from the store and he could see the kid through his window, standing in a line with a bunch of other hammerheads and pitching pennies at cracks in the cement.

"What's the matter with you?" Big Joe would lecture when the kid sneaked in through the back door. "You can't get something for nothing—any idiot knows that."

"Yeah? What about your gin rummy games at the lodge?"

"That's different." Big Joe wasn't sure why it was different, he just knew that it was.

Ritchie would shoot him a smug look and drop the bag containing Big Joe's money onto the counter; then he'd reach down and slap his pockets, which were stuffed with illicitly gained street scratch. "Listen, Dad, don't knock it—it's all in the touch."

Sometimes Big Joe had to wonder which would be worse: if the kid turned his back on him and rejected the store—the only thing of value he had to give him—or if he kept it. He could see bad news developing either way. Occasionally he took comfort in the fact that his younger son, now twenty-one (Big Joe could hardly believe *that*), had not yet walked out on him, like he was always threatening to, but on the other hand everything Big Joe had tried to teach him seemed to pass right through his brain like it was a piece of big-eye Swiss. He still, even to this day, did not know how to properly operate Big Joe's pride and joy, the meat slicer—a powerful and unwieldy apparatus with old-fashioned scales balanced on top, like the Scales of Justice, and a well-oiled blade that whistled like a guillotine—and he still wandered away from the register when there were customers in the store.

One afternoon, about a month ago, while grinding up wieners with a Chesterfield in his mouth, Big Joe had realized that maybe what they had going here was what the headshrinkers would call a "personality conflict." More out of desperation than anything else, he found himself giving the idea some serious thought. Maybe all he had to do was put Ritchie in charge during certain hours—the evening shift, for instance, when business tended to be a little slow—and then clear out and leave him the hell alone and he would straighten up in no time. History was full of success stories like this, of young malcontents with one foot in the slammer who, upon being delegated certain responsibilities—tail gunner on an army chopper, for example—suddenly developed into outstanding young men. The plan had the additional advantage of giving Big Joe some time off to relax; he was tired of putting in all those fourteen-hour days.

So he did it. He put the kid totally in charge at night and left him alone. He left him alone for about a week and then, one night, he couldn't resist stopping by the store to see how the lad was doing. In his mind he had concocted a wonderful fantasy: Ritchie standing behind the counter in a clean white apron, courteously waiting on customers while the store gleamed from floor to ceiling like a well-kept ship.

Instead, when he came around the corner and burst through the door, he saw not only that Ritchie had abdicated his position—the counter was completely vacant except for a stained rag dangling halfway to the floor—but that the register drawer was wide open, an irresistible target for anyone who happened to come in. When he saw that, Big Joe had nearly had the big one right there. He rushed over to the register, smacked the drawer shut with the palm of his hand, and looked around. Suddenly he became aware of low, suspicious-sounding voices issuing from the storage room, the doorway of which was clouded by so much smoke that Big Joe feared someone was setting the place on fire.

He picked up a roll of salami and made his way along the counter toward that small cluttered room. As he approached, a strange chant floated out at him through the haze: "One-eyed jacks, the man with the ax, trips or better to win." The phrase worked on Big Joe's brain like a whammy. Pausing a moment in the doorway, the salami clutched tightly in his fist, he whirled in and discovered Ritchie and five or six of his friends huddled around a large wooden crate, playing cards and puffing away on Big Joe's choicest panatelas, which Ritchie had no doubt passed around at some point during the game and which were now imparting to the nearby stacks of fruits and vegetables a powerful and ineradicable reek.

A guy with a splotchy red birthmark on one side of his face was snapping the cards and reminding everyone to fork up with the ante. When he saw Big Joe suddenly standing in the doorway, his whole face went red and he froze in midshuffle. The others glanced up quickly too and then, just as quickly, averted their eyes. Someone picked up a bottle of Jim Beam and hid it behind his back. Starting with the dealer, Big Joe went right around the crate, freezing everyone with an icy glare, before his eyes finally settled on his son, who was sitting directly in front of him with his back turned. He was wearing a green eyeshade and had his sleeves rolled up.

"C'mon, Stain. Deal the fucking cards." Ritchie flapped the panatela in irritation. Big Joe reached down and took it from his hand. Though not by nature a religious person, for some reason he thought of Jesus raising hell inside the Temple, and he lifted up his salami and spat a single word: "Out."

It took about ten seconds for everyone to clear the premises. A couple of Ritchie's friends slinked away with their coats pulled up over their faces, like gangsters on the six-o'clock news. Ritchie, meanwhile, just sat there, his shoulders slumped and his back still turned, foolishly twirling the visor on the tip of his finger while Big Joe went over and hurled the still smoldering stogie out the door.

When he turned around he saw that Ritchie had eased the eyeshade back onto his head. "Okay. You're right. I screwed up. So what are you gonna do about it—fire me?"

"I can't," Big Joe hoarsely replied. "You're my son."

He went away, shaking his head. He tried his best to overlook the incident, telling himself that everyone was entitled to one mistake. But there was no excusing that next time, when he found the kid sound asleep in there (he'd had to ding the shit out of the little service bell to wake him), or the night he caught him lying down in the snack-cake aisle trying to seduce his neighbor's daughter, Margie Glotz. He'd been on his way to the lodge that night when, walking past the store, he'd noticed all the lights were out. Doubling back and peering in above the Coca-Cola sign in the window, he detected what appeared to be two pairs of legs—one bare and decidedly female, the other encased in grease-stained jeans—sticking out past the rack of Hostess Snowballs, illuminated only by light the color of two-percent milk filtering in from a streetlamp right outside the door.

He barged in, setting off a noisy jangle of bells, and immediately hit the switch. The lights came on. The legs disappeared. In a moment Ritchie emerged, followed seconds later by an embarrassed Margie, still frantically reassembling her clothes.

"What's going on?" Big Joe demanded. "How come the lights were out?"

"Slow tonight," Ritchie explained piously. "Just cutting back on those energy bills."

Big Joe wiped his face with a handkerchief. He seemed to remember that profuse sweating was one of the warning signs of death. Having learned not to expect anything better from Ritchie, he went swiftly past his son and fixed his massive brows on Margie Glotz, who lived directly behind them in the house across the alley and whose father ran a hardware store a couple of blocks down the road. Big Joe knew Henry Glotz to have a perpetual chip on his shoulder. Awhile back they'd had an argument about the constant yapping of Cha Cha, a French poodle who belonged to Big Joe's mother and who had recently taken custody of Big Joe's yard, planting himself at the gate all day and barking viciously at anyone who came by in either direction.

Big Joe mopped his face again; all he needed was Henry Glotz coming after him for harboring a sex fiend. To Ritchie he said, "I'll deal with you later." To Margie Glotz he said, "I'm surprised at you." He'd never thought of her as one of those girls.

"Don't worry, Mr. Kohler," Margie said. "We weren't doing anything." She flashed her freckles at Ritchie and nudged him with her hip. "Anyway, we're practically engaged."

Big Joe said, "Not in here."

It was around that time that Big Joe started drinking a lot more than usual at the lodge and having conversations with himself. He'd have four or five belts and feel the pain sawing at his heart and he'd begin to wonder if it was all a plot, if the kid was deliberately trying to bury him. The final straw—up until tonight, that is—was when that flea-bitten menagerie started showing up in the alley behind the store. Cats, dogs, he even thought he spotted a goddamn *raccoon* out there, all hanging around like a pack of hyenas, and Big Joe had had to chase them away with a hose only to see them regroup a little farther down the alley and gaze hatefully at him with their evil downcast eyes.

He couldn't figure it out. Why now, after all these years, was he suddenly being plagued by animals? Then, one night, as he was driving past the store—he'd found himself doing that a lot too, prowling up and down the alley like a goddamn private detective—he spotted Ritchie standing out there amid this scruffy mass of beasts and throwing them scraps of meat like Saint Francis of Assisi.

Big Joe laid on the horn, dispersing the mangy mob, and then rolled down his window and stuck out his head even as the kid lobbed another hunk of sausage into the darkness.

"What are you doing?"

"Getting rid of this old meat—what does it look like I'm doing?"

Big Joe placed his fists in his eyes and fell back against the seat. The murderer in his chest was loose again—he could feel the jagged fingers wrapped around his heart—and he wondered how much longer he could last.

He took a different route home on his way back from the lodge that night. He didn't have the guts to go past his store again—he was afraid of what he might find. Lately he'd been having visions. He'd seen a taco stand, a car wash, strangers frying chicken where his own father used to sweat. He'd seen his boy dressed in shark hides, his face mustachioed and his hair slicked back, cruising alleys in a black-finned auto and staying one step ahead of the law.

He kept trudging over the frozen walk in his galoshes, his fur-brimmed cap—the kind with ear flaps—and matching winter coat, bright orange so as to give him maximum visibility if stranded in a blizzard, but it didn't seem like he was getting anywhere. He felt tired, old. The wind whistled through his molars. Self-pity covered him like soggy clothes. Failure dogged him, an amorphous black shape that rode on his shadow, matching him stride for stride. The disappointed ghosts of Milly and his father seemed to be balanced on his shoulders and he walked stooped over, lugging these and all his other burdens down the icy street like a cross.

A slim quarter moon was out, casting feeble light over the roof-tops. Goddamn, it was cold. Big Joe had had way too much to drink and he went real slow; if he fell down now he wasn't sure he could get up again, and he'd probably just have to lie there, like a huge bug, until somebody found him in the morning. All the whiskey he'd drunk had tunneled his vision and the ground seemed to slope sharply away from him, slick and treacherous, leading, no doubt, to his final resting place—a big hole with a mound of dirt shoveled on top of it and a few words etched in stone: HERE LIES BIG JOE KOHLER—IF ANYBODY REALLY WANTS TO KNOW.

2

The wind swept the alley in fierce stinging arcs, swirling clouds of powdery snow that looked to Ritchie like moon dust. It rattled the sign at the back of the building and nearly tore the thermometer off the door. It was the sort of wind that could peel the skin off your cheekbones and turn your spit to ice before it hit the ground. Perched on an upside-down dairy crate in nothing heavier than an orange flak jacket, Ritchie would not have been surprised to see penguins materialize on the humps of snow that bordered the sidewalks, but still he refused to go back inside the store.

He'd been sitting out there for about five minutes, drinking beer and feeding turkey franks to a small ferretlike dog named Clash. The reason Ritchie called him that was because nothing on the animal matched. He had the angular pointed face of a terrier and the thick matted coat of a spaniel that had been left out in the snow too long. He had only one ear, the other having been chewed to a stub in some wild back-alley encounter. He had a puppy's large floppy feet and different-colored eyes—one gray, the other yellow— that could shrewdly size up any situation and send swift messages to his paws and teeth. It was the eyes that gave away those oversized clodhoppers; the animal was not young.

Ritchie removed another frank from the ten-pack and tossed it at the mongrel, who caught it deftly in midair and wolfed it down in a couple of greedy bites. Then he sat back on his haunches and looked at Ritchie, his good ear cocked toward the sky. Ordinarily at this time Clash would've had a lot of company back there—Spot, Odd Job, Captain Zero, and assorted other animals Ritchie hadn't had the time to name, including a big black-and-white cat without any tail who would lean its battered head forward and delicately lap the canned milk Ritchie would pour into a saucepan. But they hardly came around anymore, not since the time Big Joe had put the hose on them, and now only Clash remained, looking at Ritchie with those canny mismatched eyes and Ritchie looking back, two like shapes squatting in the moonlight.

He lifted up the bottle and took another hit of beer. A couple of hours had gone by since Big Joe had attacked him, but Ritchie's ribs still ached from colliding with the cake rack and he could still feel those fingers on his throat. It was not an unfamiliar feeling. It reminded him of the way his brother Joey used to sit on him and choke him for leaving little rubber army guys scattered around the bedroom, or for uncovering Joey's stash of dirty magazines, or sometimes just for being alive.

"I thought you were a robber," Big Joe had told him, and then he'd started in on the wig—a curly black item that Ritchie had lifted from his grandma's trunk in the attic and that he'd tug on every now and then, usually when he listened to the soul station and the spirit moved him to dance—and Ritchie had tried to explain to him that a guy had to do *something* to pass the time. Maybe the old load had forgotten how boring that night shift could be. Sure, occasionally a person might stop in for some dinky little purchase—a carton of OJ maybe, or a roll of Tums—but mostly it was like gigging at Big Joe's on the moon, and Ritchie had found himself resorting to increasingly drastic measures just to keep from going nuts. Sometimes he'd put on a pair of dark glasses and pretend to be blind, or stare out the window and make bets with himself on how long it would take for the next customer to come in. When he got bored with that he'd scan the magazine rack. He'd pick up an *Enquirer* and see if Elvis had appeared to anyone recently, or flip through a fashion magazine to learn how to avoid painful intercourse, or all the different ways of removing unwanted hair. Sometimes he'd run across an article on the twelve things women find irresistible in a man—animal magnetism, intelligence, a Porsche—but as far as he could tell he didn't have any of them, so he'd skip it and move on. Sometimes he'd even find himself taking the personality tests they had in there, but after a while he quit doing that too—he always came out a loser. They don't come right out and tell you that, but he knew it.

Lately, just before he went to sleep at night, ugly ideas had been creeping into his head. He'd found himself thinking about stealing all the money in Big Joe's register and then vanishing without a trace, of becoming an anonymous figure without a past, a free man who could do anything he pleased. He'd even thought of sneaking back in the dead of night with rags and a can of gasoline and burning the store to the ground. He'd wondered how hard it would be to score some dynamite. He'd go to sleep with dreams of groceries exploding, and then, in the morning, he'd wake up and think what a jerk he was, plotting to blow up his own father's store, the store that had belonged to *his* father, Big Hans, before him. How could he even dream of doing something like that?

"Don't you see that I'm doing you a favor?" Big Joe had told him in the store one day. "This place might be your only chance to make an honest living. Be grateful you have it." Ritchie supposed he was right. He didn't exactly have a wide world of opportunity awaiting him with his vegetable education. Good Citizenship and Long Division didn't exactly open a lot of doors.

He finished the beer and then blew his foggy breath into the top of the bottle, making a little hooting noise. The sound brought Clash ambling over and Ritchie began rubbing his hands along the animal's flanks, warming his fingers in the matted fur. He supposed he ought to go in and start closing up, but he couldn't get himself to go back into the store yet. He just felt like sitting there a little longer, on the dairy crate with the dog at his feet, his nose running and his toes going numb. The alley was bordered by apartment buildings—chintzy jobs that had recently gone up. Huge fantastic icicles dangled precariously from the gutter pipes and eaves. Ritchie kept glancing beyond them, scowling down that long windy tunnel as if he were waiting for something that was unlikely to show up.

There *was* one way out, he remembered; he thought of it now as he reached into his pocket and dug out matches and his smokes. He leaned out of the wind and lit the cigarette, then turned the matchbook around with his deadened fingertips. It was the color of sand, embossed with palm trees surrounding a soft blue lagoon. The word "Oasis" was spelled out in the palm trees' branches. "For the Finest in Dining and Entertainment," the matchbook said, the number for reservations listed just below.

Ritchie was familiar with the establishment, a big fancy nightspot on the airport strip designed to look like a sheik's palace. They booked Las Vegas entertainers in there, he knew, and made all the waitresses dress up like harem girls. Rumor had it that it was run by the mob.

The reason Ritchie knew about the Oasis was because his old friend Mars was working there, operating as his cousin Nick's right-hand man. Nick was nominally in charge, but Mars claimed *he* was the guy who actually ran the joint. Ritchie could believe that. The last time he'd gotten drunk with him, Mars had been driving this sharp new van, a customized job with plush leather buckets, power everything, fur on the wheel. The desert scene etched onto the back window featured sand dunes, palms, and a trio of Arabian belly dancers; it looked like a scene from *Ali Baba and the Forty Thieves.*

The man himself had looked as swank as his vehicle. His hair was short, slicked back, and he had a thin pencil mustache sketched above his upper lip. His black suit seemed like it was polished with Kiwi; the creases in his trou were razor sharp. He looked like a big raven waiting there in the parking lot.

They'd hit a couple of the clubs along the airport strip and then Mars had started in on Ritchie about coming to work for him at the Oasis, like he always did.

"Think about it, Kohler," he'd said, regarding Ritchie down the barrel of his nose. "We're like the Marines—always looking for a few good men. Besides, what are you planning to do—grind meat for the rest of your life?"

Ritchie had frowned and ordered another mai tai. He and Mars went back a long way, ever since the beginning of sixth grade when the nun threw a quiz on important prayers and this tall skinny new guy with frizzy hair and a long pointy nose sat down in the seat next to Ritchie's and started cheating. He had the Our Father written in the palm of his hand. When the sister—a big stocky woman Ritchie often thought of as the middle linebacker of the Lord—sneaked up behind and reared back to blast the new kid with a forearm shiver, Ritchie bailed him out by pretending to throw an epileptic fit, and they'd been friends ever since.

Still, Ritchie never liked it when Mars got in his face with that Oasis stuff. Ritchie had been there. He'd seen what the place was like, and he knew he would never fit into it, not in a million years. It was the kind of place where even the busboys wore tuxedos and you had to pay a guy just to park your ride. It was the kind of place where big shots would drop more on appetizers—rare underwater shit Ritchie had hardly even heard of—than he himself pulled down in a week. Comedians he'd seen on *The Tonight Show* flew in from Vegas just to make the people grin.

"C'mon, man—be realistic," he'd said. "What's a guy like me going to do in a high-class joint like that?"

"How do I know? Tend bar. Wait tables. Can you massage? Maybe I'll put you in charge of rubbing down the stars."

Ritchie lit another cig. There was another reason he'd steered clear of the whole idea, and it had to do with Mars himself: the guy had definite criminal tendencies. Not that he was a bad individual— far from it. They'd hung out together all through high school and always had a lot of laughs. Any time you wanted action Terry Marszack was the man to call. He was generous too, always giving you things and throwing his money around.

Still, every time Ritchie would get to thinking that Mars was just a regular fella he'd show up with a load of tape decks, or a trunk full of cigarette cartons that he'd hawk in the parking lot after school. Every time he'd begin to believe that Mars was just another Joe an incident would occur, like the time six or seven guys with hammers came looking for him at McDonald's, or the time they were sitting around in his mother's apartment by the airport, smoking dope and listening to the stereo, and a slender Sicilian in a black leather jacket came up the back stairs and left a message for Mars, burying it in the door with a ten-inch blade.

"Do yourself a favor and think it over, Kohler," Mars had said to Ritchie on their way out that night. They'd had to cut the evening a little short, Ritchie remembered. It seemed that Mars had important business to take care of with some brother on the South Side he knew.

Ritchie had nodded and said that he would. It had become a ritual: Mars would always make the offer and Ritchie would tell him the same tired lie.

"And stop by the club sometime. We'll make a night of it. Grab some chow, catch a show—you got to see some of the ladies who hang out in our festive lounge. Man-eaters, Kohler. I'm talking untamed women here."

"Looking forward to it."

"I mean it, numbnut—give me a call." He'd climbed into his van and was about to pull away when he stuck his head back out the window and asked Ritchie if he was interested in an aquarium. He said he had a shitload of these fish habitats he was trying to move.

"I'm talking the colored rocks, Kohler, temperature control—top-of-the-line stuff."

Ritchie flapped his hands. "I wouldn't know what to do with it," he explained. "I don't have any fish."

Mars sucked his teeth in disappointment. Suddenly he reached back behind the seat into a shopping bag for something. "You like Aretha Franklin?"

"Sure. The Queen of Soul?"

Mars's expression turned sour. Ritchie remembered he didn't particularly care for jungle music. "Here, man." He flipped Ritchie a cassette of Aretha's Greatest. "Enjoy."

Ritchie was still staring at the matchbook when a loud rumbling noise pierced the silence at the far end of the alley, sending Clash scrambling for cover beneath Ritchie's humped yellow car. At first he thought it might be Mars himself cruising by in that souped-up monster of a van he drove, but when Ritchie glanced over he saw that it was only Margie Glotz chugging toward him in her Volkswagen bug. The car was tomato-colored, with a soft dull sheen to it, like a fruit. Ritchie had always had the impression it could be dented with one good squeeze of your hand, like something you might crush in a produce bin.

She must not have seen him sitting there because she pulled up in one of the diagonal parking spaces at the side of the building and tooted, a thin comical squeak not unlike her voice. When Ritchie got up and walked around the dumpster he saw that she was leaning forward and checking her face in the rearview mirror. She wet her lips, fluffed out her curly apricot hair. She was short and chubby, with a creamy complexion and big round cinnamon eyes. She'd had a big crush on him since they were kids, but they'd only been officially dating for about a year, ever since he'd given her a ride to White Castle one day and discovered, to his amazement, when she took off her coat, that she'd sprouted a set of knocks that were at least the equal of her notoriously stacked older sister, Cookie, whom his brother used to spy on from the bedroom window with an old pair of field glasses Rommeled to his head.

At first, when he saw her coming, Ritchie frowned and wondered what she was doing tooling past the store at this time of night, but then he remembered that it was his idea in the first place. A little while after Big Joe had choked him, he'd called her up and told her to meet him around closing time. He needed a sympathetic ear, and a soft body to lose himself in. He was counting on Margie's bounty to get the rancor out of his blood.

She was still checking her look in the mirror when Ritchie emerged from the shadows and rapped on the door. She sprang back with a startled look, then slid over and rolled the window down. "What were you doing back there, Ritchie? You scared me to death."

He ignored the question. She had her imitation suede jacket partially unbuttoned, and the front of her fuzzy white sweater was strained nearly to the bursting point. Already Ritchie could feel a powerful stirring in his jeans.

Moments later they were sitting in their usual spot, at the edge of the park by the tennis courts, ensconced beneath the bare low-hanging limbs of a maple tree. Because the heater in it worked better they had taken Ritchie's car, a little yellow Datsun he'd picked up for seven hundred dollars from a used-car dealer on the North Side who was famous for his TV spots, during which he'd ride up on a donkey and smash the windshield of one of his cars with a sledgehammer. When he bought it Ritchie had pointed out to Big Joe that the car was practically a steal, but it didn't matter: his father took an immediate and violent disliking to it. Big Joe, of course, favored huge road hogs, the type only Chicago politicians drove around anymore, and he questioned what kind of safety an auto this small could afford in the mayhem of Chicago traffic—but Ritchie knew the real reason Big Joe hated it was because it came from Asia. Big Joe didn't have any use for that continent. After all, during the war it had been an Asian who'd ambushed Big Joe on the road one day, blowing up his jeep with a hand grenade. Big Joe still had the mark of the Orient on his back, a rust-colored burn that resembled Sakhalin Island.

"You say he *choked* you?" Margie was asking Ritchie in the front seat of the car. She squinted at him, one eyebrow cocked in a skeptical arch. "What, exactly, do you mean by that?"

Ritchie lifted up a paper bag and took a hit of the Mad Dog 20-20 he had stashed in the glove compartment. "Choking, Glotz. From the Latin *chokare*—to get on top of someone, wrap your hands around his throat, and squeeze. The goal is death." He wiped his mouth on his shirt sleeve.

Margie sat back, shaking her head. "I don't believe you."

"What's not to believe?"

"Are you saying he actually knocked you down and started doing that? Is that what you're telling me?"

Ritchie nodded.

"Why?"

"Who knows? I guess he wanted to kill me. I guess, deep down inside, he hates my guts."

"That's ridiculous, Ritchie. He doesn't hate you, he loves you. He's your *father*, for Pete's sake." She began pulling the wrapper off a Baby Ruth. "Maybe that's just his way of showing you he cares."

Ritchie sighed and slumped down behind the steering wheel, which had a cracked plastic rim. He balanced the Mad Dog on his chest and looked out beyond the maple tree into the tennis courts, which were enclosed by a tall chain-link fence and covered by a hard layer of frozen gray snow. New snow fell in a fine white mist, accumulating on the narrow benches; he could see it whirling in the glow of a nearby streetlamp. Snow covered the paths and the baseball diamonds, swirled in drifting currents around the water fountain, now choked dry for the season, where he and the rest of the guys used to hang out when they were kids. Mars, Stain, Bugsy Wallace, Artie Bean, Vinnie the Fish—there were five or six of them that had always hung around together, smoking Marlboros and playing the radio real loud and calling to the girls who sauntered by. Most of the time they just pitched pennies. It was an old park tradition, a game of nerve and skill. The stakes could be anything—cigarettes, knuckle punches in the arm—but mostly they pitched for quarters. Whoever wanted in would drop two bits in a hat and then everyone would line up behind a crack in the sidewalk and toss a penny at another crack about twelve feet away; the one closest to the line won everything in the hat. Then the hat would be refilled and they'd all line up again and go the other way. Sometimes there'd be as many as eight or nine players, which meant that at least a couple of bills changed hands on every pitch.

There were a lot of good shooters who hung out by the water fountain, but Ritchie was by far the best. He had steady nerves, good balance, fingertip control. His ragged pennies could righteously chew cement. He took another glug of Mad Dog now and thought about those times, fogging up the window with his breath. It seemed like he'd been standing out by that fountain only yesterday, clear-eyed and brave, snapping off winner after winner, his pockets heavy with jack.

"So what are you going to do?" Margie finally asked him.

He shrugged. "Nothing, I guess."

"You've got to do *something*, Ritchie. You just can't let things slide like this." She stopped chewing the candy bar and thought a minute. "Maybe you should quit."

"And do what?" Ritchie said.

Margie spun around to face him, bouncing excitedly on the front seat's tired springs. "Listen, Ritchie, why won't you consider going back to school? There's this new two-year program they're starting at the junior college. It's in restaurant management—you know, like running a Burger King, stuff like that. Anyway, this friend of a friend of mine—you know Debbie, right? It's Stewie, her boyfriend—he's just started in it and he says it's really neat and I was thinking this would be right up your alley—what with your background in food services, I mean."

Ritchie fell forward, draping himself over the wheel. "Jesus, Margie, how many times do I have to tell you—I'm not going back to school. No fucking way."

Margie made a sour expression; she didn't go for the F word in any of its forms. "Why not?"

"Too dumb. Look, Glotz, just quit badgering me about it." He puffed on a cigarette and sulked near the door. Ever since they'd gotten serious, Margie had been hammering away at him, determined to straighten out his future. Her own life she had already figured out, right down to the smallest detail. First they were going to get married. Then she would finish nursing school and work with the terminally ill. Then they would have kids. Two boys. Brendan and Theodore. Didn't he think those were neat names for boys? Ritchie would shrug and say how about Rocky and Bullwinkle? He'd gone along with this business of getting married primarily because he'd thought it would get her to loosen up. But, amazingly, Margie was still hell-bent on preserving herself for marriage. Ritchie couldn't get over it. The twenty-first century was right around the corner—and here was Margie, in most other respects a modern up-to-date female, still guarding her crotch as though it were the personal hangout of the Holy Ghost.

Lately, ever since Big Joe had caught them lying down in the store beneath the Hostess Snowballs, Margie had been more guarded than ever; they'd come pretty close to actually screwing that night. To make matters worse, her old man—a small, droop-faced guy with thinning hair and a moral code right out of the Middle Ages—had slapped a one-o'clock curfew on them. Exactly five minutes before the deadline, a buzzer on Margie's wristwatch would go off and she'd disentangle herself from Ritchie's sweaty clutches and make him drive her home. Ritchie had gotten to hate the sound of that buzzer. He had needs. He felt he was entitled. He wasn't some little high school dink anymore, with fruit fuzz on his cheeks. He was mature. He had a car, a money clip in his pocket. He was working on his build. It was humiliating for a modern guy like himself to get cut off by a watch.

He slumped back against the seat again and glanced at his own timepiece, a sleek gold Bulova with a set of strange initials on it: yet another gift from Mars. Jesus. It was already close to midnight and here they were, still wasting time on stupid yak.

"What's that?" Margie said. She pointed at the bottle Ritchie lifted to his mouth.

"French wine. Here, have a glug."

She squinched up her face, waved the bag away, and bit off

another hunk of candy. That was another thing about Margie—she had no use for alcohol. He couldn't even get her drunk.

"Hey, did I tell you about Buzz?" she suddenly said. Buzz was her sister Cookie's husband, a punk with slippery hair and a Matador hiked three feet off the ground. Just after high school he'd gotten Cookie in trouble and they'd had to get married; when Joey heard the news he had been depressed for a month.

"No, what about him?"

"He got a job."

"You're kidding. Doing what—making license plates?"

"No, reading meters for the gas company. He gets to wear a uniform and everything. It's pretty neat."

"What's Cookie say?" The rumor was that they'd beaten each other up with kitchen utensils one night and Cookie had given him the boot.

"They're back together again," Margie said. "She told him he could stay as long as he went to work and didn't drink a case of Pabst every night."

"Hooray for Buzz and Cookie."

Margie shrugged. She'd always hated Buzz's guts. "Hey, I got an idea: maybe Daddy could get you a job working in the hardware store with my brother Eddie."

"Great. It's what I've always wanted, Margie—to work in a hardware store." He fished out his cigarettes and lit up again. "Look, I have a hard enough time getting along with *my* old man; I *know* I can't get along with yours."

Margie waved her arms briskly in the air. She never liked it when he smoked, especially in the cramped quarters of the Datsun. "But Ritchie—you have to at least *try* and make something of yourself, don't you? I mean, that's what life is for."

"Who says so?"

"My Grandpa Walt always said so."

"Hooray for Grandpa Walt."

"Now there was a rugged individualist. He came over here with nothing, and when he died he had over eighty thousand dollars salted away. Never spent a penny. All he did was work. Did I ever tell you?—he died right in the store. Daddy was the one who found him. He was keeled over by the varnishes, I guess. They said he had a stroke." She tapped her nose thoughtfully with the candy wrapper. "He went real sudden, but everyone agreed it was better that way—if he lived he would've been a vegetable."

Ritchie nodded solemnly. For a moment they both reflected on how it was better to be dead than a vegetable.

"I guess he showed life who was boss," Ritchie finally observed, flicking his cigarette out the window. Margie laughed and fell heavily into his arms. Pretty soon her sweater was off and Ritchie was working at the catch on her bra. He unhooked it and her wondrous breasts sprang free in the moonlight. He cupped one in each hand and buried his face in the sweet damp flesh between.

He wasn't exactly sure what happened next. All he knew was that, after the usual period of heavy groping, her jeans were suddenly down around her ankles, he was lying on top of her, and her tongue was squirming in his mouth. He could feel her breathing into him, making small gasping sounds, and he lifted himself up on one elbow and frantically unzipped his trou. His rod sprang out, ready for action. It seemed to look around a moment, swelling with pride—free at last—before Ritchie got it aimed in the right direction and fell back on top of Margie with a hungry groan.

The thrill, brief as it was, was less real than imagined: as soon as Margie felt this dangerous intruder nosing around between her legs, she made a deft and forceful movement of her hip and Ritchie found himself on the floor of the car, wedged uncomfortably under the dashboard.

"For Christ's sake, Margie."

"Don't be angry with me, Ritchie." She leaned over and kissed the top of his head. "Like I always said, we've got plenty of time for that."

He was in a lousy mood when he pulled up in front of his house, and he felt even lousier when he looked out and noticed that all the downstairs lights were still on. His plan had been to guzzle down the rest of that cheap wine, call up the Anteater—a local slut with whom he sometimes consorted—and then smuggle her into the basement, where they had an old couch. But he could see now that that idea was going nowhere. The two ladies of the house, Aunt

Hilda and Grammy Kohler, both notorious night owls, were clearly still at large and would probably remain so indefinitely.

Hilda was in the kitchen, chopping carrots into a big pot with a Viceroy in her mouth, when Ritchie hobbled in through the side door. She warned him to wipe his feet. He kicked his shoes off on the landing and threw his jacket into the hall closet. As usual, Cha Cha, Grammy's French poodle, was sprawled in there by the heat vent, but the pampered animal didn't stir for his nightly outing like he always did and Ritchie briefly entertained the delicious hope that he was dead.

Crossing his fingers, Ritchie leaned forward into the closet and whispered the dog's name. His eyes snapped open and he immediately got up, shook himself and started trotting imperiously toward the side door for his evening constitutional. By his lofty expression you'd have thought the dog was the Prince of Poodles and Ritchie his lowly footman. He acted like he had medals on his chest.

Ritchie told the dog to fuck off and went into the kitchen for a beer. Hilda glanced up from the pot but didn't say anything. She was as thin as Big Joe was heavy, with a small rabbitlike face and wiry muscles set on a narrow frame. In the den the TV blared loudly; it sounded like a *Quincy* rerun from where Ritchie stood. He watched Hilda's knife coming down, steady as a metronome: chop chop chop.

"You better go in and take care of her," she said, pausing to knock the ash off her cigarette. "She's been complaining all night."

Ritchie made a guttural sound in the back of his throat, tossed the bottle cap into the trash, and went into the den, where Grammy sat on a Naugahyde davenport the size of a rhino, her feet sunk in a basin of warm water, a book of crossword puzzles opened on her lap. She was leaning back with her eyes closed, a gray powdered wig that made her look like one of the Founding Fathers tilted slightly forward on her head. The only indications she was still living were the occasional puckerings of her toothless lips and the muffled wet wiggling of her toes.

Ritchie went over and turned the volume down on the TV set, an ancient Motorola that was the only set in the house, Big Joe being too fucking cheap to go out and buy another one.

Grammy's eyes immediately popped open and she said, "I can't hear it. Turn it up." For some time she'd been hearing these noises in her head that sounded like vacuum cleaners, and that was why she always had the TV on so loud, Big Joe once explained—to drown out the Hoovers.

Ritchie switched the volume back up and then, hunkering down in front of Grammy, slowly lifted her feet out of the water and began drying them with a towel. These were odd-looking feet his grandmother had, small and pudgy, about as wide as they were long, like feet on a baby. "Easy," she winced, even though Ritchie applied the cloth with a feathery touch. "They've been killing me all day."

Ritchie said, "You got to try and stay off 'em more." It was his wry little joke. Most people—Ritchie included—got sore feet from spending too much time on them, but with Grammy it was just the reverse. She hardly ever used them anymore and so they tended to swell up on her. They ached and throbbed. Ritchie guessed it must've been a little like the pain a one-armed guy feels in his missing arm. Grammy's feet were still there, but barely. It was like any day they could fall off.

He dried them thoroughly with the towel, sprinkled talcum powder on them, and then, starting with the left, began massaging them with slow deliberate strokes. Grammy leaned back again, an arm flung across her head in a posture of exquisite anguish, while Ritchie muttered under his breath. Handling those ridiculous feet was one of several Grammy-related duties that had fallen to him ever since the old bat had moved in, and sometimes he wondered which he disliked the most: rubbing her feet, or taking her animal for long walks in the park, or making sure she had a clean glass of water to put her teeth into at night. The teeth were the easiest, but they gave him the creeps. Every night they sat grinning at him on top of the commode, like something on *Shock Theater*. He tried not to look at them but he couldn't help himself. It was like he was under their power; he always had to look.

He finished the massage with a series of delicate big toe stretches. "There. How's that?"

"Better," Grammy muttered. "But not much."

He got up and went back into the kitchen. Hilda was still at the counter. She was peeling potatoes now, going through a big pile of them like Sherman went through the South. The peels fell to the counter in long curving spirals, which she raked into the trash.

Ritchie got another beer out of the fridge and then picked up a knife and a couple of spuds and started helping her, painstakingly knicking at the skins like an old man whittling on a bench. He and Hilda were buddies and he always liked to give her a hand. She was the only one who remotely understood him, the only one in family squabbles inclined to take his side. His father never did. It seemed to Ritchie that he'd always gotten blamed for everything, that Big Joe reserved all his love and attention for his number-one son. You could even see it in their names. Joey was Joe Junior, the apple of his papa's eye, whereas when Ritchie was born he went practically a whole *week* without any kind of handle. It was almost as if he were a dog and Big Joe were waiting to see what kind of personality he had, or if he developed spots.

Hilda was the one who finally laid down the law. The way Ritchie had heard the story, she cornered Big Joe one night in the hospital and told him he had better come up with a name for that child before it was traumatized for life. Big Joe was in the visitors' room, staring at the wall. Name some names, he finally said. Hilda started naming some and Big Joe kept rejecting every one. Too long. Too short. Too much like a sissy. Eventually Hilda threw her hands in the air and told him that if he was going to find something wrong with every goddamn name in the English language he might as well call the child Hans, then—at least that would make the old man happy, rest his soul.

Big Joe looked at her and said, All right. All right what? All right, Hans. Hilda stared back. You're not serious, she said. Big Joe said of course he was serious. She said he should name him, so that was what he was naming him—Hans. Then Big Joe got up and walked away.

So that's how he got stuck with Hans. He was sure glad he wound up with a decent middle name—Richard. Ritchie—that's what everyone called him. That's what he went by. Nobody ever called him Hans, except for his brother when he was being a prick. Every so often Joey would remind him that he was a mistake, something that came along by accident to ruin everybody's life. He didn't have to rub it in like that. Ritchie knew. He knew his mom had been sick and wasn't supposed to have any more kids. He knew what Big Joe must've felt like when she told him the news. She was aware of the risks but she wanted to have him anyway, so what was he supposed to do about it? Apologize for living?

He was a little over a year old when his mother died. Big Joe was in his late thirties. Joe Junior was six. Ritchie guessed that neither of them had ever gotten over it, and that's why they'd always held a grudge. The difference was that Joey would come right out and say it, while Big Joe communicated his resentment in other ways— sometimes by ignoring him and sometimes by a brusque impatience with everything he did, but more often (and more painful to Ritchie) by that weary way he had of looking at him, as though Ritchie were an unlucky penny that was always turning up in his pants.

"What's that?" Hilda said. She was looking at the little pile of potato slivers Ritchie had carved.

"Sorry." He picked up another spud.

She took it away. "I got a better idea. Let me handle the potatoes; why don't you go upstairs and talk to the grouch." That was another thing about Hilda—she'd always been able to read his mind.

"Why should I? It wasn't my fault. I was just standing there and—"

"Look, I didn't say it was. All I'm saying is that *someone* around here has got to break the ice."

"Fine. Let him break it."

"He won't. You know he won't. He's too damn proud."

Ritchie frowned and took a gulp of beer, rolling the suds around in his mouth. Hilda always knew how to reach him. For twenty years she'd been operating like this, trying to keep the peace.

"It's late," Ritchie said, smacking the bottle down on the counter. "He's probably sound asleep by now."

"He's not asleep. Believe me. He's too upset to sleep."

Ritchie made a pained expression and jammed his hand deep into his pocket. The matchbook was still there, lying snug against his leg; he could feel its hard edge with his fingertips. Hilda had a Viceroy going in the ashtray and the smoke was curling up in her face. She reached over and ground it out with her ringless hand. In the den a man hawked a six-record set of everyone's favorite accordion music at the top of his lungs. A few feet away, in the hall closet, Cha Cha was growling in his sleep.

"All right," Ritchie finally said. "But I'll tell you this: I'm not gonna apologize."

"Who said you had to apologize? Just stick your head in his bedroom and tell him good night."

Ritchie nodded. He took his beer and went down the hall and up the stairway, moving slowly, tiptoeing over the carpet, avoiding all the worn creaky places so as not to make a sound. He hoped to hear Big Joe snoring away as usual, listened for those chain-saw noises he always heard this time of night, but the upstairs was quiet and, just above him, he could see a thin column of light from the master bedroom shining against the wall.

The stairway angled sharply to the left just before you reached the top, and Ritchie hesitated at the bend for a moment and took another glug of beer. Right around the corner, maybe thirty feet away, Big Joe was leafing through a book—no doubt one of his Time-Life pictorial histories of war, Ritchie thought, or maybe even that moldy old scrapbook he kept in the attic filled with newspaper clippings and pictures of a trim gallant runner stepping over tacklers and breaking away; Ritchie could hear the warped pages rattle every time Big Joe turned them in his hand. He realized there was no getting past him. He really didn't want to do it, but he supposed it wouldn't kill him just to pause for a second on his way to his own bedroom and tell his father good night.

But, as it turned out, he never got to say it. Big Joe must've heard him coming after all because, just as Ritchie reached the top of the stairs, he rolled over in bed and turned off the light.

Ritchie couldn't sleep. He tried, but too many bad feelings kept washing over him, jostling him like waves, and finally he had to jump out of bed and snap on the lights and begin working out with his brother's old weights, straining and sweating and pumping iron in order to calm his blood.

After the workout he rolled the weights to the far side of the room and then crawled to the full-length mirror mounted on the door. He got to his feet and struck a manly pose. Zero. He still didn't have muscle one. Not only was he built like a prisoner of war, his face had retained that youthful innocence that appealed only to the old blue-haired gals he used to deliver groceries to. No wonder he couldn't score, not even with Margie. The longer he looked at himself the more he realized that here was a face only a mother could love.

Totally disgusted, he went over and wrenched open the window that looked out onto the alley. He felt like he was suffocating. That madhouse of a family was choking him—he had to get some air. He stuck his head out the window, breathing deeply, and then began scanning the neighborhood, looking beyond those rows and rows of slanted rooftops. For a way out.

He leaned way over and looked in one direction, then the other. Then his eyes came to a rest on a mop of curly orange hair framed in a bedroom window in the house across the way.

Margie spotted him standing there. She immediately flung down the book she'd been reading, climbed out of bed, and came over to the window. She opened it and, decked out in her pajamas, draped herself fetchingly over the sill. She waved at him and then cupped her hands around her mouth and shrilled in a voice that rang across the neighborhood, "Don't forget tomorrow night!"

Ritchie stood there, regarding her blankly.

"Dinner at my house, dummy. Eight o'clock. Don't be late. And guess what?—I'm making the whole meal myself."

"Great," Ritchie said, already feeling his stomach churning. The Glotz girls were notoriously bad cooks. He remembered the last time he'd eaten there. Margie and her mother, Glo—a robust woman, like her daughters, with a bouffant of golden-red hair—had done all the talking while Henry Glotz made vaguely threatening gestures at Ritchie with his butter knife and Ritchie sat there staring at all the ghastly dishes Margie had specially prepared for the occasion, feeling like he was part of an experiment, or the focus of some mysterious ritual that would bind him and Margie together for the rest of their lives.

Margie blew him a kiss and then eased off the sill, hopped back in bed, and shut off the light. Ritchie remained at the window, peering down over the ledge. A powdery curtain of snow was still falling; occasionally the wind would gust and make the snowflakes dance. The hard snow-packed ground below was crusted with peaks, like a field of white waves, and great drifts were piled against the fence.

Suddenly, as Ritchie was standing there, he began thinking of his friends again. He could see them all clearly, as though they had assembled in the yard and now stood beneath his window, beckoning him to join them, urging him to jump. Stain was there, married to a fat girl and selling shoes for Thom McAn. Bugsy Wallace was there, his arms full of babies, a construction hat balanced on his head. Buzz was there in his meter-reader uniform, and so was the baddest of them all, Artie Bean. Ritchie remembered the Impala he used to drive, with flames painted on the sides. Even good girls like Margie fell over when Artie strutted in his dago T. Now he was machine fodder in a big aluminum mill. He'd gained a ton. Every so often Ritchie would see him trudge past the store with a lunch pail the size of a locomotive under his arm, his ass dragging so low he looked like he needed a wheelbarrow to help him haul it along.

Ritchie fell back from the window, rubbing his eyes. No way. He wasn't about to join that group of losers, not yet, not before he'd even had a shot.

He rushed over to his pants and dug the matchbook out of the pocket. Then he seized his stolen watch. Almost two. It wasn't late. It was still early. The man never slept until dawn.

3

Louise was standing at the end of the bar in her bride-of-the-desert costume—veiled headdress, low-cut halter, billowing silk pajama pants—smoking a Salem 100 and gazing at the piano at the far end of the lounge. On the other side of the counter Vince the God shook up a batch of piña coladas in a coconut-shaped container while Paulie, the temporary, stood and watched with his arms at his sides. The usual Thursday-night crowd was on hand, massed five-deep in front of the bar, laughing and posing and getting looped on mirages. It was so loud in there you could hardly hear yourself think, but that was okay with Louise. She was a cocktail waitress. She didn't have to think.

She kept looking at the piano, which sat unattended for the moment beneath a pair of leafy fig trees. It was a Steinway. She couldn't remember the last time she'd sat down and actually *played* a Steinway. Most of the pianos she'd played—in a series of dives and honky-tonks whose names blurred in her mind—had been cheap duds, ill-tuned squawk boxes with scars and nicks and beer stains all over the keys. They looked like something a person would hide in the basement or let a bunch of kids bang on with hammers and little fists. Sometimes they reminded her of coffins. Trying to coax music out of them was like trying to raise the dead.

But this Steinway was something different. It seemed to radiate music even when no one was playing, breathe silent harmonies through its smooth curving lines. The wood was polished so bright you could see yourself in its glassy black surface. One night, at closing time, after the customers had all gone away, Teddy Drake,

the Oasis's resident Liberace, the platinum-haired oldies-but-good-
ies man, had let her sit down and play for just a moment. She was
a little rusty, but it didn't matter; even the clunkers she struck were
transformed by the Steinway into shimmering patterns of sound.

"Gimme a tea, Vinnie. Couple of mirages. Three Mick Lites." It
was Babs, the other harem girl, who'd elbowed her way to the
counter and now stood a few stools over, glancing at her checks
and blowing hair out of her eyes. Vince grunted, poured a fresh
round of mirages, and Babs carried them off on a tray. One thing
about working with Vinnie: you never had to wait for drinks. You
gave him an order, you went out and hustled a few more tables,
the drinks were always there as soon as you got back. He didn't
screw up orders or try to stiff anybody either. Louise appreciated
that. She'd worked with plenty of clowns who didn't know their ass
from anisette and who, if you got on their bad side, would deliberately try to fuck you over—but not the God. He was strictly professional. Babs was okay too, even if she did complain about her health
all the time.

All points considered, the Oasis was a first-class gig, a couple of
light-years from the toilets she'd previously worked in. The only
thing she didn't like about it was the ridiculous costume they made
you wear—every time she put it on she felt like a concubine in
some old desert saga—and who she'd had to deal with to get the
job. Mars, the weasel who'd hired her, had told her she was lucky
even to get an interview. Who knew, maybe he was right. Maybe
her luck was changing after all.

She still had a couple of minutes on her break, and she lit another
cigarette and glanced at the party that had just sat down—four girls
in gaudy clothes cruising over from the city with last year's haircuts
and hungry eyes. Secretaries probably, trying to catch a money-
market man, or housewives out on a lark. The prettiest—a thin
gawky redhead with heavy eye makeup and braces on her teeth—
looked suspiciously young, and Louise was glad she was sitting at
Babs's station. She didn't need the hassle. She'd only been working
there a month.

There were a couple of rules Louise had had to learn when she
started working at the Oasis. One was to lay off the eats. A harem
girl with excess baggage cut an unbecoming figure, Mars had ex-

plained to her when she interviewed for the job; the management wouldn't tolerate any chunkettes.

Louise didn't have any problem with that—she'd always been thin. The second rule was to never, under any circumstances, serve minors, not even if they were sitting with His Holiness the Pope. Mars had gone on to explain that, a little while back, one of the waitresses had gotten into the habit of smuggling drinks to her little sister, who one night, ripped on tequila, had lah-de-dahed out of the building, gotten into her car, and immediately plowed into a station wagon full of tourists on the way to O'Hare. There had been many severe injuries—broken ribs, crushed spleens, and so forth. A very hairy scene.

"Nick had to pay off so many people it wasn't even funny," Mars had added. "It was like the trifecta window at Arlington. His nose was out of joint for a month."

Louise had said she understood perfectly—and was there anything else? As a matter of fact there was, Mars said with a sly little grin. They were all alone in one of the back offices, ten o'clock at night, nobody around. He swiveled in his chair and, gesturing toward the liquor cabinet that stood beside the massive oak desk, asked what was her pleasure. Louise noticed the rings on his fingers, two dusky zircons that sat like plump snails on his outstretched hands. He looked into her eyes and grinned again, his face flattening into a series of sharp angles—a cartoon wolf slinking up on the chicken coop. She sat back and sighed. It seemed that all her life she'd been dealing with men like this, hustlers and geeks and small-time operators with lies in their teeth and phony dreams in their pockets—but she needed the job, she was a working woman with a kid to support and bills coming due. She remembered that the last place she'd waitressed she'd been let go on account of her "uncooperative attitude." The Oasis was the best thing she'd run across in years. It even had that Steinway. So what else was she supposed to do?

"Tell me about yourself," Mars had said, plunking a tumbler of Scotch down in front of her.

She picked up the drink and took a belt, the liquor coating her mouth like varnish. "Well, I've always wanted to work here. I grew up around here. I've been coming here for years to see the shows."

She went on, telling him more lies. She humored him, flattered him, told him exactly what he wanted to hear, but she drew the line when he made a move on her. She would lie, but she wasn't willing to do *that*, not for this hipster meatball. She was already thinking about the next club down the road when he suddenly gave her a cool indifferent look and swept some papers into his hand and told her she could start on Saturday.

Louise stubbed out her cigarette, adjusted her halter, and pasted a professional smile on her face, ready to resume her rounds. First, though, she had to take care of Teddy Drake, who'd put on a new face in his dressing room and was now waiting at the piano with a petulant pout. She asked the God to make Teddy's usual—Squirt with a twist of lemon—and then she carried it over to him on a small cardboard square and put it down on top of the Steinway, next to the vase of yellow carnations that matched the one in Teddy's lapel. She drummed her fingers lightly over the piano's gleaming surface and lingered there a moment, in the spotlight, before heading out into the crowd.

Ritchie was waiting in the lobby, standing way over in a corner by the cigarette machine with his shoulders hunched and his hands in the pockets of his shiny orange polyester coat. Mars had left a message for him at the reservation desk saying he was in an urgent meeting but would be out in five minutes. Ritchie had already been waiting at least ten, hanging back by the coatroom and staring at a framed galaxy of stars mounted on the wall. Rickles, Uncle Miltie, Wayne, Dino, Old Blue Eyes himself—all the big shots were up there, along with local celebrities and a politician or two.

The lobby was crowded. Men in expensive camel-colored topcoats kept arriving with elegant-looking ladies on their arms. They'd check their coats with the girl behind the counter and then wait for the maître d' to usher them to their tables. The women would dart into the powder room to reapply lipstick and get the wind out of their hair while the men stood under the enormous chandelier in groups of three or four, talking and laughing and flicking stray ashes off their Brooks Brothers suits. Ritchie remained in his own little corner. He didn't trust chandeliers and he didn't have a suit, having outgrown the one he'd worn to his high-school graduation, which now hung in his closet like a dead animal, next to his K-Mart floods and his wide-collar shirts.

He lit a cigarette and kept wishing Mars would hurry up and get out there. He always felt out of place at the Oasis, but especially now, when he was alone.

A man in alligator shoes walked up and began studying the cigarette machine, searching his pockets for coins. He asked Ritchie why it was that you couldn't get a decent pack of cigarettes out of a cigarette machine—everything in there was at least ten years old. "Who smokes Luckies?" the man said. Ritchie said he didn't know. He moved away from the machine and wandered back over to look at the celebrity photos again. He was staring at a picture of Sammy Davis, Jr., trying to ascertain which was the real eye, when Mars finally burst into the lobby biting on a Kool.

"Listen," he said. "You're gonna have to hang loose by yourself for a couple more minutes. I gotta run out to fucking Sears."

"What for?"

Mars spat tobacco off the tip of his tongue. It seemed that Donny Romero, an up-and-coming vocalist who was the featured entertainer at the Oasis that week, had split one of his skin-tight leather jumpsuits during rehearsal, and now he was promising to remain in his dressing room unless someone could come up with the proper support.

"It's a total zoo back there. The lard-ass is threatening to stiff us tonight and Nicky's going nuts. 'Get him something,' he finally tells me. I go, 'Like what?' Nicky goes, 'A girdle. Get him a girdle.' Can you believe it?" Ritchie was, in fact, shocked that someone of Mars's stature would be sent on such a lowly errand, but he just chalked this up to show biz.

Mars was gripping his head. "I go, 'Nick, just have one of the cooks tie a big piece of liver on him. Wrap the clown in fish.' But Nicky, he like doesn't want to hear about it. Now I actually got to run out to the nearest shopping mall and buy a girdle for the schmuck."

He led Ritchie into the lounge, brought him a mirage, and then split on his underwear mission. Ritchie sat alone at a small wicker table and looked around. This wasn't exactly what he'd had in mind when he called Margie and canceled their dinner date, telling her he'd developed a severe inflammation of his large intestine. At first he felt uneasy sitting all by himself in the crowded bar, but then, after a couple of slurps of his drink, he began to relax a little bit. He kept hitting the mirage, which came in a vase and tasted like lime Kool-Aid, and admiring the way the two cocktail waitresses moved in their harem outfits. They were working the tables briskly, taking drink orders and sauntering back to the bar, behind which a couple of guys dressed like Turkish pirates shook, blended, and poured an assortment of chills and punches. It was cool and dark in there; the lush green-black flora dripped from a recent spraying. At the far end of the room, framed by a pair of enormous fig trees, a platinum-haired musician in a velvet dinner jacket was playing the piano and singing oldies but goodies for everyone's listening pleasure.

One of the waitresses went by, and Ritchie flapped his arm to get her attention. He felt warm from the drink and warm from the candle burning in front of him in a hollowed-out pineapple. The waitress dropped off a round of drinks at a nearby table and then came over, studying him keenly as she approached.

"You want something?"

Ritchie smiled at her. "What's your name?"

"Louise."

"Another one of these, Louise." He held up his nearly empty vase.

The waitress studied him again and then looked around, as though she thought someone might be spying on her from behind a fern. "Can I see your ID?"

Ritchie frowned and reached back for his wallet. Even though he was accustomed to getting carded whenever he went out, he still didn't like it. The truth was, though he'd turned twenty-one several months ago, he still had a hard time getting drinks. Maybe it was his youthful expression, or maybe it was the meat-shop odor that always seemed to be lingering about his person like a stinky cloud. That was another thing about the store that pissed him off: try as he might, he just couldn't seem to scrub that sausage smell completely out of his skin. It was like it had sunk clear down through his pores.

He forked over his driver's license and the waitress took it in her large bony hand. She was tall and stringy, with a hard-edged mouth and big dark eyes. Beneath the veil her hair was arranged in a frosted, ice-cream-like concoction. She might've been all dolled up in that fancy outfit, but she still looked to Ritchie like a tough street chick, the sort who would pick your pocket or call you mosquito-dick if you looked at her the wrong way.

The waitress kept examining his license, glancing back and forth from the laminated card to Ritchie's face like she was an agent for the CIA. "You got anything else?"

"Like what?"

"Credit card. Passport . . ."

"Passport? What do you think I did—fly here from France?"

She smiled and snapped a halter strap at him. "Okay, how about just a credit card, then?"

Ritchie showed her his hands. "Sorry. I don't have any credit cards." He'd had a Visa card once, but Big Joe had taken it away from him after he rang up seven hundred dollars in charges at Elmo's Parts, fixing up his car. "I *am* a member of the Big Wrangler Club," he quickly added. "You want to see that?" He'd bought the card from a local steer joint so he could keep Margie happy with discount steaks.

The waitress smiled again, a brittle tight-lipped expression. She looked once more at the license, and for a moment Ritchie thought she was going to ask him what his birthday was—he'd had to parrot that on more than one occasion, as well as memorize his Social Security number—but she nodded okay, returned the card, and sashayed back over to the bar.

Some monkey, Ritchie thought. A real ballbuster. He slurped more of his drink and turned his attention to the clientele, especially the women crowded along the bars. Mars was right—Oasis ladies were something. Suddenly he found himself staring with such naked longing that he had to watch what the hell he was doing with his drink: one time he'd gulped without looking and nearly rammed the slender green cocktail straw up his nose in the process.

Showgirls—that's what he kept thinking. They had to be some-thing glamorous like that—or maybe stews. The gents who weaved confidently among them were impressive also, and Ritchie tried to picture himself as one. These weren't your typical inner-city door-knobs sporting loud medallions, chest hair, flashy satin shirts slashed to the waist. They weren't second-rate yes-men like his brother,

either. These were your bona fide pin-striped guys, your shakers
and movers, your attorneys and stockbrokers and MBA's. Still, it
was the women who kept grabbing his attention. Most of these sky
gals—if that's in fact what they were—had sleek planes of luxuriant
hair and wore the kind of bold, ultracontemporary outfits he'd seen
in the fashion magazines and which always made him stop and ask
the question: Where the hell would a North Side guy ever see a
woman decked out in one of these? Now he knew the answer: at
the fig bar in Nicky Marszack's Airport Oasis.

Finally the waitress brought over his mirage on a big silver tray.
"Three bucks," she barked, putting the frothy green vase down in
front of him.

Ritchie said, "It's on the house."

She took a step back. "Who says so?"

"Mars says so. You know who Mars is, don't you?" Ritchie puffed
out his chest. As the man's personal guest he felt no obligation to
take gas from the help.

"Of course I know who Mars is," the waitress said. She began
looking around nervously again, as if there might be a camera hidden in a nearby bush. Ritchie had run into all kinds of waitresses,
but never one as strange as this.

"Look," she finally said. "Just pay me the money, okay? I only
work here—I don't make the rules."

Ritchie frowned, dug into his pocket, and gave her the money:
two dollar bills and a bunch of grubby change. She stuffed the
money into her pants and stalked away. Ritchie watched her with
a sullen expression and decided he probably ought to mention something to Mars about this highly paranoid cocktail waitress. The guy
had a class operation going here. Too bad it had to be spoiled by
someone with an uncooperative attitude.

He was still thinking about the strange waitress, trying to remember
her name, when Mars returned with a big Sears package in his
hand.

"You got it, huh?"

"Yeah, I got it—but I'm not happy about this, Kohler, not one
little bit." He looked around and slipped the package under his coat.
"When I give it to him, I'm gonna have to have a talk with this

Romero and straighten him out. The guy's been driving me nuts, Kohler. He's been whining ever since he hit town. Nothing's right. The sound system sucks, the stage is too small. I can't even smoke a cigarette around the guy—he claims it fucks up his tonsils." Mars reached inside his coat and angrily rustled the package. "On top of everything, the guy's too fucking fat to fit into his costume, right? I got to run out at the last second and buy a girdle for the schmo. Do you know how *embarrassing* that is, Kohler? Do you have any idea?"

Ritchie rubbed his nose and told him he could guess.

"I'm telling you, man." Mars fired up a Kool. "I've dealt with some all-star assholes in this business, but big butt here takes the cake. The last I heard he was threatening to stiff us for the rest of the week. Intolerable conditions. He can't go on. One night, he says, and he takes his tonsils back to Vegas."

"What are you going to do about it?"

"I guess Nicky's having a talk with him now and explaining the situation. Nicky's good at explaining things. Not me. If it was me, I wouldn't bother—I'd ship him out tonight, Federal Express. I'd airmail his ass back to Nevada. A *girdle*, Kohler! We're talking second floor, ladies' foundation garments." He took a last quick drag on his cigarette and ground it out in the ashtray. "Well, c'mon— let's take a walk and see if Mr. Wide Load can fit into this thing."

Ritchie got up and followed Mars back out through the lobby and into the main dining room, a huge glittering hall about the size of a Bowlarama where maybe five hundred people could chow down while catching a top-name Vegas act. At one end of this expanse stood an elevated bandstand; in the center, an ornate circular fountain surrounded by small palms spewed multicolored water into the air. The place was thick with foliage. The domed ceiling had glass panels like an observatory, and assorted fig and rubber trees and similar leafy growths bloomed under the stars. The larger trees at the edges of the eating area gave way to depictions of desert exotica—sand dunes, camel caravans, flying carpets—painted across the cream-colored walls in an ascending terrain that stretched halfway to the ceiling.

The restaurant was packed and hummed with noise. At the tables, well-dressed diners studied menus the size of the Ten Commandments under large, slow-turning fans, while a small army of fezed waiters bustled through the aisles with silver food trays balanced on their fingertips. Mars knifed through this traffic with his shoulders hunched and his head craned forward, muttering to himself, while Ritchie followed a couple of paces behind, trying not to bump into things.

They walked all the way through the dining room and angled past the stage until they came to a door marked AUTHORIZED PERSONNEL ONLY. Mars pushed it open and they entered a back hallway where the offices were located. Mars said the dressing rooms were back here too. He said they had everything in them but swimming pools.

About halfway down the corridor, he paused in front of a closed door that had a star embossed on it. He rapped casually with his knuckles and stuck his head inside.

"Special delivery from Maidenform."

"Not now!" a voice shot back, and Mars immediately stepped out and shut the door.

"Nicky must still be talking to the fat-ass," he explained. "C'mon, we'll wait back here."

The main office was at the end of the corridor; Mars opened a heavy door that had OASIS ENTERPRISES etched into the glass and ushered Ritchie inside. Actually it was a suite of offices and a large reception area, which had a desk and some file cabinets at one end and an enormous leather sofa at the other. More celebrity photos and other show-biz paraphernalia covered the walls.

Ritchie followed Mars into a small inner office in the back, which was dominated by a massive oak desk cluttered with papers. On one side of the desk was a liquor cabinet, and on the other stood an exercise bike. The only other furniture in the room was a small aluminum chair with a piece of canvas stretched across the frame. It looked puny in comparison to the massive desk; it looked like it was cowering.

Ritchie asked Mars if this was his office.

"Sure." He had gone behind the desk and plunged himself into the swivel chair. He leaned way back, putting his feet up and dislodging a few loose sheets of paper, which fluttered to the carpet. "Go ahead, take a load off."

Ritchie sat down in the small aluminum chair. Through the window behind Mars's head he could look across the road and see the winking red sign of a carry-out; beyond that, the huge banked lights of an airport runway were flashing a piercing blue. The only light inside the room was coming from a high-intensity lamp mounted on the desk. He looked at the big shadow of Mars it cast on the wall.

Mars threw the Sears package on the desk and gouged his eyes. "Just another day in the fast-paced world of entertainment. You want a drink?"

Ritchie told him no thanks. For some reason he didn't feel comfortable having a drink just then.

"I'm having one." Mars reached over and grabbed some Scotch out of the liquor cabinet and took a belt directly out of the bottle. "Fucking A, what a night."

"So this is where you run the show," Ritchie said, looking around.

"The *whole* show," Mars said. Ritchie didn't ask him what he meant by that.

Mars took another hit of Scotch and then reached into his pocket and removed a set of keys. "That's it. I'm punching out." He flipped the keys into the top desk drawer and then rummaged around a minute, searching for something. He seemed annoyed. He slammed the drawer shut and then reached down to the side of the desk and yanked open another. Ritchie sat on the edge of his little aluminum perch and fidgeted. He wasn't sure where, exactly, to focus his eyes.

"*Here's* that sucker." Mars's face had suddenly brightened, like a kid who'd discovered where the Kit Kats were stashed. He had his hand stuck way down in the bottom drawer. "I knew it was in here somewhere." He brought out what he'd been searching for and held it lovingly to his face. "Check it out, Kohler. Is this a sweetheart or what?"

What Mars was cooing over was a gun, a small snub-nosed automatic, the handle inlaid with mother-of-pearl. Ritchie stared at the weapon. He'd never been in the same room with a gun before. Big Joe didn't have a gun. He didn't know anyone who had a gun, except for Bugsy Wallace's older brother, Fuzzy, who'd been in Nam and supposedly slept with an army piece under his pillow. At first

Ritchie thought maybe it was a toy, but there was an unmistakable bulk and authority to what Mars held in front of his nose that indicated the rod was not a plaything.

"Tell me this isn't one gorgeous firearm," Mars was saying. He waved the weapon, then pointed it into a corner and squinted down the sight. "Pow. Absolutely. I call this little honey the Turk."

Ritchie was about to tell him to quit messing with that thing and put it away when suddenly he heard footsteps in the reception area, heading in their direction. Mars heard them too and scrambled into action, putting the Scotch back in the liquor cabinet and stashing the heater in the desk drawer just as the footsteps came to a halt at the edge of the room.

"You've been fooling with that piece again," a voice said.

"No I haven't."

"Don't lie. I saw you reaching in the drawer."

"Okay. So I was. Big deal." Mars sulked in the chair.

The man continued to stand at the edge of the office. He was behind Ritchie and Ritchie couldn't see him, but he could see his shadow on the wall. It was bigger than Mars's shadow.

"Who's your friend?"

"Just an old buddy. By the way, I got the girdle." Mars picked up the package and flung it over. "I hope the lard-ass can stuff himself into it because I'm sure as hell not about to go out and get another one. I assume he *is* going on tonight."

"Sure he's going on. And they'll love him. The paying public will eat him up."

"I think he stinks."

"You're not the paying public," the man said. He was rattling the doorknob. "Get lost. I got a lot of work to do."

They both got up and Ritchie hung on Mars's heels as they cleared out of the office. Ritchie never did get a good look at Nick—only a brief glimpse of his slicked-back hair and his pencil mustache as he hurried by.

"Why don't you stick around and catch the show?" the big boss said to Mars as they were leaving. "Broaden yourself. Learn something."

"Screw that," Mars said. "We got better things to do."

"So which one you want, Kohler?" Mars was asking a few moments later. "The redhead or the blonde?" They were standing in the lobby again, looking through the tinted window into the crowded lounge.

"I don't know what you're talking about."

"C'mere." He motioned Ritchie closer and Ritchie came up and pressed his nose right against the glass. "See those two bimbos sitting at the bar? *That's* what I'm talking about."

"*Those* two?" He now saw that Mars was referring to a couple of lounge angels in spiked heels and low-cut dresses who were sitting on stools at the near end of the bar. They were smoking pastel cigarettes and looking bored. He'd noticed them before, and he wasn't surprised that nobody had latched onto them—who in the world would have the balls to approach such worldly-looking dishes? They both appeared to him to be at least thirty-five years old.

"Of course those two," Mars was saying. "Who else?"

"What are you telling me here? Are you saying that you know them?"

"Yeah I know them. I know everybody who hangs out in there. I'm a highly visible dude." He was impatiently cracking his knuckles, one after the other. "We're wasting time here, Kohler. Let me repeat my question: Redhead or blonde?"

Ritchie stuck his hands in his pockets and rattled his change. "Don't you think they're a little *old* for us?"

"Let's put it this way—their prom days are over, man." He came up and put his arm around Ritchie, big-brother style; Ritchie had the feeling Mars would've taken him aside, except they were standing in the lobby—there wasn't a nearby place Mars could take him aside to.

"What's the problem here, Kohler?" he began. "I thought you were interested in some serious partying tonight. I thought you came out here looking for action—correct me if I'm wrong."

"Sure I'm looking for action," Ritchie said. "Who isn't?"

"Then will you please tell me what the fuck you're whining about?"

"I'm not whining. I'm just pointing out they look a little old for us, that's all. Talk to me about a couple of younger chicks and I'm listening. But *those* two . . ." He leaned into the window and took another peek at them, bumping his head against the glass. "You're talking a couple of mature *women* here, Mars. Gimme a break. I wouldn't even know what to say."

"Say?" Mars was incredulous. "You don't have to *say* anything. Who do you think those two are in there—Dr. Joyce Brothers?" He started popping his knuckles again.

Ritchie frowned. Every so often the asshole would push him, to see how far he could go. He took his hands out of his pockets and stuck out his chest and told him okay, he was up for it.

The redhead's name was Viv. She had her hair pulled smartly to one side and pinned together with a shiny coral clip. She had the longest fingernails Ritchie had ever seen on a woman. They were the same dark red shade as her hair and her lipstick, which covered her plump mouth in a moist smear. Long graceful helixes dangled from her ears. Her low-slashed dress was vermilion.

Mars led Ritchie over and made the introductions, and then he told the ladies to hurry up and finish their drinks—he wanted to get moving.

"Where you taking us?" Shar, the blonde, reached down and adjusted her hose.

Mars slipped an arm around her waist and nearly pulled her off the stool. "Everywhere."

There were an awful lot of party spots on the airport strip. Ritchie wasn't sure they made them all that night, but they hit most of them. At each place, Mars would make a big splashy entrance, slapping backs and passing out power shakes like cigars, and then after one drink he'd hustle them off to someplace else. The ladies were having a merry time. Ritchie too. He was definitely going with it. He was gone. Mars kept buying him voodoo drinks until a jungle grew inside his head. He felt the beat of many bongos. He even danced. It was at some pineapple joint where palms shimmied under big electric fans and an island band was playing. Mars wouldn't go near the dance floor, so Ritchie went out with a pair of partners. He didn't care. He did the rumba with two older women. Glancing into the flashing mirrors he could barely recognize the madcap guy with his arms around that team of curvy mamas.

Eventually, though, the rum mist in his head burned away and he found himself in Viv's apartment, sitting on the living-room floor, painfully alert, cold sober. His hostess was in the bathroom. Before she went in she had pointed to a room down the hall and told him to make himself comfortable, but Ritchie remained on the floor, sitting on a pillow and staring at some transparent fish floating in an aquarium that bubbled in a corner.

The apartment was like an opium den—heavy dark drapes, velvet couches, pillows everywhere. It smelled of incense and nail polish. Ritchie kept staring at the fish. They hung motionless in the burgundy water. He could see their tiny hearts. His own was clattering like a mechanical monkey. This wasn't anything like wrestling with Margie in the front seat of his car, or diddling the Anteater. This was an older *woman* he was alone with, and he had no idea how to proceed, what to say. He couldn't even remember how he'd gotten there. One minute he'd been cruising the strip in Mars's van, and the next he was in a fancy apartment building and Viv was taking him to an elevator, leading him by the hand.

He was seriously considering slipping out and thumbing a ride back to the Oasis when the bathroom door opened and Viv emerged, wearing a shower curtain. At least that's what it looked like to Ritchie. It was a clear plastic wrap with birds of paradise covering all the important places.

"How come you're still out here?" she said.

Ritchie shrugged. She'd unpinned her hair, he noticed, and it hung about her face like a scented curtain. Her calves were slim, surprisingly white and delicate. Her toenails were maroon.

She yawned and said, "You're not afraid of me, are you?"

"No, I'm not afraid of you." Ritchie set his jaw. He would've liked to see her expression, to find out if she was laughing at him, but he was afraid to look up.

"Good." She yawned again. "Make us both a drink, why don't you." She gestured again to that dark inner chamber. "I'll be waiting in here."

She disappeared into the bedroom while Ritchie woodenly got up and walked to the kitchenette bar to make the drinks. A bewildering series of bottles was lined up on the counter and Ritchie picked out two and splashed them together—he had no idea what they were. He reached into an ice bucket and dropped some cubes into the glasses and then he turned himself around and started toward the bedroom. His legs had turned to butter. The liquid in the glasses had turned green. He had the distinct sensation that two people were watching him: one was telling him to drop off the drinks and get the hell out of there, and the other was telling him to stay. Ritchie listened, wondering which voice was stronger, whose advice he ought to take.

The bedroom door was partially open. Ritchie knocked with his elbow, went in, and stood on the threshold for a moment, the drinks held tightly in his fists. A candle was burning on a bedside table, bathing the room in rose-colored light. Spider plants and ferns hung from the ceiling, and two enormous cabinets, the size of mummy crypts, stood on either side of the bed, which was doubled in the mirror hanging directly behind it. On the table next to the bed sat a pink Princess telephone, a half-dozen roses in a brass urn, and a ceramic Persian cat with the candle in one of its paws.

"Just put the drinks on the table, honey," Viv whispered. She was lying in bed with a satin sheet pulled up around her, smoking a cigarette and staring at the ceiling, one arm behind her head. Her leg moved indolently beneath the covers. Her expression was catlike, serene. She looked like someone in a movie, a leading lady, unreal and unapproachable, a figment of the imagination, a mirage. Ritchie walked in and glanced at himself in the mirror. He looked like a waiter or a bellboy, someone sent up by room service with complimentary drinks. He heard one of the voices again, a voice much like his own, telling him no way, he wasn't up for it. This wasn't his movie. He was just an extra, a bit player. He didn't belong.

He came over to the bed and put the drinks on the table, next to the ceramic cat. Viv watched the smoke from her cigarette curl up toward the ceiling while he stood there with his hands in his pockets, wondering what to say.

"Listen," he finally began. "I gotta get up early tomorrow. I told my old man—"

He never finished his exit line: at that moment Viv lifted her arm from behind her head and peeled back the sheet. She'd taken off the wrap and now lounged naked on the bed, her leg still moving in that slow indolent motion, her foot arched and pointed at his crotch. Ritchie stood as if held by a magnet and swallowed her with his eyes. Her skin was rosy, her body a wondrous terrain, filled with mysterious dunes and valleys. He stared at her so long he might've been a humble tourist gaping at the Pyramids.

She smiled at him and patted her leg. "What were you saying?"

"Nothing," Ritchie croaked. He heard that other voice talking to him now, a voice that sounded a lot like Mars's, urging him to hurry, but it didn't have to tell him twice: already he was peeling off his salami clothes and lurching toward the bed.

4

Vince the God told Ritchie that the most important thing about being a bartender—besides pouring a decent drink—was to always agree with the customer. If the customer said the Cubs were gonna be shit this year, then the Cubs were gonna be shit. If the customer said the market was going up, then the market was going up.

The God turned out to be an easy guy to get along with despite his rugged appearance. He stood six-three in his pirate bloomers and, even in his mid-thirties, still had the rangy muscled physique of a Big Ten defensive end, which in fact he'd been until some sneaky flanker from Wisconsin cracked back and clipped him on a sweep one fall afternoon and tore hell out of his kneecap. He had curly black hair and this little space between his front teeth that drove the ladies crazy. Ritchie figured that's why everyone called him the God—because he was built like a defensive end and drove the ladies crazy. Or maybe it was because whatever he said was the law back there, in the lounge. Ritchie didn't know. He never asked and Vince never told him. The God was the strong silent type; he didn't believe in a lot of extra yak behind the bar. He had a hump in his nose and a jagged scar in the corner of his left eye, and Ritchie never asked him how he got those, either.

What Ritchie really admired about the God—besides his smooth touch with a highball, that is—was his mustache. It was a thick black bushy job that occupied the entire space between his nose and his upper lip. He had one helluva 'stache going for himself, and he kept it tidy and well groomed too. He combed it regularly and trimmed it nice and neat, and he didn't allow any crumbs or other foreign objects to hang out in the dense bristly hairs. Ritchie didn't know how anybody else felt about it, but he just hated to see a guy going around with like half a grinder stuck to his face.

It seemed to Ritchie that maintaining a righteous mustache was a little like tending bar—all he had to do was keep his eye on Vince and he'd pick up valuable know-how. Of course, he couldn't begin to match the God whisker for whisker, but his own 'stache was coming along pretty well. Mars was the one who suggested Ritchie grow it. He said he looked too young to be tending bar in the lounge— he didn't want people coming up to him all the time and saying, Who's your new barman, Kermit the Frog?—and if Ritchie was really serious about working at the Oasis, he ought to consider doing something about his face.

"Can you grow a mustache?" he asked, appraising Ritchie down his nose one night.

"Of course I can grow a mustache. What do you think I am—a girl?"

"Then grow one," Mars said.

At first it hardly looked like anything, just a streak of fuzz above his lip, but after a week or so it slowly began to fill out and take the shape of a bona fide 'stache. Ritchie noted its progress with satisfaction, imagining what Big Joe would say if he knew about it. Big Joe would hate his new mustache. He didn't go for face hair of any sort. Once before, Ritchie had thought about growing a mustache and Big Joe had slapped a veto on the idea. Bad for business, he explained; he didn't want a shifty-looking grocer running his store at night.

He couldn't say squat about it now, however: Ritchie was a free man. He'd quit the store and moved in with Mars. That, too, had been Mars's idea. He lived in a three-bedroom villa in an exclusive singles complex about a mile from the Oasis which he shared with Fred, a big hairy tarantula whom Mars sometimes produced at parties, coming out with the giant spider poised on the top of his head or placing it furtively on the arm of a house guest for comic effect.

"Why don't you move in with me, Kohler?" he'd suggested at the club one night. "I got plenty of space."

"I don't know," Ritchie had said. It wasn't space he was worried about. He was worried about who might show up in the dead of night.

"You're thinking about money, aren't you?" Mars had said. His face took on a wounded cast. "Did you hear me say anything about money? Just now, did the word 'money' escape my lips?"

"No," Ritchie admitted.

"Quit worrying about it then." Mars flapped his arms, clearing the air of all petty details. "Just get your shit and haul it over, roomie." He flipped Ritchie a spare set of keys. "Here—use my van."

There were a couple of things Ritchie had to get used to when he moved in with Mars. One, of course, was Fred. Ritchie and the tarantula coexisted okay as long as Mars kept him in his cage; it was when he let the huge bug out to roam loose in the living room that Ritchie had a problem. But this was rare. Fred actually had a mission in life—to guard Mars's stash. He kept some of his reserves of weed and speed and coke and pills in Ziploc baggies in the tarantula's cage, his reasoning being that nobody wants to fuck with a big spider with hair on it. Ritchie personally couldn't argue with that.

The other thing Ritchie had to get used to was the mess, Mars being a slob of colossal proportions. Ritchie himself was no stickler for neatness, but liver sausage on the ceiling? The day he moved in, the whole place was cluttered with clothes, magazines, record jackets, beer bottles, wine bottles, unopened mail, and a wide assortment of drug paraphernalia, including a large octopus-like hookah sitting in the middle of the floor. Mars never bothered with any of it. He just left everything for the gang of Spanish-speaking cleaning ladies who came in every Monday.

"Doesn't the management ever give you a hard time?" Ritchie wondered.

"Nah. They know who I am." Mars thought a minute, working a few well-oiled hairs loose from the side of his head. "The only thing they asked me to do was try and hold down the destruction." He pointed to a splintered closet door that had been torn off its hinges and was leaning up against the wall; he was currently using it as a dart board. "They weren't too happy about that," he said.

"And they asked me to stop bowling. I told them I would, but I still
do it."

He did, too. Ritchie had seen him. He had a regular set of bowling
pins and, whenever he got the urge to roll a few lines, he would set
them up against the front door. Then he would clear a path in all
the clutter and stand in the kitchen and hurl a bowling ball across
the floor into the pins. It made a helluva racket. As far as Ritchie
knew, it was Mars's only athletic activity. He claimed he needed to
do it to release tension from all the hassles and bullshit at work.

So there were a few adjustments to be made, but what was a
spider and pizza on the walls compared to walking a poodle every
night and rubbing your grandmother's feet? What was the crash of
pins and a dozen or so plundered aquariums lying about when he
could do anything he pleased? He liked his new style, liked the new
Ritchie Kohler who was slowly emerging. For the first time in his
life, when he looked in the mirror, he respected the person he saw
there. What Mars said was true—a mustache did things for him.
It made him look older, tougher, more experienced and worldly wise.
He no longer saw the eager melon face of a grocery boy staring back
at him. He saw the mug of a confident individual, a dude of action
who knew what he wanted and was ready to make his place in the
world.

The God broke him in slow. For about a week all Ritchie did was
stand behind the bar in his pirate suit and watch Vince and the
other guy, Paulie, operate. A waiter by trade, Paulie was just filling
in—Vince was the guy Ritchie kept his eyes on. He was smooth
back there. He never measured a thing. Ritchie could see that he
had every drink known to man and how to make it filed away in
his head—he'd just dash a bunch of ingredients together, shake
them up, and pour out a perfect blend. For your simpler stuff, your
manly hootches, he'd just pass the bottle over the glass. He could
feel a shot in his fingertips—he never had to look.

Babs and Louise, the two harem girls, couldn't faze him. No
matter how bizarre the order, the God could turn it out, even if it
involved food. "A pink lady, two grasshoppers, and a Moscow mule,"
Louise might yell out in that husky voice of hers, sounding to Ritchie
like she was describing a quest, and he'd look at Vince and think,

no way; but about one minute later the God would have it all out on little paper doilies, ready to haul away. It was amazing. He was so slick and fast back there that sometimes he gave the impression he had two sets of arms, like there was another guy working with him inside his satin shirt.

He schooled Ritchie in the fundamental skills of the trade, your blending and mixing and shaking techniques. He drilled him on whiskeys, liqueurs, and brandies, showed him how to handle fruit. He also passed along some fine points in dealing with the public.

"It don't hurt to go a little heavy on that first round," the God told him. "Nobody likes to get stiffed right away in a joint. You give them a good legitimate belt for openers, it loosens them up, makes them happy, then they don't care if you go a little lighter later on. They drink more that way and don't even know the difference."

"What if a guy has too much?" Ritchie gestured at a bunch of hard cases draped over the bar, the wet sleeve guys with loose ties and sloppy hairdos who were in there every night.

"Them? You can give those clowns water after eleven. They're happy if you just wave the bottle under their nose. All they want to do is not go home."

"What if a guy gets rowdy?" Ritchie wondered.

"In here?" The God sniffed peevishly. "Not in my bar he don't. Any guy causes trouble I run his ass right out the door."

For a guy who didn't know his snifters from a hole in the ground Ritchie thought he caught on pretty fast. In no time he had your standard cocktails—your manhattans, your martinis, your margaritas and whiskey sours—down cold. For the more exotic concoctions he had a cheat sheet taped to a ledge behind the counter. If a customer got a wild hair for a truly rare highball, Ritchie would consult with Vince and the God'd show him what to do. The mirages were no problem—the God kept a healthy supply in big milkshake pitchers in a cooler back there, and they poured that stuff out by the gallon. Ritchie studied glasses, mixes, twists, and peels. He practiced, watching his hands in the mirror like an apprentice magician. One day the God tasted a batch of his piña coladas and gave the high sign. He was ready to tend bar.

Mars started him on a split shift—three to eleven. He said the happy hour crowd was a little tamer; he didn't want to put him in with the wild animals right away. Ritchie guessed he also had his own reasons for doing this: the lounge stayed open until two, and if he worked with the God until last call then who was Mars going to party with?

"What about Vince?" Ritchie wondered. "Won't he mind?"

"No problem. After eleven it usually thins out pretty good back there. Vince can handle it. And if he can't, fuck it. I'm the boss, right? I'll just move Paulie back in again." Ritchie scratched his head. That was Mars for you: no problem was hard if you had the right people to manipulate.

There was one advantage to starting at three—he didn't have to immediately stick on that silly costume. Dom the day man, a dignified old gent with the gnarled face and squashed nostrils of an ex-palooka, would've seemed ridiculous in a sash and pantaloons. He wore a bow tie and a red jacket, and that's what Ritchie wore for the happy hour crew. At six, he went into the kitchen and inhaled one of the specials—his only real meal of the day—and then he changed into his pirate drag and joined the God for the evening's fleshcapades.

They made a strange combination back there—Vince with his burly Big Ten body and his solemn expertise, and helter-skelter Ritchie, all arms and elbows, dancing a funky chicken over his drinks. The God found his chaotic style amusing, but Louise, the paranoid waitress, was not nearly so entertained. Ritchie had not forgotten their first encounter, when she'd practically strapped him to a polygraph before she'd serve him a drink—nor, clearly, had she: when she saw him standing behind the bar that first night, swimming inside his sea dog costume, she'd nearly fallen off her heels.

"What are you doing back there?" she squawked. "Don't tell me you're actually a *bartender*."

Ritchie modeled his shiny new rags. "I am now."

He managed to survive the first two weeks. Then he got his paycheck. He couldn't believe it. He showed it to Mars. He thought there was some mistake.

"Take a look at this check, will you?"

Mars glanced at it. "Seems okay to me. We got your name

right . . . and Nicky signed it." He fired it back. "I don't see nothing wrong with it."

"It's way too much," Ritchie said. "Check out the numbers, man. There's an extra three hundred smackolas in there."

Mars reached over and squeezed his face. "What a guy. A regular Abraham Lincoln we got here."

"Get serious, jerk. I don't want to be ripping anybody off."

"It's not a rip-off. It's a bonus."

"A bonus?"

"Sure. You jumped ship to come with us, so I paid you a bonus. It's a common practice in the entertainment industry. We do it all the time."

"So it's okay with Nick?"

"He signed the check, didn't he? Just don't spend it all in one place, moneybags—save some for partying."

He didn't spend it all in one place. He spent it all in about five places. He went bananas in a mall and bought a whole new wardrobe. No more K-Mart floods for this boy—he went for dark power trou with razor-sharp creases. He bought shirts made in Italy and shoes turned out by a Greek. Nothing he picked up that day didn't have a fancy foreign label inside it. Even his socks came from across the sea. At the House of Suits he bought a suit—a mellow charcoal job dripping with authority, like the kind Mars wore—and then he went next door and got a haircut, trading in his mop for the sleek, slicked-back look of a serious individual. The new Kohler even spruced up his car, running it through a wash-and-wax rinse and buying a new fur cover for the steering wheel.

Pretty soon he got into a routine. He'd sleep until two and then get up and cruise with Mars over to the Oasis. He'd put in his eight hours behind the bar and then, around eleven, Mars would come by and Ritchie would change into his party duds and they'd rogue it up until morning. Ritchie was never hurting for female companionship; he could always count on Mars to have something lined up. Stews, groupies, young chicks, older women, snow queens who could freeze your heart with one icy stare—it didn't matter; females just seemed to go for the guy. Ritchie had no idea what Mars's secret with women was—he was no trip to Hollywood and he sure didn't treat them nice—but whatever he had Ritchie wasn't about to argue with it. Just hanging around with Mars gave him instant credibility as a ladies' man. All he had to do was stand there and look like he knew what he was doing and pretty soon some tantalizing knock-out would be coming on to him like he was the Sheik.

They'd leave the Oasis together and hop in the van. Up front it would be Mars and some Kim or Heather; Ritchie'd ride in back with Megan or Beth. They'd hit the clubs on the airport strip and then go back to the apartment for some after-hours fun. Mars would bulldoze the mess from the previous night's party into a corner and crank up his supersonic stereo; then he'd go into Fred's cage and bring out the flake. It was amazing how the mere mention of the stuff would get the ladies all bright-eyed and jittery—they couldn't wait to get down on their hands and knees and vacuum it up. Mars also had a nose for toot, but as far as Ritchie was concerned, he couldn't get into it. Call him oversensitive, but he'd always had an aversion to putting anything but his finger up his beak.

After the flake had been put away, the ladies would usually start talking fast and laughing a lot, flashing a happy glow. Mars would take off like a rocket. He'd spring up and start ransacking his record collection for all his favorite hammer jams, or grab his darts and fire them into the door. Sometimes he'd be in the mood to bowl. Pretty soon he'd simmer down and get this sly look on his face and whisper something to his companion, and off they'd go into his bedroom, leaving Ritchie and his April or Suzanne to amuse themselves in any way they chose.

He couldn't get over it. For a North Side Catholic boy who had always considered getting laid about as momentous as setting foot on the moon—and nearly as difficult—he could not believe the ready supply of women who were now available to him. These weren't bowsers either, like the Anteater or some of those other beasts he and the rest of the guys used to take to the drive-in or the nearest patch of woods. It wasn't like he was trucking about town squiring the She Wolf of London. Far from it: these were women who had the kind of aloof, reckless, pouting faces and lithe figures he used to drool over in the fashion magazines, and who seemed to regard getting it on as no more significant than chowing down the number seven round steak platter at the local Tenderfoot restaurant.

"Why me?" he asked Mars one afternoon. He had just spent an

evening with a gorgeous Amazon, and it made him start to wonder. Mars had plenty of other friends to hang around with—wilder, slicker, and flashier guys than Ritchie would ever be—and he was wondering what he had ever done to deserve spending a night in the sack with a six-foot woman with little stars on her nips.

"It's simple," Mars said. "You're the only guy I know I can count on if the shit ever hits the fan."

One night, about a month after he'd started working at the Oasis, Ritchie experienced his first disturbance at the club. He'd just come off his nine-o'clock break and was cooking up a batch of strawberry margaritas for some sweeties at the end of the bar—one of whom, a slender redhead with braces on her teeth, had had her eye on him all night—when an incident developed in the lobby. Several fezed waiters, including Sal, the maître d', appeared to have cornered a rowdy person near the rest rooms; they were massed beneath the chandelier, and from time to time the whole group surged in unison, as though they were keeping a large escaped animal at bay.

Ritchie stopped pouring the drinks and glanced over, trying to see who was causing the ruckus out there, but his view was partially blocked by thick ferns hanging in the window and all he could make out were the tuxedoed backs of the waiters, who formed a solid wall against the lout. Probably some drunk, Ritchie thought, dissatisfied with the service, or a cutie who was trying to beat the check; even the Oasis was not immune from stiffs.

Ritchie shrugged and went back to the drinks. He'd finished the order and was ringing it up, winking above the register at the girl with the braces to let her know that hers was on the house, when Louise elbowed her way up to the bar and told Ritchie there was someone here to see him.

"Who?" Ritchie said.

"Him. Over there." She pointed to the doorway of the lounge, where a large man now stood in galoshes and an orange winter coat, the fur brim of his hat pulled low on his forehead and flaps over his ears, still flanked by several wary attendants.

Ritchie gaped. He couldn't believe it. Not only was his old man actually standing there, looming like a big orange ghost, but it was clearly he who'd created the disturbance in the lobby; even now he

was in the grasp of two of the fezed waiters, a mountain man in
the custody of secret Egyptian police.

"Well," Louise was saying, "do you know him or don't you?" She
peered at the outlandish figure in the doorway, noting the boots,
the coat, the Elmer Fudd headgear, and then glanced at Ritchie
again. She seemed convinced he was entirely capable of being hooked
up with such an idiot.

"Never saw him before," Ritchie said, staring at the floor. Louise
gave him a skeptical look and then hurried back to convey the
message while Ritchie eased out of view and hid behind the God.

When Big Joe saw the waitress coming toward him in that flimsy
sheer getup—he could see her underpants, for Christ's sake, it
embarrassed him to look—he thought at last he would get some
satisfaction; he'd received nothing but trouble ever since he walked
into the place, beginning with that oily jerk in the Shriner's hat
who'd stepped out from behind a lectern and accosted him as he
was about to crash the restaurant.

"Excuse me, sir," the man had said. "Do you have a reservation?"
He'd looked at Big Joe as though he thought this was doubtful.

"I'm not here to eat," Big Joe had said. "I'm here to see my son."

"Your son," the man said. He tapped the side of his face. "Does
your *son* have a reservation?"

"Of course not," Big Joe said.

"Then, if he doesn't have a reservation, he wouldn't be in the
restaurant, would he?" The man smiled patronizingly at Big Joe, as
if he'd just proved a point to an imbecile; at the same time, getting
a whiff of Big Joe's breath, he deftly motioned for other, nearby men
in fezes to come up and join him.

It was then, while he was trying to explain that his son *worked*
there in some capacity and more and more Shriners kept emerging
from the shadows, that Big Joe began to think he'd made a mistake
coming there at all. He hadn't planned on coming. He'd just been
sitting at the lodge, drinking shots and playing gin with Louie the
mailman, like he always did on Thursday. It was his normal routine.
The only difference tonight was that his store wasn't open—Big Joe
had been closing early ever since the kid had quit—and Louie was
beating his brains out. Big Joe couldn't keep his head in the game.

He tried to concentrate and read Louie's cards, but his mind kept wandering and his spirits kept sagging to the floor. He didn't know why he'd been feeling so depressed. It wasn't like the kid was still a baby. He was an adult now, with a mind of his own. He'd made his decision. Besides, it was the law of nature: sooner or later every bird had to leave the nest.

He'd tried to look at it that way, even to see it as a blessing—no more animals, no more screw-ups, no more dancing in the aisles—but he couldn't help feeling like he had unfinished business, like he'd quit the team while they were on the wrong end of the score.

And so he'd left the lodge and come to the Oasis, the ritziest club on the whole airport strip, the mobster house built on juice and shakedowns and murder money, and made a complete ass of himself. Even now, the Shriners had a grip on him, ready to give him the bum's rush, while the tall young woman in her underwear approached.

"What did he say?" Big Joe asked her. It was the first coherent sentence he'd uttered since he'd walked into the joint.

The waitress took a drag on her cigarette. "He said he's never seen you before."

Big Joe recoiled. This was low. This was the pits. Everything else he might forgive—the bad grades, the lousy attitude, the screw-ups in the store, even that little Chink car he'd had the audacity of buying—but to be denied by your own flesh and blood? This was the lowest. This was fourth and twenty from your own five yard line.

"He said that? He actually said he doesn't know me?" The waitress nodded. Big Joe felt a pain burn through his chest. Bracing himself, as if he were about to bolt into a cave full of hidden dangers, he abruptly broke free of the waiters and lurched into the lounge, the buckles on his overshoes jangling and his hat planted firmly on his head, vaguely aware that all eyes were on him, that conversations stopped while people glanced up to observe this curious phenomenon, staring in amazement as though a figure out of folklore had joined them, as if Paul Bunyan himself had suddenly appeared in their midst.

He pushed past the crowd massed in front of the bar, making way through all the hot shots in their expensive-looking suits, the dollies in their pearls and shiny blouses, and confronted the boy who used to bag his baloney and lose half his nickels when he pedaled back to the store. He felt terrible. He hadn't felt this bad since Knucklehead Ford pardoned his double-crossing crook of a buddy, Richard Weasel Nixon, who'd had the gall to personally disgrace Big Joe after he'd voted for the rat three times.

"What's the matter with you?" Big Joe said. Seeing him coming, the kid had stepped out from behind a huge bastard dressed in circus clothes and now stood cringing in embarrassment behind the bar. "Where do you get off, saying you don't know me like that?"

Ritchie waved off the waiters who had followed Big Joe into the lounge; then, leaning in toward his father's face, he muttered, "What are you *doing* here?"

"It's a free country, isn't it?" Big Joe placed his forearms on the counter. "Gimme a beer."

Ritchie sniffed Big Joe's breath, which came at him in a dense fermented haze. "You're drunk."

"I know it. Gimme a beer."

"What kind you want?"

"Hamms."

"We don't have Hamms."

"What kind you got, then?"

Ritchie started rattling off a long list of available beers, few of which Big Joe had ever heard of. He held up his hand. "I don't care. Bring me anything. Bring me a shot, too."

Ritchie reached back behind the bar for a Löwenbräu while Big Joe took off his hat and looked around. He noted the fancy drinks people were drinking, some with fruit and little pink umbrellas sticking out of them. He wasn't surprised. As soon as he'd walked in, he could see that this was the sort of place where they probably didn't put any prices on the menus and, when you went to the toilet, you might have to pay a guy to hand you a towel. The joint reeked with class. Pictures of celebrities were mounted on the tinted mirror behind the bar, and the bar itself seemed to be scented with something, a sharp spicy aroma that irritated the hair in Big Joe's nostrils. Immediately to his left, a guy with a white scarf dangling from his neck was giving him the eye. "What the hell are *you* looking at?" Big Joe said, and the guy quickly turned away.

Ritchie came over with the shot and the beer. He poured the beer into a tall skinny glass, like a vase you'd put flowers in; then he wiggled his fingers at Big Joe and said, "Four bucks."

"*How much?*"

"C'mon. You heard me."

Big Joe reached into his trousers and plunked four wrinkled bills down on the bar. "You got a telephone in this establishment?"

"Why? You want to call up Louie and get a card game going?"

"No. I was just wondering if you had a telephone, that's all."

"Of course we got a telephone. There's one right over there." He pointed to the cream-colored touchtone next to the register.

"Then why don't you use it once in a while?"

Ritchie sighed. "I been busy."

Big Joe grunted and took a gulp of beer. "How much do they pay you to dress up like that?" he said, wiping suds off his lip. The kid was wearing a ruffled satin shirt, a sash, and some sort of photo-electric knickers that bagged around his ankles. He was dressed just like that big bastard he was working with. They looked to Big Joe like an acrobat team.

"A lot," Ritchie said.

"What's that on your face?"

"A mustache—what does it look like?"

"It looks like hell, is what it looks like." Big Joe had never gone for mustaches. In his opinion, a mustache was the visible proof of a character defect. Villains wore mustaches, guys who sneaked around. It was as simple as this: a man with hair on his face had something to conceal.

"Sure," Big Joe continued, his voice getting louder, drawing looks from some nearby stews. "Grow a goddamn mustache. You're working for gangsters now, you might as well hide your face."

Ritchie shook his head. "Listen. I don't have time for this. Why don't you just hit the road?"

Big Joe settled back on a stool. "Nah. I think I'll sit here and drink some more. Hey, you." He called over to the guy with the white scarf around his neck. "You got a light?" Big Joe produced a Chesterfield and the guy with the scarf extended a flame, holding it as carefully in his fist as if he were bearing the Olympic torch.

"This is all right," Big Joe said, picking a little piece of tobacco out of his teeth. "I just might stay here a while."

"Fine," Ritchie said. "Stick around. Just try not to embarrass me anymore, okay?"

"What do you mean by that?"

"You know what I mean."

"No, I don't. Look, if you got something to say to me, say it."

Ritchie didn't say anything. He just gave Big Joe a long disgusted look, turned his back, and began walking away. Big Joe's face went as orange as his overcoat. He sprang out of the stool and leaned over the counter, capsizing his beer in the process. "Hey!" He was shouting now, drawing more looks from every direction. "Don't you walk away from me. Who the hell do you think you are to walk away from me like that?"

The God suddenly intervened. He'd been watching Big Joe for some time from the other end of the bar; when the beer went over, he ambled up, blotted the spill with a rag, and informed the old-timer it was time to leave.

"What?" Big Joe said hoarsely. "Are you throwing me out—is that what you're doing?"

"If you want," the God said, "I'll call you a cab."

The two former gridiron stars stared at one another a moment, the God's face solemn, impassive, Big Joe's flashing from orange to red. There was a time when he might've taken this whole thing outside, but he was too tired now, too drunk—and the sumbitch in front of him was as big as a freight car.

"I've been thrown out of better joints than this," Big Joe finally said, just so the guy would know who he was dealing with.

"I'm sure you have," the God said. "Can I show you to the door?"

"Never mind. I can find my own way out." Big Joe pushed himself away from the counter, placed his hat with dignity on the top of his head, and then seized his shot glass and inhaled the whiskey in one fiery gulp, something he hadn't done since the Cubs blew the pennant to the New York Asshole Mets in 1969, the lousy bums.

He marched out through the chandeliered lobby and past a door-man with a big scimitar hanging off his belt. As soon as the cold night air hit him, he listed badly, and nearly took a header off the curb. He was totally skunked. He hadn't been this loaded since the day Mayor Daley died. Even then, he wasn't as loaded as this. His head roared. His eyes were fuzzy. His heart was full of pain. For a moment he considered turning around, trudging on out to the boulevard, and lying down so that buses could run over him, but instead he took a leak against the side of the building and piled back into his car.

Inside the lounge, Ritchie tried to keep busy. He poured lots of drinks and chatted with the slender redhead; he wondered when she was going to get those wires off her teeth. Later, when it began to thin out and business got slow, he still found things to do. He cleaned out all the ashtrays. He dusted off some of the more obscure liqueur bottles on the back shelf. He watered some plants. The visit from his old man had put him in a terrible mood. He was bummed for a while, but then he got over it. He had a new family now. He had Mars. He had Vince the God and Dom the day man. He had Nicky too—although he rarely saw him. He even had Teddy Drake, the lounge's platinum-haired piano man.

"Tedward," he called out, with a fanfare of arms. "Music, if you please."

5

Fog was in the air, a dirty soup that clung to streetlamps and boiled up the sides of buildings. Ritchie watched the way it hung in car beams, coating the light in thick yellow webs. He was sitting in a back booth at Pete's, an all-night diner just down the street from the Oasis, waiting for the redhead with the braces on her teeth. They'd been getting very friendly, and tonight he'd told her to meet him there a little after eleven. It was now close to midnight, but he wasn't worried—she'd probably just gotten tied up with her friends. Eventually she'd show up, he had every confidence. Ever since he'd started working at the Oasis he hadn't been shot down once.

He sipped his coffee and looked around. The place was pretty crowded, as usual, with its night-owl clientele—cabbies, truckdrivers, some traveling salesmen staying in cheap motels at the end of the strip. A young couple had come in from the nearby Cinerama and now huddled close together on the same side of the table, playing footsies in a corner booth. Pete, the proprietor, a stocky middle-aged Greek, was taking counter orders and ringing people up at the register. His son, Pete Junior, had his sleeves rolled up at the grill. He was short and stocky and looked exactly like his pop.

The place smelled of onions and potatoes and fried greasy meats. Ritchie's stomach growled. He suddenly realized he was starving, and he called the waitress over—Pete's daughter, who was also short and stocky—and ordered everything on the breakfast side of the menu. He ordered eggs, bacon, waffles, pancakes. Why wait?— that's what he was thinking. When Julia arrived—he liked her name, it was different, sophisticated, a little old-fashioned, it seemed

like he'd been seeing girls with trendy soap-opera names for a month—
the food would already be there, waiting for her. He liked the idea
of sharing an intimate breakfast with a relative stranger at midnight.
It was all part of his smooth new style.

"Am I forgetting anything?"

The waitress went over her pad. "What about sausage? You want
an order of sausage too?"

"Definitely." He handed her the menu. "You got milkshakes here,
don't you?" Pete's daughter nodded. "Bring me a chocolate milkshake. And a couple of straws."

The waitress brought the milkshake first, and Ritchie slurped on
that until Pete's son could fill the rest of the order, which the waitress
carried over on a series of plates. Ritchie stared at all the steaming
dishes lined up in front of him—the eggs, the pancakes, the sau-
sages, all the rest. He'd eaten supper at the club at his usual time,
but lately he'd found that that meal wasn't holding him and he'd
sneak into the kitchen to get a snack. One good meal wasn't enough.
In fact, lately, two or three meals weren't enough. He'd been eating
constantly. Ever since he'd started working at the Oasis, it seemed
like he was hungry all the time.

He kept staring at the food and then suddenly he consolidated
everything onto the biggest plate he had, poured ketchup and maple
syrup over the whole works, and dug in. He couldn't wait. He had
to eat. When Julia arrived he'd just order more. A couple of cabbies,
having noted the remarkable parade of food that kept flowing past
them, swiveled around and started giving him looks from the counter.
Ritchie grinned back at them, moving his eyebrows up and down.
He was in a very congenial mood. He kept picturing Julia approach-
ing along the sidewalk, the collar of her trenchcoat flared about her
neck, red-haired and mysterious, her slender figure shrouded in
fog; saw himself as her worldly guide and protector, a cigarette
dangling from his lip Casablanca-style. He wondered if she was
from another country. She rarely spoke but had the mature, composed presence of someone who'd lived life and yet still was open
to new possibilities—that's why he'd selected Pete's. He liked her
hair, her eyes. He even liked her braces. He wiped Heinz off his
mustache with a napkin and pondered his opening line.

He'd polished off the eggs and was mowing through a thick stack of pancakes when, glancing out the window, he suddenly saw a woman materialize in the haze. Ritchie leaned over the plates, his pulse quickening, and watched her cross the street. She was heading for the diner—there was no doubt about that—but it was also clear she wasn't the one he was waiting for. The walk was all wrong, for one thing—the woman was coming at a rapid pace, leaning forward in a kind of angry shuffle—and she appeared to have a huge lizard strapped to her hip. Ritchie turned all the way around and watched her walk in, surprised to see that it was Louise, of all people, the dingy waitress, who clomped through the diner in a pair of tall leather boots and took a seat at the counter near the taxi jocks. She immediately reached into the enormous alligator handbag she was toting, snatched out her cigarettes, and lit up. Ritchie noticed that her hands were trembling.

"Coffee," she barked at Pete, turning her head to emit a dense stream of smoke. "Black."

Ritchie cleared his throat and made himself large, waiting for her to acknowledge him, but she just kept sitting on the stool, hunched forward and smoking viciously, staring straight ahead. He wondered why she wasn't still at the club; maybe it had gotten slow and Mars had given her a break and let her off early. Ordinarily he would've asked her to join him, but that was out of the question tonight. No doubt Julia would be arriving any minute and the last thing he wanted was to be sitting there with another woman when she came in.

Still, he had an impulse to make his presence felt, and he got up, walked over, and slapped a five on the counter. Money was no object; he was practically overflowing with generosity and goodwill.

"Get lost," Louise growled, without looking up.

Ritchie shrugged, scraped his bill off the counter, and started back to his booth. He hadn't taken more than two steps in that direction when suddenly he felt this heavy scaly thing whack into the back of his neck. It was like getting lashed by the tail of a giant reptile. It surprised him, knocked him off balance, and he turned around to see Louise coming at him with that big alligator bag, holding it high over her head and swinging it down at him. He dove for the booth and covered up.

"*You!*" she was shouting. "*Asshole! Jerk!*" She kept smacking

Ritchie on the arms and shoulders with that big heavy bag, giving him the brute. The cabbies had swiveled around again and were watching impassively. Pete's daughter was shaking her head. *"Bastard!"* Louise hollered, clobbering Ritchie with the purse again.

It took Pete about two seconds to get over there. He came bounding out from behind the register like a small fierce dog guarding its yard. His expression indicated that he'd seen everything at least once in life, and was not impressed. Pointing a finger at Louise, he muttered in a thickly accented voice, "You. Crazy lady with the purse. Stop."

"I'll knock his stupid teeth out," Louise was saying. "I'll break his stupid face." She reared back for another attack, but Pete caught her arms. Louise struggled briefly, then she relaxed and told Pete to get his hands off her. Pete stationed himself between the two combatants and finally turned her loose.

"All right," he said. "Calm down. Everybody take a deep breath."

"Scumbag!" Louise rushed up and spat at Ritchie.

"None of that," Pete said, wagging a finger. "No spitting in Pete's." He turned and looked at Ritchie, who was still dazed from the violence of his co-worker's attack. "What's going on?"

"Beats me," Ritchie said. "All I tried to do was buy her a cup of coffee. I don't think you should assassinate a guy for that."

"Liar!" Louise shouted. She addressed Pete as if he were a jury. "This guy's lying through his mustache. You want to know what's going on? I'll tell you what's going on. This fucking degenerate just got me fired."

"None of that either. Pete don't go for that toilet mouth in here," Pete said.

"Hold on," Ritchie said. "Back up a minute. I got you *fired?*"

"Yeah. Congratulations, slime. And I'll tell you something else. I'm getting even. I swear it. I'll come back with roaches. I'll bring gasoline. I swear to God I'll burn that fucking outhouse to the ground."

Pete signaled to his daughter. "Call the cops."

"Never mind, Pete," Ritchie said. "I'll handle this." He was still trying to figure it out. He couldn't believe what she was telling him. All he'd been doing was sitting there waiting for Julia and having a snack. How could he have gotten her fired?

"Sit down." He gestured to the vacant side of the booth. "Talk to me."

"What for?"

"Because I want to find out what happened, that's what for." He glanced up at Pete, who was standing there ready to jump in like a ref if they started going at it again. "It's all right. We're just going to sit here and talk a minute."

Pete gave them a long hard look. "Okay—but any funny business and I call the cops."

Ritchie was moving some of his plates aside, making a place for her. Louise kept glaring at him, muttering to herself. Finally she slid in and sat at the edge of the booth, her legs sticking out into the aisle.

"What about your coffee?" Ritchie said. "Coffee over here for the lady." He waved at the waitress, who was mopping up a spill on the counter. Over by the grill, Pete's kid was beating the shit out of a couple of hamburger patties with a spatula. The couple playing footsies had gotten up and left. Louise meanwhile was skeptically surveying the big plate of glop Ritchie had in front of him. It looked like something a madman might eat before he went to the electric chair.

"You hungry? You want any of this?" That goulash wasn't looking so good to him at the moment, either. He'd never gotten anyone fired before, and suddenly he'd completely lost his appetite. He held up the milkshake. "Sip?"

She looked at him in disbelief. "Gimme a break."

Pete's daughter brought the coffee over. Louise fumbled in her bag and got out her cigarettes again. Ritchie produced his lighter and held a flame out to her like a peace offering, but she turned her head and lit up with a match.

"Tell me what happened," Ritchie said.

Louise's mouth tightened and she blew smoke all over his food. "Where do you get off, asking me that? You know exactly what happened."

"I do?" Ritchie scratched his head.

"What gets me is that I knew it the first time she walked in. I took one look at her and I said, minor. Somebody get that child an infant seat. I mean, who was she kidding? A girl slaps on a couple of pounds of Max Factor and teases out her hair, she might be able to fool a few idiots"—Louise gave him a pointed look—"but she can't fool me. I ought to know a phony when I see one. I used to pull that stunt myself."

Ritchie was blinking through his own personal haze. "You mind telling me who you're talking about?"

"What do you mean, who? You know exactly who I'm talking about. Your little tootsie. The one with the braces."

"Julia?" Ritchie's eyebrows flew up.

Louise shot him another look and then stubbed out her cigarette on a side order of toast. "In the first place her name is Lori. In the second place, she's sixteen."

"Sixteen?"

Louise lit up again. "She doesn't even have a driver's license, you moron, and you're slipping her all those free mirages like she's the Queen of the Strip."

She paused and glanced up at the ceiling. A couple of rusty old fans were whirling up there, chopping the smoke and looking like they might come down any minute. The place had thinned out considerably. Over by the register, Pete kept glaring at Louise with dark grumpy eyes.

"The thing is," she continued, "it didn't matter. It wasn't *my* butt. She wasn't at *my* station. *I* didn't have to serve her drinks—until tonight." She turned quickly back to face Ritchie, her body tensing, and grabbed for her purse. Ritchie braced himself against the edge of the table. For a moment he thought she might be planning to pick up the handbag and beat hell out of him again, but she only reached inside it and got out her keys.

"I *warned* you, didn't I?" Louise was saying. "I told you she wasn't legit. But you got such eyes for this little cupcake you don't even listen. 'Don't worry,' you tell me. You say anything happens it's *your* responsibility. Your responsibility!" She laughed bitterly. "What a joke."

Ritchie was staring at his food. He couldn't stand to look at that big greasy plate anymore so he reached down and stuck it under the table. Now that he thought about it, she did seem a little young.

"Listen," he began. "She was supposed to meet me here, around eleven." He leaned forward and scratched his head again. "You wouldn't happen to know if she was still planning to come, would you?"

"To tell you the truth, I doubt it," Louise said. "But you'd have to ask her dad."

"Her dad?"

She nodded. "Big oafy-looking guy, just like your old man. Arms like a butcher. Guess what? He showed up at the club tonight right after you left and dragged his baby out of there, but not before he raised eighty kinds of hell. He threatened to sue us for corrupting a minor. He promised to bring the law down on us for ruining the character of little girls. You missed it, hot shot—it was quite a performance."

"Jesus," Ritchie said. "So what happened next?"

Louise gave him that bitter smile again. "It was very simple. The guy is still raising a stink in there, carrying on like Elliot Ness, and finally Mars, your guardian angel, crawls out from the hole he's been hiding in and tries to take charge. He and Dad have a private little chat in the kitchen, and a couple of minutes later Mars comes out and says, 'Okay. Who's been serving this girl drinks?' "

"Um," Ritchie said. "So that's how it happened."

"Right, Einstein. You're finally getting the picture." She sighed and raked a hand through her hair. "It's the same old story. Some idiot fucks up, and *I* get canned."

Ritchie frowned and looked out the window. The fog had mixed with drizzle. The red neon sign on the carry-out down the street looked like it was bleeding. Those huge airport landing lights were flashing a tension-headache blue.

"I'll talk to him," he finally said.

"Don't bother."

"No, I want to. I feel bad."

Louise was rattling her keys. They were on an enormous metal ring that looked like a handcuff. She must've had ten or eleven keys on that thing. Ritchie couldn't believe anyone could have that many doors to open, that many locks.

"Let me talk to him," he said again. Louise was now staring at the cut-rate motel across the street, its lurid green-and-purple sign winking in the rain. It was the sort of place for people who were hiding out or running away or doing things they didn't want anyone to know about and would be ashamed of later. "Hey," Ritchie said. "Are you listening? Do me a favor and just stay cool. Don't do anything until I've had a chance to straighten this out, okay?"

Louise hooked her handbag over her arm and suddenly pushed herself out of the booth. "You want to know how you can do me a favor? You really interested?" She opened her fist and fired some coins at his chest to pay for her coffee. "Just stay the hell out of my life."

He finally caught up with Mars at a place called the Imperial, an old movie theater that had been converted into a heavy metal pit. He'd been trying to sit down and have a talk with the guy, but lately Mars had been involved in some mysterious business dealings on the South Side and was always on the run. Still, Ritchie kept after him. It was important. He'd never gotten anyone fired before, and ever since it had happened he couldn't get rid of this contaminated feeling in the pit of his stomach, like a residue of scum at the bottom of a pan.

The street was deserted when Ritchie pulled up in front of the Imperial. Mars had said he had something he wanted to show him there, but his van was nowhere in sight. The place looked like it was closed. It was noon, but the sky was overcast, a solid gray curtain that blocked the light. It could've been any time at all. Ritchie sat in his car and looked at the sign above him. XX the lettering on the marquee said, *Fri Sat Nite.*

He sat there a while and smoked a cigarette, and then he got out and tried the doors. He found one that wasn't locked, pulled it open, and went in. Immediately the pounding sound of jungle drums, horns, and a funky fuzz-tone bass growled out at him from inside the auditorium, and for a moment Ritchie thought he was in the wrong building, in the wrong part of town—a feeling that was reinforced when he tiptoed through the deserted lobby, past the refreshment stand that had been converted into a bar, and peeked into the dimly lit interior.

Up on the stage, a whole bunch of black guys in outer-space getups were laying down some powerhouse funk inside the empty auditorium. There must've been a dozen brothers up there. There was a horn section, a drummer, a couple of other guys beating on stuff with their hands. There were guitars, bass, and a guy with a miniature keyboard strapped around his neck. Ritchie admired their fashions: glittery gold capes, white patent leather boots, and silver mesh body stockings with the letters MF slashing across the front like lightning bolts. And hats. All kinds of hats. Musketeer bonnets. Fezes. Tams. One of the horn players had on this thing that looked like a dunce cap. It was purple and had silver crescent moons running down the sides.

Ritchie stood there and watched this spectacle for a moment, totally floored. Whoever these brothers were, they were dynamite. The music was outstanding and so was the choreography. The horns were going up and down and side to side, the percussion section was hopping, the guitar players were funk-stepping across the front of the stage. The lead singer, a sinewy dude with a mop of dread-locks, pranced and pirouetted, singing all the while in a husky falsetto.

Way down at the front, off to the side of the stage, two men conferred in shadows. One was wearing a T-shirt and the other guy had on a mink coat. The guy in the mink *looked* like Mars—starting down an aisle, Ritchie could detect that gaunt coyote profile punc-tuated by a cig hanging off the lower lip—but what had him thrown was the haircut. Just the other day Mars was still wearing his hair slicked back Dracula style, but now his head was surrounded by the curly bubble of a perm. It was teased way out, electrified. It made him look like the Bride of Frankenstein. Ritchie had to wonder where the guy was getting his hair done—the House of Wax?

Mars spotted him coming and started in right away. "You been listening?" he shouted. "You been getting a load of my new sound? I been telling Tommy T here he is now enjoying the number-one act in the city. Name another band—my dudes will waste 'em. Show me another act—the Mighty Funkateers will blow 'em away."

Ritchie took a quick glance at Tommy. He was a short, sallow-faced man in his late thirties with fatigued eyes and thinning hair. He had a nice little pot going for himself under his T-shirt, which bore the name of a currently popular New Wave band. Evidently he ran the place, and from Tommy's dour expression Ritchie guessed he was not entirely sold on the Mighty Funkateers.

"Are these brothers terrif or what?" Mars hollered above the music.

"I been telling Tommy T if he books my boys in here they'll tear the house down. He'll have to keep the people under control with cattle devices." He turned his attention back to the stage and attempted to get in a groove with the beat, hunching his shoulders and lurching in a stiff, white-guy kind of way. "I watch these guys and I can't stand still. Check out those moves. Dig the message. No more of that negativity bullshit. Soul is what's happening, Kohler. Love is where it's at."

Mars kept wiggling around and snapping his fingers; he looked like he had to go to the toilet real bad. Up on stage, the Mighty Funkateers were winding down their number. "It's clear, is it not, that this is the genuine article, no? Talent? What we have here, gents, is nothing less than the new Earth, Wind and Fire."

When the band finished playing, Tommy T said he had to make a couple of phone calls and excused himself. Mars waved his arms at the Mighty Funkateers and told them to take five.

"Jerk-off," he muttered, gesturing with his head to the backstage area, where Tommy T had vanished. "He tells me he doesn't think the brothers'll go over here. He says he doesn't think this particular type of music will appeal to his clientele. Bigotry, that's what it is. Nothing short of racial prejudice. I hate that shit."

Ritchie glanced up at the stage, where the Mighty Funkateers were taking a break. They were smoking cigs, tuning their instruments. A couple of guys had taken off their hats. In the back, a percussionist had slipped on a pair of shades and was glugging a can of Bull he'd hidden behind his bongos.

"So, what do you think of my new do?" Mars said after they'd taken a couple of seats in a side row. Ritchie made a noncommittal movement of his shoulders. "I know, it takes a while to get used to, but I needed a change. I was tired of that Shock Theater look. I mean, who needs the hairs of cruelty? I'm not entirely satisfied with it, though." He reached up and mashed down the top of his hair with a fist; it immediately sprang back up, like foam rubber. "I'm thinking of going to the island look. Braids. What do you think, Kohler—would I be bad as a Rastaman or what?"

Ritchie grinned at the idea. *"That* I'd like to see."

"So what's your impression? You're a good judge of talent, Kohler; what's your opinion of my act?"

"Honestly?"

"Of course."

"I think they're dynamite. I don't know about those hats, though."

"Tell me about it." Mars wagged his nose. "I been trying to explain it to them about the hats. Here I lay out an extremely large investment for sharp outfits and they got to go out to State and Lake on me and get hats. For personal expression or something." He cupped a hand to his mouth and spoke confidentially. "That's one thing about dealing with these people—you got to put up with hats."

Ritchie shrugged. He didn't care to comment one way or the other on this observation.

"I love the music though," Mars continued. "I always used to think it was trash. I never had ears for that Zulu beat and a bunch of spear chuckers shouting and jumping up and down. I'm a white guy, right? I don't have no feel for Africa.

"Then, the other night, I'm over in soul town, doing some business with this brother I know? So we make our transaction and then the brother asks me if I feel like getting down. He says he knows this dynamite band and he wants me to ride over with him and check 'em out. I say, 'Brim'—that's the brother's name—'I really don't know if that's advisable.' I'm a little concerned about my whereabouts, dig. We're talking Stoney Island Avenue. Congoland. Where I am you got to go all the way to Indiana before you see another white man. But Brim, he like vouches for me, see. He says as long as I'm with him, I'm cool. You got to catch this brother, Kohler. He's only about five-eight, but solid, like the Merchandise Mart. Goes around in this Zorro hat. A dangerous individual, take my word for it. He can like kill with his vocal chords. Definitely a nasty bro." Mars nodded, testifying to the black man's badness. "So I decide, what the hell. Plus I'm wired. I'm wasted. I'm just fucked up enough to run this noise up the flagpole and see what happens."

"So you went ahead and checked it out."

"Fucking A. Brim's got his Seville parked out front so I hop in and go along for the ride. It's Brim and his lady up front, and I'm in back with like one of the Pointer sisters. We ride over to a gin mill near Jackson Park where this band is playing. So we go in and right away I'm thinking, Christ almighty Marszack, what have you walked into? Picture it, Kohler. The place is packed. Wall to wall color. Everyone all dressed up like it's the heavyweight championship of the world. I'm looking around. I'm praying to God to see another white person in there, but it's no dice—I'm the only Caucasian in the joint. You should've seen the looks these brothers give me when I walk in, Kohler. It was *chilling*, man. It was truly spooky. Brim's got a table reserved right up front and I stroll through the joint with all these evil eyes on me and I'm thinking, Marszack, you're in for it now."

"Sounds extremely hairy, Mars. If it was me, I gotta tell you, man—I'd of been looking for the back way out."

"There *was* no back way. So we go over to the table and order some drinks and wait for this band to show up. I'm figuring it's just gonna be another South Side shine act. Rhythm and blues. Or, worse, jazz. I hate jazz. I'm figuring on listening to one or two numbers, to be polite, and then getting my butt out of there. I'm sitting there with this big shit-eating grin on my face praying to God I can get back home alive."

Mars produced a pack of Kools from somewhere inside his mink coat and lit up under the big No Smoking sign. Tommy T had not reappeared and up on the stage the Mighty Funkateers were looking increasingly bored and restless. "So anyway we're sitting there and pretty soon this huge pack of brothers comes out and gets on stage and starts tuning their instruments. It's like a whole fucking *orchestra* up there, the Uganda Philharmonic. They set up and then they break into their opener and right away the place goes up for grabs. You should've seen it, Kohler. People are boogeying at the tables; they're going crazy on the dance floor; they're testifying in the aisles. I'm a show-biz veteran, right? I thought I'd seen everything, but I've never seen an act like this. I couldn't believe it. I'm listening to 'em for maybe five minutes, and I'm completely blown away!"

Mars paused and closed his eyes briefly, recapturing the moment. When he opened them again, they were filled with zeal, that born-again glint of a true believer. "I'm telling you, man, it was truly incredible. It was like a religious experience. I was inspired. I was fucking uplifted. I was filled with brotherhood and goodwill. I slapped hands. I gave away toots and money. I *danced*. Dig it, Kohler: I, Terry Marszack, actually went out onto the dance floor and wiggled

my ass around." He stared at Ritchie to see if he were fully com-
prehending this wonder, but Ritchie wasn't. No matter how hard
he tried, he couldn't picture Mars boogalooing in a club full of
brothers. It was like trying to imagine a square circle or something;
it did not compute.

"So you know what else I did? I bought the band." Mars held up
a power fist and said, "You are now looking at the chief fiduciary
officer, promoter, business manager, and clean-jumping soul brother
of the Mighty Funkateers."

Ritchie couldn't keep from chuckling. It was funny. Even Mars
seemed tickled by this improbable sequence of events. "I'm a changed
man, Kohler. Who needs all that hostility? Be mellow, roomie. Dig
it: Soul is the only way to go. Plus," he added out of the side of his
mouth, "your black entertainment dollar is greater than the white
buck on a per capita basis—and that's a fact, Jack. Now if I can
only talk some of these honky bigots like Tommy into booking my
dudes in their clubs—if I can make *that* crossover—there's no
telling how far we'll go. The sky's the limit, my man. I'm talking
tours, recording contracts—some day you may turn on the set and
see yours truly on American Bandstand!"

"Yeah, but will I know you? You're going for the look, right? How
do I know you won't go out and get yourself a different name?
Kareem Abdul Marszack . . . Terry X . . ."

"Nah. That name shit is out. I *am* taking dance lessons, though.
Some of the brothers in the band are teaching me moves." He
shuffled his feet, flapped his arms, bobbed his head up and down;
he looked like a guy with a serious motor control problem. "I don't
quite have the feel of it yet, but not bad for a white guy, huh? I
been watching and studying. It kills me the way those bros can
dance." He gestured toward the keyboard player, who was leaning
back against one of the amps. "You see that guy? Monroe? He can
dance better than me with a goddamn *piano* hanging around his
neck." Mars's countenance suddenly took on a bleak expression,
like the one he sometimes got when contemplating a truly unapproachable scam. "But I'm getting there," he added. "You give me
a couple more months and I'll be pushing Michael Jackson."

He paused and glanced irritably around. Tommy T had still not
reappeared. Up on stage the Mighty Funkateers were looking dis-

gusted and sullen. Monroe, the keyboard player, was catching forty against the amp. The horn section had broken out a deck of cards. Ritchie thought he could detect an undercurrent of hostility emanating from the black musicians, the possible beginnings of a mutiny in the ranks. What's this motherfucker still waiting on? they seemed to be thinking.

Mars checked his watch. "Do you believe this guy? Who does he think he is—Ed Sullivan? Five more minutes and I take my act elsewhere. This ain't the only club in town." He turned to Ritchie. "So—what did you want to talk to me about? I hope it doesn't have anything to do with money because if it does, man, I can't help you. I'm way overcommitted at the moment. I got no liquidity."

"Forget about money," Ritchie said. "This is about Louise."

Mars gave him a surprised look. "Haven't you heard? The bitch is history. I fired her the other night."

"I know. I heard all about it."

"It was a distasteful scene, Kohler. Very embarrassing. You may not know it, but there was a little girl in there. A baby. Couldn't have been a day over sixteen. So she's sitting in the lounge, getting sloshed, and *I* got to deal with an irate daddy." He pinched the bridge of his nose. "Shouldn't have happened, Kohler. I warned her about carelessness like that."

Ritchie had eeled around in his seat. "That's what I want to talk to you about. It wasn't her fault."

Mars lifted his eyebrows. "Whose fault was it then?"

"Mine. Louise was just an innocent bystander. I told her it was okay. It was *my* idea to serve the girl drinks."

Mars was studying him carefully now, as though he was suddenly not quite sure who he was dealing with. "So what are you saying here, roomie? What am I supposed to do, fire *you*?"

Ritchie sat back and blinked. "No, of course not. I just want you to give Louise her job back, that's all I'm saying. It's only right."

Mars shook his head. "No can do."

"Why not? It isn't fair, man. Like I told you, it wasn't her fault."

"I don't care whose fault it was. Look, I got a responsibility to the organization. A major fuck-up occurs, somebody's got to answer for it." He had assumed that smug self-righteous tone that never failed to irritate Ritchie. "Furthermore, I got a certain profile to maintain, you know what I'm saying? My reputation is at stake. I take this waitress back just because I got a soft spot, pretty soon I'm just another hamburger back there. People'll lose their respect."

Ritchie wrung his hands. That nasty feeling was bubbling up in the pit of his stomach again, like a bad Whopper he'd eaten for lunch. The dark auditorium suddenly seemed even darker, invaded by a thick gloom that obscured even the exit signs. "So you won't consider it, huh?"

"No way." Mars sat back and folded his arms across his chest, imitating a cliff. Abruptly he reached out and biffed Ritchie's shoulder, big-brother style. "Hey, what are you so worried about? She can always get another job, right?"

"Yeah." Ritchie's hands felt clammy and he wiped them on his pants. "I guess."

"Of course she can. Now, if you don't mind, I got more important things to worry about—like how I'm going to deal with *this* rude hard-on. I mean, who does he think he is to make me wait like this?"

Mars glanced at his watch again. Suddenly he stood up and clapped his hands to get the Mighty Funkateers' attention. "Okay, blood," he announced, his voice ringing through the cavernous auditorium. "Let's pack it up. We're splitting. Meet you at McDonald's, brothers. McRibs on me."

6

A museum of losers—that's what the bus station reminded Louise of. A subterranean assembly hall for the down-and-out, the star-crossed, the desperate and luckless with no place else to go. The last stop at the end of the road.

She sat in the cafeteria, smoking a cigarette and watching that parade of losers go by—servicemen and winos, indigent women toting babies, senior citizens with shopping bags and confused raisin faces, seedy guys reconnoitering for love. Threadbare individuals with cardboard luggage slept in plastic chairs in the waiting area; some fed quarters into the TV machines. Across the way a bunch of teenagers were goosing the video games, which emitted strange electronic beeps and gurgles and flashed their nasty colors into that dingy underworld light. A greasy white pimp in a plantation hat hung loose by the telephones, waiting for the next Hound from Iowa to come in; ten feet away, a security cop slouched at the baggage counter and shot the breeze with a clerk. Above it all, the PA system kept broadcasting garbled information, intoning departures and arrivals no one could understand.

Louise took two Anacin and checked the time. She had that big alligator handbag packed on the seat beside her, but she wasn't waiting for a bus. She wasn't dressed for highway adventure. Wearing a purple knit pullover with a scooped neckline and tight black leather slacks tucked, dominatrix style, into her boots, gold chains and hoops, her blond Oasis hair cascading to her shoulders, Louise was dressed for a different sort of cruise. Her friend Terri had said it was all taken care of—just slip the rent-a-cop twenty and he'd

look the other way—but her date was late and she wondered if
there'd been a fuck-up, if Terri had neglected to remind him or he'd
forgotten the place. Once before Louise had done this and the guy
hadn't shown up at all, but that didn't surprise her. If there was
one thing she'd learned about men it was when you needed them
most they were never around.

Look for Mister Whipple—that's what Terri told her. She said he
looked just like the guy in the toilet paper ad. Sweet, considerate,
pushing sixty, he'd have a room reserved in a nearby hotel, some
hors d'oeuvres and bubbly, a bit of small talk, and then he'd spill
his heart out and maybe cry in her arms. Dress butch, Terri reminded her; every so often he liked to be dealt with firmly and told
what a bad little fellow he was, which he wasn't, just a lonely old
widower who liked to pick up pretty young strangers in bus stations
every now and then. Easiest two fifty she'd ever make in her life,
Terri told her. Usually he didn't even want to get laid.

Okay, Louise thought, so where was the old rooster? She was
paying a baby-sitter and didn't have all night. She looked out into
the lobby again. A black guy with a steel brush in his head bopped
by. A young pregnant woman with stringy blond hair was feeding
crackers to a two-year-old. Louise kept her eyes on the greasy pimp.
He reminded her of the guy who'd greeted her in this very station
when she first hit town many years ago, just eighteen, from a small
burg in Indiana, with eleven dollars, a toothbrush, and a can of
mace in her jeans. She'd always heard that the city was a cold
unfriendly place, but she didn't find it that way at all; on the contrary, it seemed to be crawling with solicitous individuals who were
eager to help an attractive young girl who'd just wandered in from
the sticks—starting with a thin pockmarked mulatto in a mohair
coat who moved in on her with an offer of guidance and free ac-
commodations the minute she stepped off the bus.

Louise told the mohair to fuck off. Despite her innocent expression she was no Pollyanna. She knew the score. She might've been
a small-town Hoosier, but she'd already had an excellent education
in human behavior provided by her mother Lennie, and Lennie's
older sister Lucille. It had been just the three of them sharing a
trailer on the outskirts of Michigan City—there wasn't any Pop. The
only thing Louise knew about her father was that his name was

Howie and he worked for the railroad and had a profile like Alan Ladd. Evidently the profile was what had caught Lennie's attention: Alan Ladd was still big back then.

The way Louise understood it, Howie and Lennie got together in his Studebaker one night and the next month Lennie was late. Howie had promised her love and devotion etc., but when Lennie went to the train yard to tell him the news, she learned that Howie was no longer around. He'd taken the choo-choo west, they said, to the coast, with the idea of breaking into pictures as a stunt man; he'd always had a talent for falling down. If she wanted to see Howie she should watch for him in the latest Paramount releases. She did, too. From then on, every time Lennie saw Alan Ladd fall off a horse on television she'd grab Louise's hand and say, "Look, honey—there's your dad!"

Lennie worked in a pesticide plant on 421 while Aunt Lucille took care of Louise. She was too delicate for work. She had asthma and brittle bones. Lennie drank a lot, but not Lucille; she didn't approve. She was a lady. She wrote poetry and listened to the Texaco opera show on the radio on Sunday nights. She wanted Louise to be a little lady too and dressed her in ribbons and pinafores. She read poetry to her and made her walk around with a book on her head. She also made her take piano lessons, which Louise didn't mind; she liked music, plus it was a way to get out of the trailer. But as far as that lady stuff was concerned—forget it. Poetry was for wimps and she wasn't about to walk around all afternoon with the collected works of Edna St. Something-or-Other balanced on her noggin.

Lennie, meanwhile, had boyfriends. Lots of boyfriends. Railroad guys with names like Jake and Skeeter stitched above the pockets of their locomotive suits. Sometimes Lennie went out at night and didn't come home. Sometimes, when Lucille was at a revival meeting praying for the sick and speaking in tongues—she'd gotten the Lord after He cured her of her asthma one night, appearing to her in the dizzying camphor fumes above her bed in the guise of a gigantic healing moth—Lennie would bring a railroad fella home with her and they'd have a trailer party. Louise didn't care for these railroad guys but she didn't begrudge Lennie her fun. She was a teenager then and knew what life was all about.

One night, inevitably, things got out of hand; curses emanated from Lennie's bedroom and then a man came out sans his overalls. He had a big Adam's apple and a bottle of rye. It seemed that Lennie had passed out on him at an inopportune time, leaving him with a neck hickey and a full head of steam. He saw Lennie's girl watching TV all alone on the sofa and decided to cozy up with the idea of introducing her to his boiler. Louise tried to explain to him that she wasn't interested; the railroad man tried to persuade her that she was. They debated the issue on the sofa for a while, and then the man pushed her down and got on top of her. Louise learned an important lesson about love that night; all you had to do was lie very still and pretend to be elsewhere, and it would be over in a minute.

On the day she turned eighteen, Louise taped a note for Lennie on a bottle of Wild Irish Rose and rode the Hound to the Windy City. For the first couple of days, while she got her bearings, she slept on the subway, keeping one eye open for the predators who roamed at night. She drank from water fountains and ate crackers out of machines. In case of emergency, she always had the mace.

Eventually she got a job waiting tables in a Wells Street hash house and ran into a gay street mime in Lincoln Park who offered her a place to crash. He also introduced her to other free spirits—poets, musicians, magicians, street artists who entertained on downtown corners and made their living passing hats. The mime asked her if she could carry a tune and Louise said sure and he hooked her up with a blues trio who played every day in the park. From there she went to saloons and coffee houses—any place where they had a piano and needed a person to make pleasant background noise. She'd do forty minutes and then wait tables and then do a stint at the piano again. She wouldn't dance and she wouldn't wear lewd costumes—if they wanted that they could get someone else. She wasn't looking for a big break, either. A few bucks in her pocket—that's all she wanted—and a decent roof over her head.

Then one night she was discovered. She was singing in a Clark Street dive called Torchy's when a slick-looking stranger walked in. Louise noticed him right away. He didn't resemble the rest of the burnouts in there. He was wearing an expensive Italian leather jacket and had a real nice haircut—it was obvious he spent a lot of time on himself. He took a table right up front and started watching Louise, smoking long brown cigarettes and drinking Perrier. Louise noticed that too, and the way he kept staring at her with a coolly appraising look, like she was something on exhibit he thought about buying.

As soon as she finished her set, he came right up to her and said, "My name's Pierce Davis. Let's talk."

"About what?" Louise said.

"About your future."

"My future."

Pierce Davis nodded. "You got potential, baby. I got opportunity. I think we can work something out."

She had a break coming so she decided it wouldn't hurt to sit down and have a drink with this hot dog and listen to what he had to say. The first thing he said was being discovered by Pierce Davis was the luckiest night of her life. Oh really, Louise said—why's that? Because you got talent, Pierce Davis said. Pierce Davis knew talent. He had it himself—having been a musician of mucho talent before he decided to focus on the entrepreneurial end of the business. He said he had a talent for that, too. He had mucho contacts in the industry, he told her, and was, at that very moment, in the process of assembling a monster band composed of the best talent in the city. He was talking state-of-the-art here, top of the line. A recording contract was a distinct possibility, he hinted, synched with a ten-city Midwest tour as an opener for Tina Turner. Everything was mellow except for the lead singer—and that's where Louise came in.

"I must've been in fifty dumps like this, looking for someone," Pierce Davis told her. "You're it, baby. You're the best I've heard."

Louise almost laughed out loud at this. She wasn't stupid. She knew when she was being hustled. Still, there was something about Mister Big Talk that made her keep listening. He had that sharp jacket and that slick way of expressing himself—plus he had these eyes. They were freaky green and had a way of seeing right through you. They reminded her of the way a cat can stare and stare at you until you think it knows exactly what you're thinking and pretty soon you aren't sure who's in charge anymore—you or the damn cat.

"So what's the story here, doll?" Pierce Davis finally asked her. "You ready for the big time or you want to keep singing in toilets the rest of your life?"

Louise told him thanks for the offer, maybe she'd give it some thought. Pierce Davis immediately got a disappointed look in his eyes. He had a talent for that too, Louise was to discover. Getting his feelings hurt. He could be terrifically sensitive when he wanted to be.

"What do you think," he protested. "You think I'm trying to shack up with you or something? You think *that's* what this is all about?" Louise told him the thought had crossed her mind. Pierce Davis shook his head and flashed that wounded look again, like he was crushed she would even entertain the possibility. "Trust, baby," he went on. "In this business trust is everything. Without trust you don't have squat. Look at what happened to the Beatles," he pointed out.

Louise had another drink with Pierce Davis and decided to take a flyer—she figured she didn't have much to lose. He waited for her to get off work that night and then drove her to his apartment. He had recording facilities there, he told her; it was strictly business—he needed to get a demo of her voice. Those recording facilities he'd mentioned consisted of a cheap Sony which he had her hum into while he accompanied her on the guitar. Their relationship remained strictly business for about an hour—which was as long as it took Pierce Davis to green-eye Louise out of her pants. Trust, he reminded her when she told him that this hadn't been part of the deal; without that, a relationship wasn't worth a nickel.

She lived with him for almost three years, and the closest she ever got to the big time was when he finagled a couple of backstage passes to a Grateful Dead concert at the Horizon. The band, the recording contract, the ten-city Midwest tour—none of that ever materialized. Sure, every once in a while there was talk of getting an act together, but Pierce always ixnayed the deal. The drummer was an ego tripper, he'd complain; the bass player's fuzz tone got on his nerves. He hailed from a family of rich ninnies in Glencoe who were willing to underwrite his career; when that source finally went dry, they lived on whatever Louise could scare up waitressing and playing coffee houses. She'd put in fourteen-hour days while

Pierce remained in their two-room flat beside the el tracks, writing incoherent song lyrics on sheets of toilet paper and noodling on his guitar. It seemed that everyone they knew was some type of creative genius. They hung around with poets and dancers, and musicians who were reinventing the saxophone. Artists too. Lots of conceptual artists. People who worked exclusively with linoleum, that sort of thing.

Louise was never really sure why she kept staying with Pierce Davis. Maybe she just needed to believe his lies. Finally it was Pierce himself who broke off the relationship. He said this crummy town was smothering him—he had to go somewhere he could breathe. The coast, he said—that's where the action was—and then he split for LA to become a major recording artist while Louise stayed behind. She pleaded to go with him, but he insisted on hacking it alone. "Too rough," he said. "Trust me, baby. I'll call the minute something breaks for us."

So she did. She trusted him. She trusted Pierce Davis and waited for his call right up until the time she checked herself into Cook County Hospital to have his child.

The voice on the PA was babbling again and suddenly there was a flurry of activity in the waiting area. People got up and grabbed their shopping bags and funny-looking suitcases and started shuffling over to one of the gates to stand in line. Louise wondered where all the losers were going. She watched them through the grime-streaked window, seeing a faint reflection of her own face superimposed on the glass.

Mister Whipple was now forty minutes late, but there was nothing she could do about it; she'd just have to sit there and wait for him to show up. She lit another cigarette and ran a hand down the back of her neck, reflecting on the fact that she'd been waiting for men who needed to be forgiven all her life. When she was little she used to sit by the window for hours and wait for Howie her dad to appear, visualizing him riding into the trailer park on a big white horse, like Shane, and sweeping her up and taking her to the mountains and the wide-open spaces. Then, years later, when she was in labor, all alone and out of her mind with pain, she kept waiting for Pierce Davis to rush into the delivery room in a surgeon's mask and take

charge in there—he'd always claimed he would personally deliver
their kid. He knew when she was due and had promised to be with
her, but he never showed his face. Afterward, while she was re-
cuperating in the hospital, she tried calling him a bunch of times,
but all she ever got was a stupid recording: "Pierce Davis isn't in
right now. He's busy being a major recording artist. Please leave
your message at the tone." She left him a message, all right. She
said, "In case you're interested, you've got a son, you sonuvabitch."

Eventually he did get back to her, a few days after she left the
hospital. Louise couldn't believe what he was calling about: the
child's name. After all he'd put her through, he still had the nerve
to insist on providing a name for the baby, and a fucked-up name
at that—Garcia. "Garcia!" Louise said and Pierce Davis said sure,
after Jerry Garcia, you know, from the Dead. Louise told him to get
bent, she wasn't naming any kid of hers Garcia. Pierce Davis said,
"Okay—what about Pierce, then?" and Louise told him not a chance,
she wasn't naming him after a slimeball either.

Joey—that's what she wound up naming him. Joseph Gallenko.
No middle name. She didn't know any man she respected enough
for that and so she decided to save it in case she ever did run into
somebody. But this was looking more and more doubtful. Maybe
someday, when the boy was old enough, he could pick one out for
himself.

He was seven now, growing up fast. Already he was in second
grade. That was something she'd been thinking a lot about lately—
Joey's education. She'd been checking out schools in the suburbs
and seeing what they offered. A nice private school would be ideal,
but she knew she'd have a hard time swinging that, especially now,
when she was hurting for cash. But maybe someday. She wanted
Joey to get a good education. She wanted him to have a future, and
not grow up to be an ignoramus, like his mom.

At first it seemed like he was going to look like his father, but
now he was beginning to look more and more like her. He was tall
and slender, just like she was, and he had her eyes. He was smart
too. Everyone said so, including her best friend, Jessie, who took
care of Joey when Louise was at work. She had a boy too, Dexter,
who was just about Joey's age, and she was always telling Louise
about some sharp observation Joey had made or showing her some-

thing the two kids had built—a wooden magazine rack, an artificial heart carved out of a melon, a cardboard bungalow for Zeus, Dexter's dog. That was the thing about Joey—he was a builder. He always went around with a little rubber hammer hanging on his hip. Lately he'd developed an interest in how everything in the world worked and was continually tinkering with Louise's hair dryer, or crawling under the kitchen sink to investigate the pipes.

"You don't have to worry about what he's got upstairs," Jessie would say, slinging her long dark braid around. "Believe me, honey— that kid's sharp as a tack."

Thank God for Jessie, Louise thought. Like Terri, she used to be a wigged-out woman of the street before she got her act together, and now she had a real nice thing going, baby-sitting five or six kids in the neighborhood and selling her needlework to some of the local shops. And, unlike the slimeball—who in all these years had never called or visited or even sent a fucking nickel even though the guy was doing all right for himself from what she gathered, managing some all-chick band on the coast called the Tease—Jessie had always been there for her, reassuring her when she would worry herself sick about Joey's nutrition—it seemed like the kid would go for months living exclusively on a diet of Froot Loops and Oreos— or stay up late at night imagining that he had dire diseases, rare maladies they have special drives for.

She didn't do that anymore. She observed his good teeth and sturdy limbs and no longer worried about him dying from a lack of zinc, no longer saw a dreaded germ in every one of his coughs and sneezes or bolted up in the middle of the night to see if he were still alive. She was a more confident mom now, and a good one too, she believed. It was the only thing that really mattered to her—that she be a good mother to Joey. It was more important now than ever given that she was about the only family he had. The pesticides and the drinks had finally caught up with Lennie—she was slowly pickled and Black Flagged to death—and that left only her crazy sister, Aunt Lucille. Lucille wouldn't mind getting her hooks into Joey, Louise knew, but she wasn't about to let that happen any more than she would turn her child over to his slimeball of a father, or to Howie, the snake of the West.

One lucky break—that's all she needed. One ray of sunshine and she'd be back on her feet again. Maybe, if it were bright enough, she could get out of that stinking city altogether and take Joey to the mountains and the wide-open spaces, where everything was clean and safe. Maybe she could even set up a little business for herself like Jessie had. Why not? Okay, so she wasn't the smartest cookie on the block, but she had willpower. She could do it. Watch kids, sell some of her sketches—something nice and wholesome like that. No more Mister Whipples. No more hipster geniuses. No more idiot bartenders who corrupted babies and got you canned.

Her friend Terri was wrong. The man didn't look like Mister Whipple. Louise thought he looked like Captain Kangaroo.

He was standing in the gift shop, partially concealed behind a rack of paperbacks and peering across the lobby into the cafeteria, where Louise still sat. He was wearing a gray trenchcoat—Louise wasn't surprised—and an Alpine hat with a little yellow feather in the band. Louise could see the feather sticking up above the paperbacks. The only other people in the cafeteria were an elderly couple eating something with gravy all over it and a guy in a baseball jacket who was at the table behind her, passed out face-down on a *Trib*. Still, the man seemed to be looking for some sort of signal. Louise lifted up a thin braceleted arm and patted the back of her head. The man watched her and then disappeared behind the rack again.

He bought something small in the gift shop—breath mints, maybe— and then edged across the lobby and stepped into the cafeteria. He glanced furtively around and then came over to her table and sat across from her, a lugubrious frown on his jowly face.

"I'm late," he said. "Please forgive me."

"That's okay."

"I got lost in traffic." The man thought a moment, drumming his fingers on the table. "No, that isn't true. I didn't get lost. I just wasn't sure I wanted to come."

Louise shrugged and lit a cigarette. She didn't know her next line so she decided to keep her mouth shut and let the old guy do the talking.

"I don't know why I make these arrangements," he was saying. "I keep doing it, but I know it's wrong."

"No, it isn't," Louise ventured. She had a lot of time invested in this codger, and badly needed the dough.

"Sure it is. Look at me. Sitting here, in the bus station of all places, talking to someone I don't even know." The man glanced piteously at his reflection, and stroked his mustache. "A man my age, doing this—it's ridiculous. I shouldn't be here, not at all."

"Listen," Louise said. "You're here already, right? Why not make the best of it? I got an idea—let's just the two of us go somewhere nice and talk."

"You mean that?" He peeked at her. "You'd really like to talk to me?"

"Absolutely. That's what I'm here for."

The old guy's face grew downcast again. "Of course. You're only willing to talk to me because I'll pay you to—that's the only reason." He stuck out his lip.

"That's not true," Louise added quickly. "I'm always willing to listen. Just think of me as a friend."

The man seemed to be comforted by this. He popped a breath mint in his mouth. "By the way, my name's Gordon," he said.

"Pleased to meet you, Gordon. I'm Mary Anne." She felt greatly relieved suddenly. This wasn't going to be difficult, not at all. The guy was old enough to be a grandpa—it would be like spending a few hours at the home.

"Listen, Gordie, now that we're properly acquainted, shouldn't we go?" She grabbed her purse.

"Not yet." Gordon reached out and patted her hand. His own was as soft and fleshy as a baby's. "I want to tell you something about myself first—just so you'll know the type of individual you're dealing with."

"Okay." She sighed and sat back in her chair, stifling a yawn. She'd told Jessie two or two-thirty; she didn't have this kind of time.

The old guy, Gordon, smiled and took off his hat. He had about twenty-five hairs left, which he combed straight across the top of his head. His scalp was shiny, very clean. He began talking, telling her things, intimate things about his life, while Louise sat there and pretended to listen. Every so often she glanced out into the lobby to see what was going on. A thin, dark-complected man who fit the general description of a terrorist was stuffing something

wrapped in newspapers into one of the lockers. Another man stumbled out of the rest room gripping his head. The pimp in the plantation hat was yanking a handle on the candy machine. The escalators
kept going up and down.

". . . and then, when she got sick, I didn't even have the decency
to visit her in the hospital," Gordon was saying. "I'd drive over and
spend maybe five minutes with her and then tell her I had to go."

"Nobody's perfect," Louise said.

She lit another cigarette and glanced back out into the lobby.
Gordon kept talking. Suddenly she saw something on the escalator
that nearly made her fall out of her chair. She stared, stupefied, at
a strangely garbed figure who had bolted into the station, observed
him as he scrambled down the slow-moving stairs and hit the floor
running. He stood in the middle of the lobby for a moment, looking
around wildly, and then his glance penetrated the cafeteria and he
shot up his arm and waved.

". . . and then, right when she was dying . . ."

"Jesus Christ," Louise muttered. "I don't believe it."

He was making his way over now, pushing through a big clump
of people who'd just stepped off a bus. The idiot had obviously
hustled here directly from the club because he was still decked out
in the picaresque regalia he worked in—blousy satin shirt, pantaloons, and that ridiculous red sash wound around his middle. He
looked like someone out of a swashbuckler opus, the half-pint side-
kick who can't even hold up his sword.

He darted in, flushed and puffing. "Thank God I caught you
before you left town."

"What are you talking about?" Louise said. "I'm not leaving town."
She narrowed her eyes. "How did you find me here, by the way?"

"I called your apartment and a woman told me you were already
at the bus station." Ritchie frowned and looked her over, noting
especially the heavy rouge on her cheekbones and the super-tight
leather slacks. Come to think of it, she wasn't dressed like any
Greyhound passenger he'd ever seen.

"If you're not leaving town, what the hell are you doing here,
then?"

"None of your business, nozzlehead." She turned her attention back to her client, who was immobilized in the chair, like a cripple, his legs dangling helplessly on the floor. "C'mon, Gordo—we're outta here." She got up and grabbed the back of his chair and began shaking it, trying to get him to move.

Suddenly Ritchie seized her arm. "Hang on a minute. We need to talk."

"About what?"

"About your *life,* that's what." Irritated, he frisked himself for his smokes. "Listen, I gotta be honest. When I talked to him and explained what happened the other night, he didn't seem too interested . . . but let me work on him some more. I can't promise anything, but I think we still got a shot."

Louise was looking out beyond the baggage counter to the boarding gates, where a couple of buses squatted on the pavement like huge silver bugs; one had its motor running and she could smell the diesel fumes, taste them in her mouth. "How can I make this clear to you? I don't want you to talk to him for me. I don't want you to do anything for me. I want you to go away."

"But I came all the way over here to see you."

"Look." She regarded him as though he were some new type of pest they hadn't yet found a spray for. "You want to make amends for what happened the other night. You feel bad about it. Okay. I understand. You want to know how you can help? Seriously?"

Ritchie nodded.

She moved closer, as if to whisper: "You can *stay the fuck out of my life!*"

Ritchie winced; his ear had temporarily shorted out and he pounded the side of his head to rewire the connection. Louise meanwhile had hooked her alligator bag over her arm and was clomping through the lobby. At first Ritchie thought she was leaving the terminal entirely, but she was only headed for the powder room; he and the geezer with the mustache and the funny hat sat at the table and watched her slice through the ticket line and bam open the rest room door.

"She's still mad at me," Ritchie finally said.

The old guy nodded. "I can see that." He was staring at Ritchie in confusion, nervously rubbing his hands. "Um, what role do you play in this, sir—if I may ask? Boyfriend? Irate husband?" He regarded Ritchie's clothing. "Gypsy half-brother, hot blooded, quick-tempered, fiercely possessive of your womenfolk?"

"This?" Ritchie gestured at his blazing shirt. "This doesn't mean anything, chief. I'm just a bartender. They make me wear this stuff at work."

The old guy paused and thought a moment. "A bartender."

"That's right."

"Then, in a sense, you're paid to listen to people, aren't you?"

"I guess. But mostly I let Vince handle that department. I just make the drinks." He looked irritably in the direction of the ladies' room. They had important things to talk about and he wondered if she were planning to stay in there all night.

"Pardon me?" Ritchie said. The old guy was mumbling again.

"I *said*, I suppose it all started when I was a child." The man spoke solemnly, but there was a mechanical quality in his tone, as though a tape recorder were running inside his head. "I have a brother, a few years younger than me. Once, when we were kids, I was supposed to leave a key for him in the mailbox. He was playing ball. I was home alone. I went to a friend's house next door and I didn't leave the key. I took it with me. It started raining. Positively pouring. My brother came home. He ran up the front steps and reached into the mailbox for the key, but of course it wasn't there. *I* had it. I watched him from my friend's window with the key *right in my hand.*"

Ritchie shrugged. "That's nothing. Listen to *this*. Once, I threw a dart at my brother. Stuck it right in his leg. He *deserved* it, the son of a bitch."

The old guy's face became agitated, deeply troubled. For a moment Ritchie thought he might start to cry. "Please listen. You don't understand. I walked out on my mother. I never loved my wife. Thirty years we lived together and it was like two strangers in the same house. And then, right at the end, when she was dying—"

"Look, mister." Ritchie sat back, reclaiming his personal space. He had no idea where the geeze was going with this line of yak. Furthermore, there was something about the guy that had been bothering him, and he finally realized what it was: the guy's mustache. It looked almost exactly like his own and made them seem related in some obscure way. "I don't want to be rude, but I'm really not interested in hearing this at the moment. I got a lot on my mind."

The man pursed his mouth, the hair above his lip bunching like a caterpillar. "You mean you're not part of the . . . arrangement?"

"What arrangement?"

The old man suddenly became indignant. He seized his hat. "I don't have to stand for this, sir. A deal was made. Please tell your friend I find the situation totally unacceptable. Good night." He got up from the table, jammed his hat on his head, and left.

Ritchie watched the small rumpled figure march through the lobby, ride up the escalator, and disappear through the heavy glass doors. He still had no idea what the old guy had wanted, or how he'd offended him, but then again he wasn't surprised. The bus station was full of strange rangers, damaged individuals who'd fallen through the cracks. You never knew what you'd run into. You sit around minding your own business and pretty soon you're listening to some doorknob's whole life story: it was just like being at work.

Louise, Ritchie noticed, had finally come out of the toilet and was talking to someone on one of the pay phones. Her back was turned but Ritchie guessed she was in the middle of a tedious argument; every so often her shoulders would slump and she'd flap her hand in the air.

It looked like she was going to be on the horn for a while, so Ritchie got up, grabbed a food tray off the counter, and started going through the cafeteria line. He selected the mystery meat special, and then added two coffees and a couple of pieces of coconut cream pie. He paid the register attendant—a tall, lanky woman with saffron hair and a big mole on her cheek—grabbed a bunch of ketchup packets off the condiment rack, and then hauled his tray back over to the table and prepared to dig in. His stomach was howling. It seemed like he hadn't eaten for weeks.

He was squeezing a big glob of ketchup onto the mystery meat when Louise came back over, tossed her bag on the table, and pitched herself wearily into a chair. She'd redone her makeup, coated her face with powder and rouge. She looked like she was wearing a mask.

"They can't find his lizard," she announced, rubbing her eyes.

"Pardon me?"

"Joey's got this stuffed lizard, okay? Sleeps with it every night. Won't go to bed without it. Now it's lost somewhere, my friend Jessie's turning the apartment upside down, but she can't find it, and Joey's throwing a fit. I tell him, 'Sleep with the raccoon tonight. Can't you, just this one time, sleep with the raccoon?' Joey says, 'I don't *want* to sleep with the raccoon. I want my lizard.' " She pushed two large shiny bracelets back up on her wrists. "I'm telling you, man: kids."

Ritchie looked over at her. "You got a kid?" For some reason he'd never thought about Louise having a kid. She didn't seem the type.

"Yes, I have a kid. Something weird about that?" Her eyes scanned the area. "Where's Gordo?"

"You mean the old guy?" Ritchie buttered a roll. "He just split."

"What!" Louise jumped up and began looking desperately about the terminal. "You're crazy. He's got to be here somewhere. I'll have him paged."

"Didn't you hear me? I just told you, he left a couple of minutes ago, while you were on the phone."

"Why? Did he say where he was going? Details, idiot." She pounded the table with her fist.

Ritchie put down the roll. "Look, all I know is that one minute the guy's sitting there, talking at me, and the next minute he's bent out of shape. He keeps wanting to know if I'm part of some arrangement. 'What arrangement?' I said."

Louise slumped over and laid her head on the table, like she was offering it to an ax.

"You got to be careful who you talk to in places like this," Ritchie admonished her. "I think the guy has serious problems." He took a bite out of the roll. "What were you doing sitting with the old coot anyway?"

Louise was rummaging in her handbag for smokes, her hands pecking like hungry birds. "Never mind. You wouldn't understand."

"Sure I would."

She paused and glanced up at him with a morbid grin. "He was my *date*."

"Your date?"

"That's right, dimwit. We were on our way to a hotel room. Just the two of us—you get the picture?"

Ritchie chewed slower and slower, and then he stopped chewing entirely; he felt like he had little bits of cardboard in his teeth. "Wait a minute. Let me get this straight. You and the geezer. In a hotel room. For money. Is that what you're telling me?"

"Sure. What else?"

Ritchie shivered; it felt like something hairy had crawled up his neck. "Jesus, Louise. That's awful. How could you even consider doing something like that?"

"What do you think—I was going to *marry* him? Grow up. It's a simple business transaction. We go there, we talk a while, I tell him what a bad little rascal he is and put him to bed. That's it. I probably don't even have to diddle him—that's how easy it is—and then you barge in here and fuck everything up, as usual." She bit savagely at a fingernail.

Ritchie, meanwhile, was taking the whole thing in. He sat back with his arms folded across his chest. "That's disgusting, Louise. Shacking up in a hotel room with some dirty old stranger—how can you say that isn't the pits?"

Louise stopped chewing her finger and thought a minute. "It doesn't have to be a stranger." Suddenly she leaned toward him, a crafty look in her eyes. "What about you, for instance?"

"What about me?"

"You wouldn't mind sleeping with me, right? Okay. I'll sleep with you for two hundred dollars."

Ritchie swallowed and slumped in his chair. "C'mon, Louise . . ."

"What's the matter? You a fag or something? You want to sleep with me or don't you?"

"Jesus, Louise. For Christ's sake . . ."

"It'd be worth it, man, believe me." She was leaning across the table and whispering in a low husky voice. "I guarantee you would have a real good time."

Ritchie didn't want to hear any more, so he picked up his knife and fork and stared at the mystery meat. It was dark brown, almost black, with a thin border of greenish-looking fat around the edges. He guessed it was Swiss steak. Louise had dropped that phony harlot act and was staring out into the lobby, where the pimp in the plantation hat was chatting amiably with a young blond girl in a denim jacket who'd gotten off the bus.

Ritchie cut a piece of meat and placed it cautiously in his mouth. Louise had turned back to watch him.

"Something wrong?"

"How can you eat at a time like this?"

"I'm hungry." He chewed the meat. It didn't taste like Swiss steak. It tasted tangier, like something wild that had been run over.

"My life is falling apart and you're feeding your face."

"C'mon, Louise. Your life isn't falling apart."

"It isn't, huh? I don't have a job. I don't have any money." She reached behind her, to the table where the guy in the baseball jacket was still passed out, and snatched part of his newspaper. She held it up, showing Ritchie the date. "Check it out, man. It's the tenth already."

"So?"

"So I haven't paid my rent. My goddamn landlord is going to throw us out in the street."

Ritchie shook his head. "No, he isn't. He just can't throw you out into the street. He's got to give you notice before he throws you out."

"He already has, shit-for-brains. 'One more time, Gallenko'—that's what he told me. 'One more time and you're gone.' "

She balanced her chin on her fist and stared out into the lobby again. At the baggage counter, the pimp and the blond girl were waiting in line. Ritchie had given up on the mystery meat special and was sizing up the pie, wondering if he could eat it. He knew he had to eat something to stop the gnawing, but he also knew it probably wouldn't make any difference. His stomach felt like a deep bottomless well; no matter what he put into it lately it never seemed to fill.

"Here." He took a couple of plates off the tray and plunked them down in front of her. "I got you some coffee and a piece of pie."

She slid them right back. "Don't talk to me. I don't want you to ever talk to me again, okay?"

Ritchie frowned. He picked up his fork and started jabbing it into the pie, punching little holes in it. Louise kept staring into the lobby.

The pimp and the blond girl had disappeared into the city, but most of the same people were still there. Some were coming and some were going. Some were just killing time.

Ritchie took a sip of coffee and rolled the bitter liquid over his tongue. His conscience had started bothering him again, getting right up in his face and poking a finger at him, like a jerk at a party who won't leave you alone.

"How much is it?" he finally said. Louise looked at him. "Your landlord—how much is he gouging you for?"

"Five and a quarter."

Ritchie took another sip of coffee and thought some more. Then, to his astonishment, he heard himself say, "I'll pick it up."

Louise laughed in his face. "Get serious. You're not paying my rent. It's completely out of the question."

"Why? I got you into this mess, didn't I? It makes sense. You need money and I've got money. When you're on your feet you can pay me back."

Louise looked at him again, this time with a funny little smile on her face, like he was a riddle she couldn't quite figure out. "Listen to Saint Francis here. What do you think I am, a charity case? Forget it, jerk. I pay my own freight—any way I can."

"I'm not going to start arguing with you about *that* again," Ritchie said. "Listen, do yourself a favor and think it over. In the meantime, here—eat your pie."

He shoved the plate toward her again and she surprised him by picking up a fork and actually cutting out a tiny wedge. Ritchie did likewise with his. They sat there a little longer in the Greyhound cafeteria, decked out in their funny costumes, eating their pie and occasionally glaring at one another like two people on a bad blind date, all dressed up and no place to go.

7

Louise lived in an old gray stone apartment house on the North Side, not far from Loyola. The building had a tired, top-heavy posture. Dried-up ivy clung to the walls. There was a drugstore on one side of it and a laundromat on the other. Across the street, the big green-and-red sign of a 7-Eleven glared against the sooty evening sky.

Ritchie went into the building, found Louise's name on the mailboxes, and buzzed her apartment; then he waited in the foyer for a moment with a small goldfish bowl poised in the crook of his arm. The goldfish was for her kid, Joey. At first, when he stopped at a department store to buy a present for him, he hadn't been thinking fish. He was thinking more along the lines of a stuffed animal, or Mister Potatohead.

But then, when he glanced across the aisle into the small pet department, he quickly changed his mind. He'd always had an attachment to goldfish. When he was a kid he used to win several every year at the annual parish carnival by lobbing Ping-Pong balls into an array of bowls set up on a card table. It was just like pitching pennies. He'd go up to the goldfish booth, get his three chances for a dollar, assume his well-balanced, flex-legged stance, and let the ball roll off his fingertips. He was a winner every time.

The clerk covered the fishbowl with a piece of plastic and then Ritchie paid him and headed for Louise's. He wasn't sure why he'd stopped to buy a present, but then he didn't know why he had agreed to baby-sit for him in the first place. He didn't have to—he'd paid his dues. As far as he was concerned, his conscience was clean.

Furthermore, he was no baby-sitter. He'd never baby-sat for anyone in his entire life. He didn't even like kids.

"Baby-sit?" he'd said when Louise called him up at the Oasis one afternoon. "You gotta be kidding."

Louise said she had an audition lined up that weekend at a neighborhood club, her regular baby-sitter was going to be out of town, and now she was desperate to get somebody. She said did he think she would even consider asking a meatball like him to baby-sit if she wasn't desperate?

Ritchie made a harsh sound at the back of his throat. "What night?"

"Sunday."

"Sunday! Sunday's my day off."

"I know it," Louise said. "That's why I'm asking."

"I can't Sunday," Ritchie said. "I got a date." It was something Mars had had cooking for quite a while. A couple of Oriental girls he'd spotted coming out of the airport one day. Stews with Singapore Airlines or something. They only came to town once a month. Oriental chicks, Kohler! Mars had said, gripping Ritchie's arm. Schooled in the love arts. Trained to serve. Master and slave girl. He wasn't sure but he thought they also might be twins. "No way," Ritchie said to Louise. "It's completely out of the question."

"Okay," Louise said. "Suit yourself. I'll just have to cancel. I guess you don't want your money, huh?" She was referring, Ritchie knew, to the large sum he'd loaned her in another inexplicable moment of weakness.

Ritchie took the receiver away from his ear and glared at it. He smacked it against the top of his head. *Oriental* girls. Dedicated to please. Unfathomable positions. "All right, goddammit," he finally said. "What time?"

"Eight o'clock. Don't forget, Einstein, and don't be late."

She buzzed him up and then greeted him on the second floor landing dressed all in black—black leotard top, black skirt, black mesh stockings. Ritchie had to wonder where she was getting her clothes— Beatniks Anonymous? For the first time he saw her without her blond Oasis wig. Her real hair was relatively short. It was dark, like her eyes, and wavy. Together with the clothes, it gave her a gloomy and aggrieved appearance. She looked like a skinny refugee from some faraway war-torn land.

She was glancing curiously at the fishbowl he carried up the flight of moldy stairs. "What did you do—bring your pet?"

Ritchie frowned. "This is for the kid." Suddenly he wished he hadn't brought a goldfish; it was seeming more and more to him like a bad idea, like a feeble attempt to bribe the child. He hid the bowl behind his back. "Where's the audition?"

"Little joint over on Devon. Mostly college kids. Eighty different kinds of burgers and peanut shells all over the floor. The guy asked me if I can do Madonna and I said sure and he said come on over and he'd give a listen." She shrugged and glanced indifferently down the stairwell.

"Are you feeling all right?" Ritchie said. She looked to him like she wasn't feeling very well. She seemed flushed and sweaty, like she was running a fever. The hair about her temples was damp. Her voice, he'd noticed, sounded huskier than usual.

"I feel okay. Just a little nervous, I guess."

Ritchie put his hand on her forehead. "You're hot."

She immediately jerked away. "Don't touch me. Where do you get off, touching me like that?"

"Open your mouth."

"Why?"

"I want to see your tongue."

She defended this organ by pursing her lips and clenching her jaws tight. "You're not seeing my tongue," she muttered. "My tongue is none of your business, dig?"

"How's this in here?" He probed the glands in his neck. "Are you glands swollen?"

"Your brain is swollen." She moved aside and held the door open for him. "Hurry up and get in here, will you? I'm running late."

Louise wasn't much of a housekeeper—Ritchie could tell that right away. Her apartment was small and cluttered, with odd-looking secondhand furniture scattered here and there. If Margie Glotz lived in the ideal sitcom house, then Louise lived inside a garage sale. The main piece of furniture in the living room was a decrepit-looking sofa mounted on cinderblocks with a big trunk in front of it that served as a coffee table. On the trunk sat a candle burning in an empty wine bottle and giving off a scent like church, like the incense they fling around at Benediction. Next to that was an ashtray the size of a hubcap; it was so full you'd have thought somebody had been cremated in there. A series of sketches covered the peeling wall: a child, a handsome Indian-like woman with a long braid of hair, a thin gloomy-looking woman standing on a pier and staring at a frozen lake. Ritchie glanced at all the dirty dishes that were piled up in the kitchen. He spotted a large green stain on the counter that seemed like it might be alive.

"Nice digs." He felt right at home in this mess. "Where's the kid?"

"In his room. C'mon, I'll introduce you."

She led him down a hallway to a partially closed bedroom door, from behind which issued gruff threats and piercing battle noises. She knocked once and opened the door. Peering in, Ritchie observed a serious-looking dark-haired boy of about seven wearing floppy tennis shoes, cords, and a purple-and-white Thundercats T-shirt. He was sprawled on the floor with a couple of GI Joes, who appeared to be systematically bayoneting each other in the eye.

"This is Kohler, honey—the guy I was telling you about?" The boy glanced up once, without expression, and then continued playing with his army men. Louise turned to Ritchie and said, "Go in and talk to him—I gotta finish getting ready."

She hurried off into the bathroom while Ritchie stood in the doorway a moment, holding the fishbowl awkwardly in front of him with both hands, like a prom favor. "Mind if I come in?" The youngster glanced up again and Ritchie took a good look at him. His resemblance to his momma was striking. He had her features and her coloring, her dark expressive eyes. The kinship was evident right down to the hostile look he trained on Ritchie, which, like a derringer, was no less threatening transmitted in a miniature edition.

"So what's up?" Ritchie chirped. "I see you got some GI Joe action going here. A-one. I used to have a couple of those dudes myself." This was true. He'd gotten in on the GI Joe craze right at the end of his own boyhood and used to haul those giants out at the end of a big battle of rubber battalions, sort of like his own version of thermonuclear escalation.

The youngster didn't respond to this overture so Ritchie switched gears. He scooted down on the floor and, putting the goldfish bowl between them, said, "Look. I brought you a fish."

Joey turned and sneered at the bowl, as though Ritchie had set a stinking pile of dogshit down next to him. "A goldfish. How queer is that?"

"It's not so queer once you give him a name."

"Get serious. You don't name a fish."

"Sure you do. I used to name all my fish." This also was true—but he didn't know why he'd bothered. They never lived very long. Like two weeks. He'd kept them in his room, on some spread-out newspapers at the foot of his bed, and one by one they'd started bellying up on him. Dave was the last to go. Or was it Tony? Maybe he forgot to feed them or maybe he fed them too much—he couldn't remember. Or maybe his big brother had something to do with it. It was possible. He'd always hated Ritchie's fish.

"How about Dave?" Ritchie said. "Dave is a good name for a fish, don't you think? Or Tony—that's good too."

Joey turned away and shook his head, as if he'd just encountered the biggest fool on the entire planet. Ritchie shrugged and moved the fishbowl aside. "Okay. You can name him later." He picked up an armored personnel carrier and began gliding it rapidly across the carpet.

Joey reached out and snatched it away.

"Hey, I thought we were going to play together tonight," Ritchie squawked. "I thought we were going to have fun." Acting on a strange impulse, he moved in a little closer and threw his arm around the boy, almost like a dad. "What do you say, kiddo? Can we be pals?"

Joey moved out from under him and gave him an answer, the first language he'd addressed directly to Ritchie's face: "Eat shit and die, banana-head."

Moments later, Ritchie was knocking stuff around inside Louise's refrigerator, looking for something decent to eat, when she stepped into the kitchen. "Don't you have any hamburger or anything?" The only meat he'd found in there was a ten-pack of Oscar Mayer wieners, which he'd removed and placed on the counter beside a stack of dirty dishes.

Louise was staring at him in amazement. She had picked up the package of hot dogs and was holding it against her head like an all-beef compress. "You should see a doctor about your appetite," she said earnestly. "I think there's something seriously wrong with you." She slid the franks back into the fridge.

Ritchie meanwhile had opened her freezer, which was layered with ice three inches thick. "Here we go. Fudgesicles, Louise. Nature's perfect food." He reached in and seized one of the frozen treats.

"Sure," Louise was saying. "Make yourself right at home. How did it go, by the way—with Joey."

"Not real good." He had ripped the paper off the Fudgesicle and spoke with a chocolate tongue. "To be perfectly honest, I think the kid hates my guts."

"That's how he always is at first. Don't worry about it—he just doesn't take very well to men."

I wonder where he gets that from? Ritchie thought, then he said, "He's kind of rude, don't you think? Maybe he needs a little discipline."

Louise shot him a tight-lipped look. "Don't you dare try anything while I'm gone—I'm warning you, Kohler."

"Relax. Don't worry about it. All I'm gonna do is sit around and watch television and eat."

Louise continued to glare at him. She had put on her blond Oasis wig and was sporting lots of eye makeup. Ritchie decided he preferred her in short hair and without all that paint, but either way she still didn't do anything for him; she wasn't his type. Now an exotic tomato from the Far East—that was another matter entirely.

"You touch one hair on his head and you'll pay, Conan," Louise was saying. "I don't go for any of that physical stuff."

"Of course not," Ritchie said. "What do you think I am—a monster?"

At that moment Joey's door opened and the youngster came out and tiptoed to the edge of the living room. He carried a large stuffed yellow lizard in one hand and a toy rifle in the other; moreover, as if this weren't threatening enough, his face was totally concealed behind a savagely grimacing plastic werewolf mask.

"Behave yourself, honey," Louise crooned. "I'll be home as soon as I can."

She went over and gave him a peck on the top of his head. Then she got her coat out of the closet and headed for the door, pausing to wrench her alligator handbag off the sofa. Ritchie braced himself and took a step back. He'd grown to fear that scaly thing.

"Here's the number if anything comes up." She handed him a scrap of paper. "I shouldn't be gone long."

"Take your time. No problem."

"He usually goes to bed around nine-thirty. If he wants a snack, there's apples in the fridge."

"Got it."

She stood there fidgeting a moment, trying to think if there was anything else. "No rough-housing and nothing violent on television. Be firm—but nothing physical, understand?"

"I said don't worry about it, okay?" He escorted her to the door. "Have fun. Break a leg." She glared at him again on her way out. "It's a *saying,* for Christ's sake." He frowned and shut the door behind her.

When he turned around he saw that Joey had disappeared. Searching the apartment, he finally found the lad lying in ambush in the hall closet, the tip of his toy rifle sticking out between a couple of coats.

"So," Ritchie said loudly. "It looks like it's just you and me, huh pardner?" He clapped his hands. The sound rang through the hallway like a pistol shot. He couldn't believe what he was doing, standing there in a strange apartment and talking to a boy hidden in a bunch of coats.

"Hello in there," he began uncertainly. "You want to do something with your big buddy Kohler here? You feel like—"

Before Ritchie could finish, Joey thrust out the stuffed lizard and, holding its large triangular head upright, muttered in the manner of a ventriloquist, "Tell it to Mister Slime."

"I don't want to tell it to Mister Slime," Ritchie said. "I'm talking to you. In the first place, come out of that closet."

The coats parted and Joey emerged. He stood cautiously in the closet doorway and fidgeted his leg, like at any moment he was going to make a break for his bedroom. He was still wearing that ridiculous dime-store wolf face. Focusing on the fierce dark eyes peering back intently through the slits in the mask, Ritchie said, "You got a football? You feel like playing some football or something?" They didn't have to go outside; he figured if the kid had a football they could fool around with it right there in the apartment. He remembered how Big Joe used to do that with his brother sometimes, when Joe Junior was a kid. Big Joe would clear the furniture aside. Then he'd get down on his knees and he and Joey would go at it for a while, Joey lugging the ball and trying to get past him into the dining room for a touchdown.

"We could clear out some of this furniture and play right here," Ritchie continued. "What do you say?"

Joey didn't say anything, just gave a barely perceptible shake of his head.

"Don't like football, huh?"

"No," the youngster said.

Ritchie thought, That's cool. Football was violent. Kids could get hurt, develop unsportsmanlike attitudes. He was in charge here—he had to consider stuff like that. He remembered that when Big Joe and his brother played, Joe Junior hardly ever made it to the dining room. After ten or fifteen minutes he'd invariably start crying and Big Joe would start yelling at him for being a baby and Hilda would fly out from the kitchen and bawl both of them out. In retrospect, the whole thing didn't seem like a very healthy experience.

"Okay, we'll skip football," Ritchie said. He looked around and spotted a stack of Louise's records propped up against the stereo. "How about listening to some music? I'll bet your mom has some pretty good records we could listen to." She was a musician and he was her kid, right? He figured maybe the youngster had music in his blood.

Joey didn't even bother giving this idea an answer. He just stuck his toy rifle out into the hall, like a divining rod, and began following it, edging a little closer to his room.

"Don't go too much for music, huh?" Even as Ritchie said this he was thinking, Use your noodle, Kohler: How many seven-year-olds listen to Lena Horne? "Okay, we'll skip music. Maybe there's something good on TV." He went over to the set, a small black-and-white portable, snatched the *TV Guide* off the top of it and brought it back with him, but Joey had already scampered off and disappeared into his bedroom, leaving Ritchie standing there like a door-to-door salesman, a peddler of unwanted merchandise—vacuum cleaners, kitchen gizmos, apocalyptic religious pamphlets proclaiming the end of the world.

Ritchie thought, Well, I tried. He'd given it his best shot and the kid had rejected him. So be it. The only reason he was there at all, he reminded himself, was to make sure Joey didn't set fire to the building or fall out a window and break his neck—it didn't say anywhere that he actually had to *entertain* the little snot.

Having given himself this pep talk, Ritchie went back into the kitchen and opened up the fridge again. Louise had a couple of Old Styles in there and Ritchie started to reach for one, but then he thought better of it: he was on duty here and probably ought to steer clear of brew. Instead he got another fudge bar out of the freezer, went out into the living room, and switched on the TV, which sat on a little stand in the corner of the room. He began twisting the channel selector rapidly back and forth, searching for something he could stand to look at. He was hoping there might be a good creature feature on Channel 32 but there wasn't—only a boring talk show hosted by an obnoxious local TV personality. He kept flipping the dial but all he could come up with was a Bob Hope special on one of the networks, a George Burns movie on another, and a documentary about China on the public station. He hardly ever watched educational TV—it was way too much like school—but he left it on anyway and sat down on the cinderblock sofa and licked moodily on his Fudgesicle, wondering how long Louise would be gone.

Sitting in that dark quiet room, Ritchie suddenly began to realize how loud it was in the apartment building; it seemed like other people's noise was coming at him from all directions. Someone in the apartment below was listening to one of those twenty-four-hour religious stations—he could hear the radio preacher's voice rising like hot air through the vents. Above him the thump thump thump of heavy metal music pounded on his head. Down the hall, a man and a woman were shouting at each other while a baby methodically cried. It was—all of this racket—your typical metropolitan babble, a Windy City lullaby. Ritchie tried to tune it out and concentrate on the China program. It showed the Wall, it showed the fishing ports, it showed all these Chinamen wearing the same kind of suit and riding around on bicycles. Ritchie figured there had to be a couple of billion bicycles in that nation. They had bicycles up the ass.

He kept watching, but then the program abruptly made him think about the Oriental foxes he'd passed up that night—total abandon, undreamt-of delight—and he ground his teeth and jumped up and quickly turned the dial, switching back to the talk show hosted by the obnoxious local TV guy. It was the type of show where people could call in anonymously and register all sorts of vicious opinions. Ritchie leaned forward and listened, hoping at least to hear some good insults, but the topic didn't seem very promising. The guest on the program was a spry, bearded man with the zealous manner of someone who was hawking a new kind of therapy, like hanging upside down. Ritchie watched him hold up a copy of his book and smile sincerely into the camera. The dust jacket had an enormous picture of his head on it; it was almost exactly the same size as his real head.

Disgusted, Ritchie got up again and bopped the little metal knob with his fist, shutting the TV off. Then he went over and stood by the window a moment and looked up at the sky. A thin, waxy moon was visible, hanging directly above the smudgy rooftops of nearby buildings. In the distance, the skyline of the city loomed impassively, the white bricks gleaming, the windows slashed with brilliant light. Below, in the alley, a big gray cat squatted motionless on a fire escape like a Slinky. The streets were oddly deserted. It was Sunday night, Ritchie remembered, and he guessed that everyone was home now, where they belonged. He thought about that for a minute and immediately certain feelings started stirring inside him, shadowy things he couldn't quite put his finger on or describe but which were there nonetheless, darting just below the level of his awareness, ready to jump up and make him sad and a little crazy if he ever gave them a chance.

He quickly turned away from the window and decided it was time to check on the kid. Tiptoeing down the hall, he stood outside Joey's

closed bedroom door and listened. Those noises were coming from
inside the room again, battle noises filled with screams and shots
and loud explosions. The sounds made him feel lonely. They echoed
deep inside his head. It seemed the kid had some swell GI Joe action
going in there, and suddenly Ritchie found himself wishing he could
play too. He could make good noises—machine guns, grenades,
dive-bombing airplanes. It was no fun being left out, standing all
by yourself in the hall.

Another wave of gloom hit him and he realized it had nothing to
do with exotic women from the Far East and all that spicy action
he was missing; on the contrary, it was being triggered by the boy
behind the door. He now understood that he'd wanted Joey to like
him, and that's why he was feeling so blue. The kid seemed to have
spunk, that old fighting spirit. He didn't take any shit. The truth
was, he reminded Ritchie a lot of himself and it disappointed him
that the kid hadn't even given him the time of day, that he so
obviously considered him a jerk, a banana-head, el supremo turkey.

He remained there in the hallway for quite a while, his shoulders
slumped forward and his hands deep in his pockets, absently jiggling his change. It was a nervous habit he had—putting his hands
in his pockets. Big Joe always used to yell at him for it. He'd come
back from a grocery delivery loaded down with change and Big Joe
would say, "Take your hands out of your pockets, will you?" He
must've said that to Ritchie a thousand times. He thought it looked
like hell. Ritchie supposed his old man believed he was doing something in there, handling himself. But he wasn't. He was just jiggling
his change. It was comforting to him. What the hell were pockets
for anyway if you couldn't stick your hands down in them and jiggle
your change?

Some guys hate carrying change in their pockets. Ritchie knew
people like that. Mars, for instance; he wouldn't pocket so much as
a dime. Not Ritchie. He'd always carried a lot of change, always
liked the feel of it, the weight of loose coins against his leg. He was
used to it from his old days as a delivery boy—that and pitching
pennies. It was good to have your pockets full when you were pitching. The added weight anchored you down, gave you a solid foundation. You could make a better pitch if you wore a few ounces of
metal on either thigh. Plus it indicated you were winning, on a roll.

Heavy pockets meant prosperity, success. Pitching pennies was the one thing he could do better than anyone, and ever since he was a kid the chink of coins in his pockets had always sounded like music to him.

He dug his hands way down in there and brought out what he had—a couple of quarters, two or three dimes, a nickel, and a whole bunch of pennies. He must've had ten or eleven of the semi-worthless things. He transferred the other coins to the kitchen table and held the pennies in his palm. They made a nice heavy mound, a little pyramid of copper. He started picking through them, looking for ones that were ragged and scuffed up. He found a couple that looked like they'd been chewed in a garbage disposal, and he put the others aside and kept just the two, the sorriest-looking ones of the lot. You couldn't do anything with pennies like these. If you tried to fork them over as currency, people would look at you like, "What the fuck are these?" If you put them in a gumball machine, they'd probably jam up the works. They were just about useless—for anything but pitching, that is.

He went back over and switched on the hall light. Then he stood at one end of the tiled corridor and began pacing, stopping when he'd reached what seemed like two lengths of city sidewalk. There was a seam in the tiles just about where the crack in the sidewalk would be. He walked back to the other end and eyed the distance—it looked just about right.

He held the coins, bounced them, rolled them over his fingertips to try to get the feel of them. One was a little heavier than the other and he knew it would be the better of the two. If he were in among competitors, pitching for money, that would be the one he'd start with. But the other one wasn't bad either. A shooter with any skill at all could make it bite a line.

He took his stance, loosened up his arm and wrist, and quickly cast both pennies, one after the other, trying to get the range. Neither pitch was worth a damn, each an easy loser. Ashamed of himself, he went over and scooped them up and tried again. These throws were better; one actually cozied up to within an inch of the seam. Of course, this wasn't the same as real pitching. He wouldn't believe it was. The tile was soft and dead, for one thing; a pitch here wouldn't kick on you like it would on city cement. Plus you didn't have a cold October wind blowing in your face or smoke from burning leaves stinging your eyes and blurring your vision. You didn't have Chicago grit to contend with or dog dirt waiting in the grass to foul up your rollers or Big Joe yelling at you to get your butt back to the store. You didn't have to line up beside a couple of hot shooters either, older guys who could put the fear in you and turn you into mush. No, there weren't any of those swell things in that narrow hallway, but for the time being it would have to do.

He started pitching serious. He must've pitched for ten minutes in the hallway, keeping track of how he was doing. He was doing okay. His phantom opponent had the lighter coin. The guy was good, but Ritchie was better. He began finding the range with his gouged-up little sluggo, zeroing in on the line. He got into a rhythm. He was sweating a bit, feeling loose. The coins chinked with monotonous regularity onto the faded tiles.

Probably it was the noise of the coins that brought Joey out— that and Ritchie's running commentary. Whatever it was, eventually those loud battle sounds subsided in the bedroom, the door opened a crack, and Ritchie knew the kid was watching him. He just kept pitching. The door opened a little wider. The youngster must've removed that silly wolf mask because each time Ritchie went by to scoop up the coins he could see an eye peeking out at him beneath a tangle of curly black hair.

Finally the kid opened the door entirely and watched, without cover, from the edge of the room. Except for those intense dark eyes, his attitude was skeptical, his head slightly inclined, as though Ritchie were an old dog trying to teach himself a new trick. His expression indicated that what he was observing—a grown man tossing pennies at cracks in the floor—was the lamest thing he had ever seen in his life, but after a few more moments he couldn't keep from asking this weird new baby-sitter just what he thought he was doing.

"Pitching pennies," Ritchie said, bending down to gather up the coins again. "Haven't ever seen anybody pitching pennies before, huh?" The youngster frowned. "I guess not. I guess it's too low now for you hip modern kids." He toed the mark and made his pitches. One of them bounced up and kissed the seam in the tiles and he snapped his fingers—"Liner!"

Joey scowled. But Ritchie could tell by his eyes that the kid was interested.

"Listen," he said. "You wouldn't want to try a few, would you?

Joey shook his head. "It looks dumb."

"It's not dumb if you're winning. I've only been pitching maybe ten minutes and already I'm a coupla bucks ahead."

Joey shifted his weight and jammed his hands into the pockets of his corduroys—a good sign. Ritchie would've bet all his pennies that the kid was dying to pitch a few.

"Come on and try it," he said, offering him one of the coins.

Joey moved his shoulders around and then shuffled out into the hallway. Ritchie handed him a penny and explained the rules. They were simple enough: the one closest to the line wins.

"Go ahead."

The kid put the penny in his fist and flicked it out haphazardly, without really aiming. It was a lousy pitch, landing a good three feet in front of the line.

"That's terrible," Ritchie said. He threw his in with barely a glance. "You lose."

Joey stuck out his jaw defiantly—another good sign. The kid was a competitor. "Gimme a break. It was my first one."

Ritchie handed him back his penny and gave him a few tips. "Okay. In the first place, relax. You're way too tense. Do this." He wiggled his arms and shoulders like a silly goose. Joey looked at him like he was nuts, but he went ahead and did it. "Now," Ritchie continued, "take your stance. What you're looking for is good balance. You want to be up on the balls of your feet, leaning forward, but not too far. I shouldn't be able to do this, for instance." He gave him a little poke in the center of his back and the kid nearly fell over.

"Cut it out, jerk. Quit poking me."

"I'm just trying to teach you, is all. Okay. You got your stance. Not bad. Now the grip." He showed Joey how to grip the penny, wedging it gently between the thumb and the first two fingertips. "Ease up," he said, feeling the tension in the boy's wrist. "Don't squeeze so hard. That's a penny you got in there, not a titty."

Joey suddenly grinned up at Ritchie and his face went red. Another good sign. The kid was sharp. He knew titties.

"Now," Ritchie said, "the release. You want to give it a nice easy backhand toss and let it roll off the fingertips—like this." He tossed out his own penny. Joey watched it bounce once and graze the line. He looked impressed. This big turkey frank can do something after all, he seemed to be thinking.

"Okay," Ritchie said. "Now you."

Joey took his stance, flexed his wrist a couple of times, his eyebrows knitting in concentration, and let fly. The pitch was decent, landing about a foot behind the line. He beamed and glanced up at Ritchie for approval.

"Not bad," Ritchie said. "Not bad at all. Too bad it's a loser though." He went over and scraped both coins off the floor.

The smile slid off Joey's face. He stuck his jaw out again and said, "Wait here." Then he hustled off to his bedroom and came back an instant later carrying a big ceramic frog with a plug in its butt. He brought the frog over to the kitchen table and pulled out the plug, releasing a cascade of coins—quarters, dimes, nickels, and lots and lots of pennies.

"Well, what's this?" Ritchie said. "All right. Looks like we finally got some action going here."

Joey piled up all his pennies into a big mound and Ritchie gathered a few of his own and they got down to it. They pitched for twenty solid minutes, concentrating, working hard. Naturally Ritchie could've taken his little nest egg off him without any trouble, but he didn't do that. He pitched just well enough to make it interesting. He didn't want to discourage him, but he didn't want to give him the wrong idea either. The kid had to learn. He had to take his lumps, just like everybody. Ritchie would win one, and then he'd let Joey win one. Ritchie would win two and then Joey would win one. Ritchie would rattle off four or five in a row and Joey would start calling him jerk and asshole. Ritchie was getting to like him more every minute.

They were still pitching when Louise returned. They heard the door open, but neither of them turned around to say hello. Louise walked slowly up behind them and then stood there and watched for a while; she had a big furrow running up the middle of her forehead.

"What is it?" she finally said.

"We're pitching pennies," Ritchie said.

Joey said, "C'mon, Mom—haven't you ever seen anyone pitch pennies before?"

"Go ahead, hot shot," Ritchie said. "It's your turn."

The youngster made his pitch.

"Wait a minute," Louise said, her voice even hoarser and muddier sounding than it had been before. *"Gambling?* Is that what this is? I'm gone for a couple of hours and you're teaching my child how to throw his money away?"

"Hurry up, Kohler," Joey said impatiently. "What are you waiting for?"

Ritchie made his pitch. He flicked it in there stiff—a winner.

"Prick!" Joey shouted.

"And language!" Louise said. "What kind of mouth is that?" She stalked into the living room and flung her handbag onto the couch, then stalked back over rolling up her sleeves. "I can't believe what's going on tonight," she muttered. "First I get shot down by some two-bit college yo-yo—and then I come home to this?"

"It's just a game," Ritchie said. "Don't take it so seriously, for Christ's sake."

Louise's gaze drifted to the kitchen table. She observed the big ceramic frog and the mound of pennies which, at that point, had diminished considerably. *"Kohler?* What's this? You mean to tell me you're actually taking his savings?" She made a fist and belted him hard in the shoulder for this villainy.

"Jesus, don't worry about it. I'm gonna give it back." He was rubbing his shoulder; for a skinny person she could hit hard, almost as hard as Margie Glotz. "I take it you didn't get the job, huh?"

"What do you think?" she croaked. "This is the first shot at a lounge job I get in months—and I come down with a case of laryngitis."

"Hang in there," Ritchie said. "Something's bound to break for you soon."

"Yeah," Louise said. "Like my neck."

"Will you guys quit blabbing so much?" Joey was glaring at them with his hands on his hips. "Go ahead and make your move, Kohler—I feel a hot streak coming."

8

Dave lived. The goldfish thrived in his new habitat, on a TV tray in Joey's bedroom, near the windowsill. Ritchie was the one who suggested the fish be put there, where he could get some light. He figured maybe that was the problem with all the fish he'd had as a kid: not enough light.

"Look at this little dude," he'd say to Joey from time to time. "Don't you just love him?" He'd grab a box of fish food and tap a few crumbs into the bowl. Sometimes he'd watch Dave swimming around in there, swishing his little tail, and he'd wonder if the fish was lonely. "Tell me the truth," he'd say. "You think Dave needs a friend?"

"Sure. Why don't we get him a cat?" Joey made a lot of wise-ass jokes like that, but Ritchie could tell he was becoming fond of the fish. He liked his new pal Kohler too, Ritchie realized—maybe too much. Ever since he'd showed him how to pitch pennies that night, the youngster was always pestering him to come over and teach him new things. He wouldn't let him alone. He'd even call him at the Oasis and tell him jokes.

"Hey, Kohler," he'd say. "What has one eye and rides a big white horse?"

"What?"

"The Lone Potato. You coming over tonight?"

"I can't. I gotta work."

"Hey, Kohler."

"What?"

"What's black and white and red all over?"

"Um . . . a newspaper?"

"No. A mashed penguin on the side of the road. What about tomorrow night?"

"I don't know. We'll see."

"Hey, Kohler."

"What?"

"What's green and goes hoppity bump, hoppity bump?"

"I give up."

"A frog with a wooden leg."

Ritchie understood what was happening here. He appreciated that the kid was going through an important stage and needed a guy he could copy and look up to—but why him? He didn't need the job. He was just your average speed, your two-dollar hunk of baloney—the kid would be better off picking someone else as Acting Dad. But the youngster seemed to be stuck on the idea. He wouldn't let Ritchie alone. It was getting a little embarrassing. Nine o'clock on a Thursday night, the busiest time of the week, the lounge packed, Teddy Drake flaming at the piano, the air thick with laughter and cigarette smoke and Ritchie up to his eyeballs in drinks—and the phone would ring and Vince the God would grab it in his meaty hand and then turn to Ritchie and say, "For you."

"What?" Ritchie would bark into the receiver.

"You're coming over Sunday, aren't you?" Joey would say, his voice squeaky with expectation.

Ritchie would gnash his teeth. He and Mars always had dates on Sunday. Stews, or dancers, or a couple of live-wire physical therapists that Mars had spotted at a rodeo club one evening, wrestling in mud.

"You *promised,* Kohler," Joey would squawk. "You're not ratting out on a promise, are you?"

"I don't know. I'll see if I can make it."

"Hey, Kohler."

"Now what? I'm busy."

"What has whiskers, big ears, and doesn't even remember to bring you a present once a year?"

"You got me. The dumb Easter Bunny?"

"Uh uh. My real dad."

————

He started coming over a couple of times a week, bringing things. He brought a peewee football and some boxing gloves, huge pillow-like objects that more closely resembled puppets than the manly tools of self-defense. They stuck these on and went at it for a while, Ritchie down on his knees and showing Joey the proper way to keep his dukes positioned and how to work off the jab. Louise didn't go for it, but Ritchie explained that it was a nasty world out there and it was important for a kid to know how to protect himself.

He brought other stuff, toys. He brought a Hot Wheels speed shifter track and a GI Joe Cobra FANG gyrocopter, ideal for rapid hit-and-run rocket strikes. He brought a couple of plastic swords and they dueled in the living room, scrambling over furniture like swashbuckling guys. They pitched pennies in the hallway. Louise wasn't too thrilled about it, especially when the toilet language started to fly, but she decided to let it slide after Ritchie pointed out that the game was teaching Joey responsibility and sound fiscal man-agement: he had no capital to play with if he couldn't get his al-lowance, and he couldn't get his allowance if he didn't keep his room tidy and brush his teeth after every meal.

One Sunday afternoon when Ritchie came over, Louise's friend Jessie and her own kid were there. Jessie was a tall big-boned woman with a long braid of hair that she slung around like a lariat. Ritchie liked the way she shook his hand. She gave him a good firm grip— not the bone crusher she appeared to be capable of, but certainly not one of those halibut shakes you got entirely too often nowadays. Her boy, Dexter, sat on the floor playing with a large gray dog named Zeus. He had one of the plastic swords in his hand—a bright glowing yellow thing—and was hitting Zeus on the head with it. He wasn't hitting the animal hard; he was just tapping him with it, like he was knighting the beast.

"Don't hit the dog like that, honey," his momma said.

"Zeus doesn't mind," Dexter said. "He can't feel a thing anyway." This statement appeared to be true: whether by age or affliction, or both, the animal seemed almost totally insensate.

Dexter and Joey got out the GI Joes while the moms sat on the sofa, drinking coffee and shooting the breeze. They made no effort to involve Ritchie in their conversation, so he went over and talked to the dog, periodically lifting up the animal's large veiny ear to see

if anything were registering in there. He was feeling left out until
Pie showed up with the Smokey Robinson record. A chubby little
Oriental girl with jet black hair, she was heavily into dance music—
like the kind Ritchie used to listen to in the store—and as soon as
she put the record on, all three youngsters congregated in the middle
of the room and started doing the robot and the freak and all sorts
of other funky gyrations. Ritchie got in on it too; it'd been a long
time since he'd had a Smokey Robinson party.

"C'mon, you guys," he called to the women, who were evidently
too cool to get out there on the rug and shake it. "Doesn't anybody
want to bump?" Jessie produced an awkward smile while Louise
flashed him her what-a-jerk expression—lips pursed, eyebrows arched
high up on her forehead, eyes rolling from side to side like they
were framing him in a kind of parenthesis. Ritchie had encountered
this look so often he could see it in his sleep.

She still didn't have much use for him, that was obvious. She
merely tolerated his presence because of the boy. That was okay
with Ritchie—the feeling was mutual. Their relationship remained
strained, uneasy, strictly cats and dogs. They didn't have a lot in
common. They didn't like the same beverages, for instance, or the
same TV shows. Ritchie liked malt liquor and situation comedy;
Louise went for melodrama and vodka with a twist. They didn't have
the same taste in art. Ritchie enjoyed pictures of flowers, horsies,
meadows, sunsets—anything with bright cheerful colors. Louise
had a more austere sensibility and disfigured the walls with her
gloomy cityscapes, her stark sketches in black and gray. She'd gotten a job as a counter girl at Walgreen's and it hadn't done much
to improve her disposition. While Ritchie and the kid would be
playing Hot Wheels in the hallway or goofing around in his room,
Louise would be curled up on that cinderblock sofa with her sketch
pad open, drawing something dismal: the fire escape, cats browsing
in the alley, the sooty rooftops of the buildings down the street. She
would stay there for hours, sipping Smirnoff's and filling that big
hubcap with cigarette butts. It seemed to Ritchie she filled that
thing to overflowing at least twice a day.

"Can't you cut down a little?" he'd say, coming over and opening
a window. "It's like a smog alert in here, for Christ's sake." He
himself had suddenly, one day, given up the habit for no considered

reason. It was just one more thing about himself he didn't understand.

"Tell it to the surgeon general." She'd retaliate by immediately lighting up another cig. "I happen to have a lot on my mind, Mister Lung Association, so let me alone."

She seemed to realize she was becoming more indebted to him now than ever, and this rattled her, threw her off key. He could not believe how cold she was. Once, while making a snack for himself in the kitchen, he accidentally brushed her hand with his while she was drying the dishes—it was like touching an iced trout—and she had immediately snatched it away. Another time he came into her bedroom to give her an important phone message and she nearly murdered him with a butcher knife. True, the circumstances were unusual—it was early in the morning and she probably wasn't used to having a man sleeping over at her place—but was that any reason to pull a blade?

He'd slept there only because one of his tires was flat and he didn't feel like monkeying with it in a rainstorm; he certainly didn't have any desires on her skinny bones. Joey was delighted at this turn of events, but Louise reacted as though she were being forced at gunpoint to harbor a ten-most-wanted guy. They stayed up late that night watching a creature feature on television, Louise drinking steadily while Joey and Ritchie made wisecracks at the set; then, when the movie was over, she hustled Joey off to his room, threw a couple of moldy blankets at Ritchie, and went to bed, taking the vodka with her. Ritchie wasn't sure but he thought he could hear her pushing a heavy object up against her bedroom door.

That cinderblock sofa was hard and lumpy. It was like crashing in a gravel pit. He slept fitfully, tossing and turning until early in the morning, when he came fully awake at the sound of the telephone. Confused, he sprang up and answered it with urgency, but it was only Walgreen's calling. They wanted Louise to come in as soon as possible—somebody was sick.

Ritchie mumbled okay, he'd give her the message. He hung up and tiptoed to Louise's bedroom. He knocked softly, asked if she was decent. Receiving a groggy reply, he attempted to push open the door but was met with resistance; she did, in fact, have a big piece of furniture wedged up against the door, and he had to put his shoulder into it to get this obstacle—a chest of drawers—to budge enough to let him slip into the room.

Louise was sunk way down in bed with the blankets pulled up around her face. There didn't appear to be anything substantial under those covers; she looked like she weighed about as much as the pile of dirty laundry Hilda used to make him carry down to the basement every time she did the wash. On the floor beside the bed was the bottle of vodka. It was almost completely shot.

He leaned forward and touched her shoulder. "Psst, Louise. Your boss just called . . ."

She opened one heavy-lidded eye and looked at him; suddenly she flung off the covers and, reaching under her pillow, produced the butcher knife and brandished it menacingly, the blade glinting in the early morning light.

Ritchie thrust out his arms. "Jesus, Louise. It's me. Kohler."

"Keep back," she warned. "How dare you barge in on me with a hard-on?"

He'd slept in his underpants, not exactly your vintage Fruit of the Loom, and had jumped off the couch with his customary morning boner. "You mean this?" He gestured at his offending turgidity. "This doesn't mean a thing, Louise. It's totally innocent." Even as he spoke his pecker was deflating to its normal harmless state.

Louise waved for him to get his private parts out of her face. "Put your pants on, will you? Jesus."

"Forget about my pants and listen up a minute." He gave her the Walgreen's message. Groaning, Louise dropped the knife and sank back down under the covers again, wrapping a pillow around her head. She looked terrible. Her face was swollen and there were dark patches under her eyes. No doubt about it, Comrade Smirnoff was exacting his revenge.

"Look," Ritchie said. "You'll feel better once you get some food in your system. Why don't I make you breakfast and in the meantime—"

"Stop it!" Louise pressed the pillow tighter to her ears. "Why are you always talking about food? I mean, Jesus *Christ*. I drank a whole jug of vodka last night and now you charge in here with an erection and tell me I gotta go right to work. You want to know what I would really like? You interested? Give me three Excedrin and then bury me. Just put me in the ground."

"I'll make some eggs," Ritchie said. "How do you like them?"

"In an Easter basket, covered with chocolate."

That afternoon, on his way to the Oasis, Ritchie heard a voice whispering in his ear. He dimly recognized it; it was the voice of reason, trying to penetrate his thick skull like Radio Free Europe. *What do you think you're doing, schmuck?* the voice was saying. *Why are you getting into this?* Knives, nastiness, playing race car with a seven-year-old—who needed it? *He's not your kid.*

The answer was simple: he was stuck. The kid looked up to him. He'd been abandoned once already, and who knew what crippling emotional damage Joey might sustain if Ritchie ran out on him too? So how could he hit the bricks? The truth was, he wasn't even sure he wanted to. He actually enjoyed spending time with the kid. If he did say so himself, he'd finally found something he was pretty decent at—being an acting dad. He even read to the youngster. Joey had a bunch of little books stashed in his toy box, and every so often Ritchie would read him a story before he went to bed. When they had run through all those and Joey wanted some books with a little more meat on them, Ritchie went to the library and picked some up. He could hardly believe it. Here he was, the same Kohler who, before, would've set foot in a library only for shelter in the event of all-out atomic war, now coming out of the stacks at the neighborhood branch with an armload of Newbery Prize winners and checking them out—hold on to your hat—with his very own bona fide library card.

He began to think of things to do, places to take him. Chicago was a great big city—they ought to get out and take advantage of it once in a while. He could take him to a Bears game and to Santa's Village. He could take him to the planetarium and to the museum of natural history, where they had Chicago's all-time favorite gorilla stuffed inside a glass cage.

"Hey, Louise—Joey ever see Bushman?" They were in the car on their way to Lincoln Park Zoo. A mild Sunday in late October. The leaves on the trees were changing color, but the sun was still warm; he could feel it on his arms as they headed south on Lake Shore Drive. Behind them, Joey rode in Jessie's car with Dexter and a bunch of other kids.

Louise looked at him. "What are you talking about?" She sat glumly by the passenger door chaining cigs.

"Bushman," Ritchie repeated. "The gorilla they got stuffed in the museum. He's one of the most popular gorillas who ever lived."

"No shit." She stared out the windshield.

"We'll have to take him to see Bushman one of these days. Santa's Village, too." He changed lanes to get around an old slow guy wearing a straw hat. "What kind of Halloween costume you think he'll go for? They got all this real expensive junk now, but I personally think the old stuff is better." He reflected a moment on his own trick-or-treating days. "He could go as a big rabbit or something. Or a ghost. Just throw an old sheet over him and cut out little holes so he can see, and there you go. I went as a ghost," he added. "I did that a couple of times."

Louise lit another cigarette. "He's not going trick-or-treating," she said decisively.

"Why not?"

"Where you been, lamebrain? There's too many lunatics now. They put stuff in the candy. A kid goes out and comes back an hour later with a bag full of rat poison and razor blades."

"Yeah," Ritchie said. "You're right about that." You couldn't be too careful nowadays. Every Halloween, the papers were full of all kinds of evil stunts these cranks and weirdos were pulling. "Good thinking," he said to Louise as they drove along.

They parked about half a mile past the zoo entrance, waited for Jessie and her crew to join them, and then walked back along the waterfront. The lake was calm, as calm as Ritchie had ever seen it, and that warm sun hung over it like a giant tangerine. Music blared from a hundred radios. Kids on skateboards went by. So did long-distance runners, lovers, elderly couples walking elderly dogs. The zoo was crowded; bullshit weather was right around the corner, and it seemed like everyone in the city was out, enjoying one last nice autumn afternoon. Ritchie looked around, pleasantly observing his fellow Chicagoans, Americans, residents of the good old USA. They had big solid bodies and big grinning homely faces. They strutted proudly in their polyester pantsuits, in their denims and Sansabelts and ill-fitting dago Ts.

The animals, as usual, seemed bored, even churlish; you couldn't get a trick or a lively look out of any of them to save your life. The big cats hid inside their craggy habitats. The monkeys did a lot of stuff you wouldn't want your kid to see. They played with their dongs and ate their own cage apples. Still, Ritchie was in a very agreeable mood. At a refreshment stand he bought everyone snow cones and then, a little later, he popped for hot dogs and Cokes.

"We ought to do this more often," he said to Jessie. "Get out and see the sights, I mean."

"Sure," Jessie agreed. "There's a lot of neat stuff to do along the lake."

"Absolutely." He crammed half a hot dog in his mouth. "What I want to do," he mumbled, "is take Joey to see Bushman. You know— that famous gorilla they got stuffed in the museum down the road?"

Jessie gave him a blank look. "The planetarium is cool," she said after a while.

"No doubt about it. All those stars and planets and stuff. Hey, Louise . . ." He looked around but Louise wasn't there. He spotted her sitting on a bench about fifty yards away, smoking another cigarette and staring moodily at some rare type of antelope, one of several unlucky species on exhibit that day. Habitat disappearing. Grazing lands drying up.

They went to the planetarium. They went to the museum and saw the mighty Bushman, who'd just gotten a new fur job and drew large crowds like an old-time movie star. On Thanksgiving they ate a duck. It wasn't bad, with Stove Top stuffing and some cranberries on the side.

A funny thing happened, though, while Ritchie was eating din-ner—a wave of melancholy suddenly engulfed him. There he was, munching away and enjoying the festive occasion, and then he found he couldn't swallow; he was all choked up. He was missing an all-day bacchanalia in one of the Oasis's private party rooms, starring Mars and a host of harem girls, but that's not what he was mooning over. No, what he'd started thinking about were all the Thanksgivings he'd sat down at the dining-room table with Big Joe and Junior and Hilda and Grammy. He thought about all the grub that was spread out there—the giant Butterball turkey and the sweet potatoes and the corn and the hot buttered rolls and all the other stuff. There wasn't enough room on the table for all these dishes— they'd have to keep one item passing at all times. He thought about all the yelling and commotion going on, the elbow fights with his brother, the damn dog nosing under the table, and the big argument every year about who was going to say grace. He sat there with his modest piece of duck and his little mound of stuffing and suddenly he started feeling sorry for himself, dewy-eyed over those Thanks- giving feasts of his youth. He found himself missing Big Joe and his crabby disposition, Hilda and her Dutch apple pie. He missed Grammy Kohler finding something wrong with everything on the table. He had to admit it: he even missed his asshole brother and that idiotic little dog.

"What is it?" Louise was saying. "Something wrong with the food?"

He shook his head. "Everything's yummy. Love this duck." He forked up a piece and chewed for a while but it was no dice—he could barely get it down. Abruptly he threw his napkin off his lap and said, "Excuse me a minute, " and went over to the telephone.

He dialed the number but nobody answered. It must've rung at least ten times before Big Joe himself picked up the phone. Ritchie could picture him standing there with his belt loosened and gravy all over his chin. In the background, he could hear laughter and the clamor of table talk above the drone of a football game.

He spoke in a small, uncertain voice. "It's me. Ritchie."

There was a long pause. "We're eating," Big Joe finally said. "What do you want?"

It was a good question. He didn't know what he wanted. It'd been a long time since he'd talked to his family, and he supposed he just wanted to say hello. Fourth and inches, the football announcer was saying. In the distance Ritchie thought he could hear Hilda, but her voice was faint, barely detectable, like she was living on a planet a million miles away.

Big Joe spoke again. "You still there?" His voice wasn't exactly angry and it wasn't exactly cold. It wasn't anything, just an empty sound, a nullity, the vocal equivalent of a total eclipse of the sun.

Ritchie said, "Happy Thanksgiving," and hung up the phone. He wasn't sure, just before he took the receiver from his head, if he'd actually heard Big Joe wish him the same, or if he'd only imagined it.

He sat back down at the table and put his napkin on his lap and stared at his plate. Joey and Louise were looking at him.

"You okay?"

"Sure. I'm fine. Pass the stuffing." He spooned a wet clump onto his plate and then picked up his knife and fork again, but it was useless. His stomach was knotted up.

"You don't have to eat your dinner if you don't want to," Louise said coolly. "It's just a lousy duck."

"I said it's okay, didn't I?" He shoveled in another piece and chewed desperately. "Yum."

"I knew I should've made a turkey," Louise said. She was poking at the duck with her fork. Joey meanwhile had sawed holes in a couple of sliced beets and was wearing them like a mask over his eyes. "I mean, who has duck on Thanksgiving?"

"The duck is fine!" Ritchie shouted. "What do you want—a signed affidavit?"

They sat there in silence for another moment. Then Louise got up and pushed her chair out of the way and began clearing the table in a hurry. "You done over there?" Before Joey had time to answer she snatched his plate out from under him and clattered it into the sink. She discarded Ritchie's the same way. Then she got an apple pie out of the oven and plunked it down on the table in front of them, along with a couple of fresh plates. She wreaked havoc in the pie with a spatula, gouging out a pair of ragged pieces and dumping them onto the plates. Ritchie and Joey looked at each other while she slid the plates at them and stood there with a defiant expression, a fist at her hip.

"Dessert's served, pilgrims. Dig in."

Ritchie forked up a mouthful and tasted it. It was good. She'd even put cinnamon on it. Okay, maybe it wasn't quite as good as Hilda's Dutch apple, but it was definitely a piece of pie a guy could be thankful for on a dreary Thursday in late November. He took another bite and thought, let the old man have his own damn Thanksgiving. He liked it fine right where he was.

9

The first Sunday in December they took Joey to a big downtown department store to see Santa Claus. Before they went, though, Ritchie did his homework. He checked out this particular Claus. You had to be careful about your Santas nowadays—that was his reasoning. Times weren't the same. They were letting all sorts of unqualified persons don the jolly red suit—bums and winos and the like. So he checked it out. He didn't want to take Joey to a Santa who had Mogen David on his breath. He wasn't too crazy about some of these cheesy beanpole Santas who were walking around either. If a guy wanted to be Santa he should make an effort to jolly up and look like Santa; he shouldn't be some scrawny guy with a pair of Coke-bottle lenses who looked more like a tax man for H&R Block.

This Santa passed the test and so they piled into the car and headed downtown. It was an overcast day and big wet flakes of snow were falling, the kind that disappear as soon as they hit the ground. The store was crowded, but it wasn't that vicious mob you get at the end of the season, during the rush, when someone'll pull a rod on you over a tube of wrapping paper. They walked around the store for a while, looking at the decorations and all the holiday window displays. "God Rest Ye Merry, Gentlemen" was being piped through the speaker system. Everyone seemed friendly and of good cheer.

Finally they wandered over to see Santa. He was stationed in a corner of the store, installed on a throne and giving audiences like the Pope. Ritchie had to hand it to Joey. When it was his turn to go up, he didn't hesitate or flee in terror, like some kids do. He marched right up to the jolly old soul, parked himself on his lap, and whipped out a list. It was fairly comprehensive and contained a number of outlandish requests, like a real helicopter, and a rocket-powered sports car, and a horse. He went through the whole thing while Santa smiled and periodically came out with a "Ho ho ho."

"Take a picture," Louise said, elbowing Ritchie in the side.

"Oh, yeah." He'd almost forgotten he'd brought his camera. He instructed Joey to sit up straight, then he zeroed in with his Polaroid and took the shot. The colors were a trifle garish, but it wasn't bad. He'd even managed to coax a smile out of Joey, which was surprising when you considered the solemnity of the circumstances: a big downtown department store, scores of people watching, the youngster perched on the knee of a living myth.

"Nice," Louise said.

"Lemme see." Joey snatched the snapshot and studied it gravely. "It's okay." He handed it back to Louise and then began tugging on Ritchie's arm. "C'mon, you guys. You promised I could look at tanks."

"Just a second," Ritchie said. "I want to get a picture of the two of you."

"Kohler," Louise said. Like many women, she had an aversion to having her picture taken. But with her, Ritchie had the feeling it wasn't vanity; it was like she was afraid the camera might capture something she didn't want exposed.

"C'mon. It'll only take a second." He directed them to stand near the head of the line again so he could get Santa in the background. Then he took a few steps back and, peering at them through the small black box, began studying the shot from various angles and distances like a professional. Actually he was a terrible photographer and didn't want to chop off anybody's head.

"Hurry up, Kohler. This is embarrassing."

"Quit rushing me. And stand closer together, will you? You're too far apart."

Louise moved in closer and crouched down a little so her head was about level with the boy's. Ritchie crouched too. As he framed the two of them in the view finder he couldn't help noticing how lustrous Louise's hair looked, shining like rich chocolate in the bright Christmas lights. Her skin had some natural color in it. He'd never seen her looking so . . . nice.

"Smile, Louise."

"I am smiling." But even as she said this, a fuller, truer smile broke slowly across her face.

That night Ritchie decided to go out and get a Christmas tree. There was a stand on a corner about a mile away, and he figured on running over there and beating the rush. A nice full-bodied Scotch pine was what he had in mind.

"Why don't you wait until it stops snowing," Louise said. She glanced out the window; it was coming down pretty hard.

"Nah—it'll only take a couple of minutes."

Joey said, "I'll come with."

"No. I want to surprise you guys." It was an old Kohler tradition: the man of the house always went out and got the tree. Big Joe used to do it every year, and before him, Big Hans. "You got ornaments and stuff, don't you?" he asked Louise.

"Of course I got ornaments."

"Then get 'em out. I'll be right back."

He put on his coat and barged out into a blizzard. The wind was whipping in off the lake, bringing with it fierce gusts of snow that blew sideways across the city. Ritchie drove straight into the storm with about twenty-five bucks in his pocket. It wasn't enough. The guy at the corner stand was asking at least thirty for his skinny Christmas trees.

"You're kidding on these prices, right?" Ritchie said to the salesman, a husky ethnic with a blue beanie and a three-day growth of hair on his jaw.

"Why would I do that?" the guy said. He was stamping his feet and pummeling his sides to keep warm. He didn't seem all that interested in Ritchie's business. "Look. My price is thirty. Take it or leave it."

Ritchie left it. He got back into his car and drove around, skidding along the icy streets, but at every lot he encountered more of the same. At one place they even had police dogs, and barbed wire strung along the perimeter of the lot so no one would steal their precious Christmas trees. *Barbed fucking wire!* He couldn't believe it. What ever happened to goodwill toward men?

The snow kept slanting down. The wind howled. He kept on driving. He was beginning to think this old Kohler tradition wasn't all that it was cracked up to be. He could see why Big Joe sometimes came back in a real bad mood. At one point he thought about packing it in and running out the next day and picking up one of those artificial trees that came in a box, but then he visualized what they looked like—pitiful things with toilet-brush branches that you screwed into a plastic frame. They were supposed to look forever natural, but the minute you pulled one out of the box it looked like it was dead. It would be mortifying to put up a tree like that. People would laugh out loud at it. No way. He wasn't about to buy a tree you could scrub the toilet with—he'd promised Joey and Louise the real item. Big Joe always brought home a real tree and damned if he wasn't going to do the same.

The wind kept howling, blowing him farther and farther into the city. Suddenly Ritchie found himself in a familiar neighborhood. Through the whirling gusts of snow he recognized the Catholic church Hilda used to take him to, and his old grammar school. He began going slower, his eyes taking in everything, all the landmarks of his past—the drugstore and the local post office, the DQ and White Castle, Henry Glotz's hardware store, the park.

A guy behind him was blowing his horn and Ritchie stuck his arm out the window and motioned him to go around. He had come to a complete stop in the middle of the street, directly across from the store. It seemed smaller than he remembered it, more dingy and dilapidated-looking. The paint was flaking and the wind had ripped some shingles off the roof. The big sign facing the alley hung precariously, like at any moment it might break off too. It seemed to Ritchie that the store had aged badly, like some men do, and he wouldn't have been surprised if a particularly strong gust leveled it to the ground.

He idled there another moment, squinting into the snow. The interior of the store was dark, and Ritchie could see the little Closed sign in the front window. Big Joe must've figured nobody but an idiot would be out tonight and closed early. He was probably right, but still Ritchie was irritated that the place wasn't open. He rolled up his window and drove on.

There was a Christmas-tree lot around the corner and over a few blocks, by the fire station, but Ritchie didn't go that way. Instead he drove in the other direction, turning down a residential street lined with two-story brick houses. Some had red and green Christmas lights strung above the door. Ritchie drove to the middle of the block and stopped when he came to a house with a big plastic Santa on the lawn. It was Margie's house. He remembered that one Christmas one of his friends had sneaked up in the night and glued a big carrot to Santa's crotch, giving the St. Nick an obscene vegetable hard-on. He probably thought it was funny, but Margie didn't and neither did Ritchie. He'd snapped off the carrot and later he'd found out who the wise guy was and made him eat it, Elmer's glue and all.

He put the car in neutral and again rolled his window down, visoring his hand to his forehead to keep the snow out of his eyes. He squinted above the bushes in front of Glotz's picture window to see if anyone was home. Margie's bug was parked out front, but he couldn't see her. He couldn't see anyone. Maybe they were all watching TV in the den. Maybe Margie was in the kitchen making a fruitcake. Every Christmas she made a fruitcake and carried it over to Ritchie's house in a brightly colored tin. "Merry Christmas," she'd say and lift off the top of the tin and there it would be, another fruitcake, grinning up at everyone with a little date and raisin face. "Thanks," Ritchie would say, feeling his stomach churning. They ate it though. Eventually, by the end of the holidays, the whole thing would be gone and Ritchie would carry the empty tin back across the alley. Margie would ask how was it and Ritchie would say great, not having the heart to tell her they gave the last third of it to the dog.

He put the car in reverse and backed up a few feet so he could get a better angle on the kitchen. That was when he noticed the other car. It was a sleek red Buick with fancy wheels and something lacy hanging from the rearview mirror, parked right behind Margie's car. Ritchie knew all Margie's neighbors; none of them would have a car like this. He backed up a little farther and noted the Loyola sticker in the Buick's rear window, which exactly matched the one in the rear window of Margie's little red bug.

He stared at the two cars a little longer—they seemed to be almost touching—and for a moment thought about getting out and bamming Margie's door and asking her what the story was on this Buick, but he didn't. It wasn't his business who she rode with anymore. He rolled up his window and pulled away, a lot faster than he'd meant to; when he got to the end of the block and turned the corner he slid about thirty feet and then fish-tailed into the alley, the back of the Datsun scraping a chain-link fence bordering someone's yard. He maneuvered away from the fence and gunned it again, churning through the unplowed alley until he came to the back of his own house. He stopped there, his engine still racing, and glanced across the snow-blown yard into the kitchen, where Big Joe sat in a chair by the window, reading a newspaper and drinking a beer. Behind him, Hilda was chopping something up at the counter with a cigarette in her mouth. Maybe it was the poor visibility, or an optical illusion, a mirage fashioned by the storm, but Big Joe seemed much older to Ritchie, his hair thinner, his face thinner, the flesh about his neck and chin baggy and gray.

He would've liked to stay longer, to look harder and see if his eyes were telling him the truth, but at that moment a small angry black shape came charging toward the fence, yapping loudly, and Ritchie put the Datsun in gear and quickly drove away.

Inside the kitchen Hilda hollered at Big Joe again. "I said, the dog's barking." She was chopping up carrots with a Viceroy in her mouth.

Big Joe looked up from the newspaper and glanced into the yard. Nothing was out there but wind and snow and the damn poodle, still yapping by the fence.

"So what. Let him bark."

Hilda put the knife down. "You better get him in here. You want Henry Glotz to call the cops again?"

"He did that?" Big Joe took a gulp of beer. "He actually called the cops?"

"Sure. Don't you remember? You were sitting right in that chair." She picked up the knife and took another carrot out of a bag. "You better do it—it'll cost you plenty if they have to come again."

Big Joe grumbled and put the newspaper down. Then he pushed himself away from the table, got up, and went to the closet to put his coat and his hat and his galoshes on. The coat was still damp from his walk home and his boots were still cold and slick on the bottoms. There was a little puddle on the floor of the closet where they'd been sitting. Already it seemed like it had been winter forever, and winter had just begun.

"Don't snow in Florida," Hilda had reminded him when he came in that night and Big Joe had said fine, if she liked Florida so much she ought to go down and live there. She could mail him a postcard and tell him how it was.

When he went out the side door, the wind nearly tore his hat off and he could barely see the poodle through the surging gusts of snow. He took a couple of steps into the yard and hollered at the animal, but the dog just kept standing by the fence, looking out into the alley and barking at a ghost. Big Joe clapped his hands but the dog still didn't come. He wished he knew Ritchie's whistle. The kid had had a way of sticking two fingers in his mouth and producing a whistle so high and shrill that it completely paralyzed the beast, like a police siren. He'd do it two or three times and eventually the dog would slink over, like he was under arrest. But Big Joe could never get the knack of this sound; every time he tried it he felt like an idiot.

He finally had to bribe Cha Cha in by saying the word *cookie*. He didn't even have to say it loud and the dog immediately turned around and bounded after him into the house. He followed Big Joe into the closet and into the kitchen too, barking eagerly, his little tufted tail jutting and his teeth slightly bared.

"All right, already," Big Joe said. He reached for a package of Fig Newtons on the table, got one, and broke it in two. He gave half to Cha Cha and ate the other half himself. In the den, a shoot-out was taking place on a cops-and-robbers television show; the sound was so loud it seemed like they were opening up right in the house. Big Joe grumbled again, got another cookie out of the package, and went in to turn the volume down.

Grammy Kohler was sleeping on the davenport, her feet in a basin of water and that ridiculous powdered wig balanced crookedly on top of her head. It seemed like she'd been sleeping more and more lately. Sometimes he'd look at her and wonder if she was dead. She wasn't, but sometimes he wondered what was the difference: the only time she showed any life was when he yelled at Cha Cha for chewing on his slippers, or when she wanted him to rub her feet.

"Where's Ritchie?" she'd say every time he did that, which was nearly every night. She'd look around like she'd just noticed he was missing, as if the feeling of getting her feet rubbed had triggered some dim recollection of her grandson, as if her memory were in her toes.

"Don't you remember?" Big Joe would say, putting one foot down and reaching for the other one. "He ain't here anymore."

"Where is he?"

"I don't know where he is. He's gone."

He tiptoed over to the television now and slowly turned the volume down. He stood there a moment and looked at her, waiting for her eyes to open. He waited a long time. Finally, just when he was beginning to worry, Grammy's eyes snapped open and she told him she couldn't hear the television set; reassured, Big Joe turned the volume back up and eased out before she could ask him to rub her feet.

He walked back into the kitchen and got another beer out of the fridge, and then he went out into the living room and looked at his Christmas tree. It was a pathetic-looking tree, set in a nook by the picture window, its scrawny scarecrow arms pointing every which way. He'd only had it a couple of days, but already it had lost half its needles; they were scattered all over the floor and he kept stepping on the goddamn things. He hadn't wanted to buy this diseased tree, but the guys at the fire station were charging outrageous prices this year—thirty bucks and more. Big Joe had never paid thirty bucks for a tree his whole life. "Whataya got for twenty?" he'd asked them and they'd hauled out this weed from the back of the lot.

"Hey Hilda," he hollered now. "Where the hell are the ornaments?"

"In the basement, where they always are." She paused a moment. "Why?"

"Because I want to decorate the Christmas tree, that's why."

"Now?"

"Sure, now. Why not now?"

"You're too drunk. Wait until tomorrow—you'll just wreck it if you do it now."

Big Joe took another gulp of beer and stared at his Christmas tree. It was the worst tree he'd ever had—even Hilda said so—but it was still better than one of those lousy artificial jobs she'd been after him to buy.

"Go get the ornaments," he hollered again into the kitchen. "I'm tired of looking at this thing. I'm either gonna trim it tonight or throw it out."

Hilda sighed and went down to the basement and got the boxes of ornaments. She got the tinsel and the Christmas lights too. Big Joe got another beer, took everything out of the boxes, and began decorating the tree, using the same system he always used: first the lights, then the ornaments, then the tinsel. He didn't go for food on the tree or any fancy extras, like mangers or that frost you sprayed out of a can. He always used the same lights and the same orna- ments—only the tinsel changed from year to year.

He considered himself an expert tree trimmer and had tried to pass his know-how on to his kids. Joey had picked it up right away, but Ritchie had been stubborn and it took him a while to learn it right.

"Not that way," Big Joe would mutter, removing a big clot of tinsel the kid had heaped onto a branch. "What do you think this is—spaghetti?" He'd reach into the silver mass and delicately pluck a single strand. "Like this. Hey, are you watching?"

"Yeah, I'm watching," Ritchie would say. "But I still think it's too slow."

He'd learned eventually, though, and the tree always turned out fine. Of course, then Big Joe had a lot more tree to work with than the sorry-looking thing he had now. Back then he had big Scotch pines and sturdy evergreens, the sort of tree you could be proud of and stand by with the rest of your family and have your picture taken and mail it with holiday greetings to all your friends.

He had the lights and all the ornaments up and was working on the tinsel when suddenly the bell rang at the side door. Big Joe put down his beer—it was his sixth or seventh of the night, he couldn't remember—and went to answer it. He opened the door and there stood Margie Glotz with the biggest human being Big Joe had ever seen. He wore a crew cut and some type of letter jacket, and just kept going up and up into the storm, like a sequoia. The guy must've been seven feet tall.

"Sorry about the dog," Big Joe immediately blurted. He figured Henry Glotz had sent Margie over with this goon to beat him up.

"The dog?" Margie glanced at him uncertainly.

"I brought him in as soon as I heard him," Big Joe said. "It won't happen again."

"We're not here about the dog," Margie said. "I just wanted to bring you something. Merry Christmas, Mister Kohler." She took her arms from behind her back and thrust a cake tin at him.

"What's in it?" Big Joe said.

Margie laughed. "It's a fruitcake—don't you remember?"

"Oh, yeah." Big Joe looked at the tin and felt something grumble in the pit of his stomach. "Listen, don't just stand there in this goddamn weather. Come on in. I want you to see my Christmas tree."

Margie peered up at the giant. "Okay. But we can only stay a minute."

They came in and followed Big Joe into the living room. "Take off your coats," Big Joe said. He gestured at Margie's friend. "You want a beer?"

"No thanks. I'm in training."

"Herbie's on the basketball team," Margie said.

"Sure," Big Joe said. "Big guy like you—what position?"

"Center."

"Can you dunk?" Big Joe said. "Can you slam it right through there?"

The big guy nodded and moved his shoulders around.

"Attaboy!" Big Joe said. "Hang on a second. Lemme get you a beer."

He went and got the big guy, Herbie, a beer and they all stood around looking at the Christmas tree. Hilda came out too and Big Joe handed her the cake tin.

"It's a fruitcake," Margie said. "Go ahead and open it."

"We'll save it for later," Hilda said.

"So," Big Joe said to Margie. "What have you been doing these days? I haven't seen you."

"Studying mostly. I'm in the nursing program at school."

"Attagirl."

"You heard from Ritchie?"

There was a brief silence and then Big Joe said, "Not for a while."

"He's probably been real busy," Margie said.

Big Joe looked at her. "Doing what?"

"Oh, you know. Things. The holiday season is always real hectic, right?"

Big Joe nodded, pulling on his lip. "I thought maybe you heard from him."

"No," Margie said. "Not for a long time."

There was another silence, broken only by the wind battering at the window, the gunshots coming from the den.

"So," Big Joe finally said. "What do you think of my tree? It's real," he pointed out.

"Very nice," Margie said. "It's one of the better ones I've seen this year."

"It's coming along," Big Joe said. "It'll look real good once I get it all decorated." Suddenly a thought flashed in his head. "Hey, I got an idea—why don't you kids help me finish it?"

Margie glanced quickly at her friend and said, "Um, I don't know, Mister Kohler. I really think we—"

"Sure. Stick around a minute and gimme a hand. Hilda, get this guy another beer."

"No thanks. I'm—"

"What's your name again?"

"Herbie."

"C'mere, Herbie. I want to show you something." He motioned for Herbie to join him by the window and Herbie ambled up and stood next to him, towering over both Big Joe and the tree.

Big Joe had a hunk of silver in his hand. "I want to show you how to put on this tinsel. Most young fellas like yourself just whip it up there like it was spaghetti, but that's wrong. There's a right way and a wrong way to do everything—am I right?" He knew he was, but there was something wrong with his voice. It sounded muddy and strangled, almost desperate.

"That's right, sir," Herbie said.

"Here. I want to see you do it. Do it right." Big Joe handed him a single length of tinsel and watched as Herbie reached down to hang it on a branch. Big Joe watched like it was the most important thing in the world.

Herbie draped the tinsel delicately over a branch, and then stepped back sheepishly, as if he'd just scored on a clever lay-up.

Big Joe smiled and thumped him on the keester. "Attaboy!" he cried.

When Ritchie finally got back to the apartment, Louise was waiting for him on the landing, regarding him furiously through a tangle of hair. "Don't ever do that to me again," she said.

"What are you talking about?" Totally exhausted and covered with snow, he was coming up the stairs slowly, leaning forward under the weight of the tree, carrying it on his back like Jesus had.

"Where were you all this time?"

"Getting this stinking tree—where did you think I was?"

"For *three* hours. Where'd you have to go—the North Pole?"

"Just about." The guys by the fire station hadn't been open and he'd picked the tree up at a lot way the hell over on the West Side. It wasn't what he'd been looking for at all—a skinny evergreen, not even five feet tall and kind of caved in on one side—but by then his Christmas spirit had vanished entirely and it was the only tree he could afford. Even at that he'd gotten into a shouting match with the bandits who were running the place. They wanted twenty-five dollars for this piece of shit. Ritchie offered them twenty. They settled on twenty-two and he paid them their blood money and told them to haul it over and stuff it in the back of his car.

"Have you ever heard of the telephone?" Louise was saying. "Couldn't you at least have called and let me know where you were?"

Ritchie stared up at her in amazement. Her face was gray, drawn with worry, and she held a drink in her fist.

"God almighty, Louise. I was gone for a lousy couple of hours."

"I know. But I thought you were stranded in this blizzard or something—or in a wreck. I thought maybe you weren't—" She broke off abruptly and frowned down the stairwell. "Just don't do this to me again, Kohler, that's all I'm saying. Next time call or something. Let me know."

"All right already," Ritchie said. "Help me get this in." She hurried in and got a broom and helped him brush the snow off the tree, and then they tipped it on end and shoved it through the door.

All the commotion awakened Joey, who bounded out of his bedroom and rushed over to inspect the tree.

"What are you doing up?" Louise said. "It's late."

"I'm not sleepy." He was circling the tree, sizing it up from various angles. From the look on his face, Ritchie guessed he didn't think much of it, that he'd been expecting more—something on the order of the gigantic glowing fir they set up every year in front of the White House.

"Is this the best you could do?" he finally said.

"Yes it is," Ritchie growled. "Get out of the way." Joey moved aside and Ritchie lugged the tree over and planted it in the stand Louise had set up in the corner of the room. It didn't look any better in the stand than it had on the lot; if anything, it looked worse.

"You got something I can wear?" he said to Louise. He was beating on his sides and blowing on his hands to get warm. His teeth chattered. His clothes were soaked. He could no longer feel his toes. "A robe. A blanket. Anything."

Louise brought him her flannel bathrobe and a bunch of blankets, and Ritchie hobbled into the bathroom to change. When he came out he saw that she'd filled a basin with warm water for him to stick his feet into, and had poured him a drink. He sat down on the couch, eased his feet into the basin, and waited to thaw. Outside, the snow kept coming down and the wind kept blowing, knocking at the windows like it wanted in. Joey was squatting by the tree, staring at it gloomily.

"Do we have to have this tree all Christmas?" he said. He had a couple of shiny ornaments in his hands and was scraping them together.

Ritchie said, "Something *wrong* with it?"

"It looks terrible," Joey said. "I want a different tree. This tree sucks."

"Watch that," Louise said.

Ritchie wiggled his toes. "Lookit. This is the tree I went out and got for you, so you better get used to it. I'm not about to go out and get another one."

"That's right, honey," Louise said. "Kohler went to a lot of trouble to get this tree. Anyway, it'll look better once we put the ornaments on."

Joey reached up and hung one of the ornaments on a branch. Then he sat back and studied the effect. The lone ornament looked bad, dangling there. It looked pathetic.

"No, it won't," he said.

"You can't go by just one ornament," Louise said. "You've got to put them all on."

"So let's do it," Joey said. He was reaching into a paper bag and withdrawing boxes of ornaments. In another bag were packages of tinsel and a couple of strings of Christmas lights.

"Tomorrow, honey," Louise said. "It's too late to start that now."

The youngster stuck out his jaw. "I don't want to wait until tomorrow. I want to put the ornaments on right now!"

Louise glanced at Ritchie and sighed: there's no stopping a kid once he gets an idea in his head. She nodded okay and Joey immediately sprang into action, digging into the boxes with both hands. Sensing his expertise was needed, Ritchie lifted his feet out of the basin and went over to assist him. Louise poured three eggnogs, spiking two of them with a generous dose of rum. She switched on the radio to a station that played Christmas music and then joined them by the tree. Ritchie tasted his grog; it was good. The music was corny but nice. He didn't care that he looked ridiculous, decorating a Christmas tree in a woman's flannel bathrobe; he was thawing out, finally feeling like a human being again. He was even beginning to sense a spark of that holiday spirit returning, beginning to believe that the trip had been worth it despite his encounter with the strange red Buick and the imposter at the kitchen table, sitting in Big Joe's chair.

There's a right way and a wrong way to trim a Christmas tree—that's what Big Joe always said. The wrong way was to just fire everything on there haphazardly, like you were blasting it on with a shotgun. Big Joe had taught Ritchie that you can't trim a tree in a hurry—you have to take your time. First you put on the lights, stringing them under the branches so the cords don't show. Then you put on your ornaments and your bells and your Styrofoam wise men and Santas, keeping an eye for symmetry in color and shape. Big Joe was never one for putting food on a tree, but if you wanted to hang up some candy canes or popcorn balls or whatever, now was the time to do it. Last, you put on your tinsel for that overall shiny effect and to cover up any eyesores. The trick with tinsel, of course, was to put it on delicately, strand by strand.

"Not that way," Ritchie said to Joey. Like most kids, he was applying the stuff in great silvery hunks. "Like this." He picked out a single length of tinsel and draped it daintily over a branch.

Joey sneered at this method. "Too slow." He seized another glob.

Ritchie grabbed it away from him. "Not so fast. Look, if we're going to trim this tree together, let's do it the proper way—right, Louise?"

"Right." She had found a tiny glass bell and was holding it in her hand, searching for the precise spot to put it. Her eyes were bright, keenly focused, and the rum had brought a soft glow to her cheeks. Ritchie had never seen her look so . . . real.

When they were finished, Joey plugged in the lights and they all stepped back and regarded their work.

"Admit it," Ritchie said, turning to Joey. "It's a pretty decent Christmas tree."

Joey yawned. "I guess it's okay."

"Okay? I think it's a lot better than that. I think it's A-one—don't you, Louise?"

"Uh-huh." But when he turned around he saw that she wasn't looking at the tree at all. Instead, she was looking at the two of them, Ritchie and the kid, staring with an expression of grave intensity, as if she were afraid that if she blinked once or looked away they might disappear, and the tree with them, and all she'd have would be the wind.

10

Nobody listened. There was a singer up there, pouring her heart out, and nobody even heard. Ritchie gulped his beer and glared at a couple of drunks at the next table who were talking football at the top of their lungs. At a booth across the aisle a party of six was playing some sort of trivia game, hooting at each other's stupid answers. They had the board spread across the table, the little plastic cards, everything. At the bar, some fat guy wearing an electric blue suit and big square sideburns wooed the cocktail waitress with Polack jokes. Ritchie worked his jaws. There was a singer up there, goddammit, baring her soul, laying her heart right there on the piano, and nobody but him heard a word.

He was in a dive called Cozy's Too, a little out-of-the-way club about half a mile from the river, under the Kennedy overpass. Louise had asked him if he'd ever heard of it and Ritchie said no. He'd had a hard time even finding it. He'd missed it on the way over and driven right up to the river and had to turn around. Even where he sat he could still smell that rank river smell, seeping in through the door. The road outside was full of holes and the city had covered some of them with sheets of metal that thumped and rattled every time a car went by. Which wasn't very often. It seemed to Ritchie nobody would come down here unless he was lost.

Two nights, the guy had told her, forty bucks a pop. Louise had told him the going rate for professionals was a hundred, and the guy had said who did she think she was, Peggy Lee? All he wanted was someone to fill in until the jukebox was fixed. He said he didn't even *have* a piano. He had to borrow one from his cousin, who ran the original Cozy's on the other side of the drink.

The piano was small and tinny-sounding, dented in on one side like it had fallen out a window some time; evidently the cousin kept it in a warehouse as a tax dodge. It amazed Ritchie that Louise could coax any music out of it at all. But what amazed him even more was her voice. It was low and husky, a little on the sultry side. From what he'd heard so far her taste ran to blues and bittersweet ballads which she sang in a languorous, wistful style. He'd hustled there from work primarily to give her moral support—he hadn't expected to be actually *moved*. Now if only these louts would start paying attention . . .

She finished her set with a Mel Tormé number and whispered thank you into the mike. Ritchie looked around again; he was the only one clapping, a loud defiant sound that rang like machine-gun fire through the club. There couldn't have been more than twenty-five people in the whole place, most of them sitting alone in shadows. Someone finally gave a right answer in the trivia game and the players bleated in amazement. Up at the bar the guy with the side-burns was giving the punch line to one of his jokes—it's working, it's not working, it's working, it's not working—and pounding his hand on the counter.

"Welcome to the Ritz," Louise said. She'd gotten a drink and come over to join him. Ritchie ordered another beer.

"Well, what did you think?"

"Seriously?"

"Of course."

"You were terrific. I just wish these idiots would pay attention to you, that's all."

Louise shrugged and lit a cigarette. "That's show biz. You have to get used to it."

"I know. But do they have to be so *rude*?" He turned to the hilarious trivia players and asked them to keep it down.

"Listen," Louise said. "You're not planning to start something in here, are you? I got one more night in this pit."

"No way. You're looking at a perfect gentleman. All I'm saying is that when you're at the piano everyone ought to shut the hell up."

She smiled and sipped her drink—Sprite with a twist of lemon. She was wearing that same black ensemble Ritchie had seen her in before, only she was filling it out better and not looking so much like a prisoner of war. She'd left her blond wig in the closet tonight and gone with her natural hair, which was combed all to one side in a long tumbling wave and left the other side of her face exposed. Ritchie followed the delicate line of her jaw all the way up to the ear, small and intricate as a seashell. He'd never noticed how pretty her cheekbones were, nor how, when she smiled, her eyes seemed to turn a richer shade of brown.

"So what did he tell you?" He meant the proprietor, a thin rat-faced guy, who, at that moment, was bamming the top of his cigarette machine, trying to get it to work. "Can he use you again—or did he finally find someone to fix his box?"

"Not yet. He's still waiting. But he told me tomorrow is it. He says he can't afford live entertainment."

Ritchie glanced again at the patrons; they looked like what might be left over after atomic death. "I can see that. But in the meantime what's he gonna do for music?"

"Bring his stereo in."

Ritchie shook his head. Two more people had come in, a man and a woman, each dressed in identical fast fish outfits, even those big seafood platter hats. Ritchie remembered there was a Captain Billy's right around the corner.

"Jesus, Louise." The couple had brought in a box of shrimp nuggets and lots of little cups of sauce. "How do you find these places?"

"I don't. They keep finding me."

He stuck around until she finished her last set and then they left Cozy's Too together and he followed her back to her place. Jessie was there, knitting something and watching television. In front of the set Joey and Dexter were curled up on a big sleeping bag, sound asleep on the floor.

Jessie said, "How'd it go?"

"Let's put it this way—it's not Park West." Louise dumped her coat on the sofa. "But at least it's forty bucks."

Jessie stuffed her knitting into a shopping bag and nudged Dexter, who immediately sat up and put on his shoes, then his coat, never once opening his eyes.

"See you tomorrow night," Louise said, slipping Jessie some money. Jessie nodded and steered her little sleepwalker out the door.

Ritchie helped Louise put Joey to bed and then he pulled out a bottle of wine and they stayed up half the night drinking and talking. Louise told him things. She told him about her life in the trailer and about the hipster weasel Pierce Davis and a lot of other personal stuff. She said it had taken her a long time to get over it when the genius left her—he'd seriously messed up her head. Ritchie said it didn't matter; just about everyone he knew had been messed up at one time or another. It was part of living. Then he told *her* something.

"Try this out," he began. "All this time you've known me I've never told you my real name."

"What?"

"It's true. I've deliberately concealed it from you."

"No kidding," Louise said. "I'm appalled."

"You think it's Ritchie," Ritchie said. "But it's not."

Louise took a sip of whatever it was they were drinking at the moment—straight vermouth, Ritchie supposed. They'd polished everything else off. "What is it, then?"

He looked her right in the eye and said it. "Hans."

"Hans? Are you serious, Kohler? Your real name is Hans?"

He nodded. "There. It's finally out."

"Hans," Louise said to herself. She kept repeating it. "Jesus, Kohler. It's bad. It's really awful."

"Tell me about it," Ritchie said.

"It's about the worst name I ever heard." She was smiling. Then she laughed. She sounded just like she sang when she laughed. "It's even worse than Louise."

The next night, during his break, Ritchie decided to stop in at the back offices to see Mars. He hadn't been seeing much of his roomie lately. He'd been spending a lot of time with Louise. The white soul man had been real busy himself, running all over town trying to hustle the Mighty Funkateers. Sometimes he'd drive to the South Side and meet with that black guy he knew. Ritchie couldn't remember his name. He really didn't want to remember his name, and he didn't want to know any details about his business either.

Ritchie told Vince he'd be back in a couple of minutes and slipped out of the lounge. As soon as he hit the lobby he could hear the music—a loud twangy C&W sound. The featured performer at the Oasis that week was the Princess of Appalachia, everyone's country sweetheart, Miss Jubilee Jones, who, as Ritchie ducked inside the showroom, was running through a rendition of her smash crossover hit, "Made in the USA." She was tiny and blond, with the hard-edged glamour of a minor beauty queen, and she had one of those high squeaky voices like maybe she'd been doing helium just before the show. She pranced across the stage before a packed house in a red-white-and-blue cowgirl outfit that glowed in the dark. She looked like a performing X-ray. Ritchie avoided gazing at her straight on.

He skirted the edge of the giant room until he came to the door that led to the back offices, pushed it open, and walked down the long carpeted hallway, past the dressing rooms of the stars. He had his hands in his pockets and a secret inside his head. Ever since he'd heard Louise sing at Cozy's he'd been thinking about it, but he hadn't told her what he planned to do. He wanted to keep it a surprise.

He just hoped Mars was in the mood to listen—that was the main thing. Nicky was away again, out in the desert on a long business trip, and evidently the effort of helping run a major nightclub operation while being a clean-jumping soul brother at the same time was overtaxing Mars's assets. Lately he'd become a very disagreeable guy. He'd been doing a lot of bowling in the apartment; the pins were always scattered all over the floor. His darts were stuck in the woodwork. He complained of phlegm in the chest and an unceasing case of postnasal drip. His nose was red and swollen, like the honker of a fading middleweight. His face was more gaunt and weasel-like than ever, and he seemed to be losing pounds, shriveling up inside his power duds.

He'd been taking it out on people too, abusing busboys and cocktail waitresses, yelling at the chefs. He'd even fired Teddy Drake. It was something he'd wanted to do for a long time. The only problem was that Nicky liked the guy. They were tight. Mars claimed that Teddy was back in the office every other night, polishing Nick's shoes with his tongue.

But Nicky was away, and when Teddy came to Mars about re-negotiating his contract—more money, a bigger dressing room, special cleaning service for his capes—the soul man had hit the ceiling. He was through being Mister Nice Guy—that's what he told Ritchie. As acting boss, he gave the song stylist five minutes to gather up his glitz and clear his ass out of the building.

Oasis Enterprises was shut down for the evening. The reception area was dark and empty, but a shaft of smoky light was coming from the partially open door of Nicky's private office and Ritchie knew the acting boss was in. He had to wonder what he was doing in there, however; the smoke was so thick in the doorway you'd have thought Mars was torching paper, setting fire to all of Nicky's books.

But it was only a cigar. When Ritchie peered into the room he saw Mars leaning back with his feet up on the desk, enveloped in smoke, puffing away on the biggest stogie Ritchie had ever seen. The cigar sat in the middle of a grin as wide and sharp as a sickle.

"Kohler! Come on in. Join the celebration." Mars lifted a drink and toasted him.

Ritchie stepped in, hacking at the smoke with his arms. "What are we celebrating?"

"Life. Specifically, mine." He clinked the ice cubes in his glass and took another wallop. "It's finally happening, Kohler. Me and my bros. You remember my jerk-off friend from the Imperial, don't you? Tommy? Mister Rudeness? I've finally persuaded him to book the brothers for three nights this week—with an option for more."

"Congratulations."

Mars took the cigar out of his mouth and admired it for a moment. He had the attitude of a plantation king about to bestow great favors on his slaves. "This is only the beginning, Kohler. I see unlimited opportunity. I dream big dreams. Six months from now you'll be seeing me in Hollywood, doing business with record moguls. You'll be finding the brothers in *Billboard,* hitting all the charts. Monster—that's what I'm talking about. I'm optimistic. I'm feeling very co-pacetic. Here, man, enjoy . . ." He flipped Ritchie a cigar.

Ritchie caught it and stuffed it in his pants pocket. He planned on celebrating later.

"Sit down, roomie. Drink with me."

"I can't. I'm on break. I gotta get back."

Mars chuckled. "Listen to him. He's gotta get back. What an employee I got here. Remind me to give you a raise." He reached for the bottle of Scotch on the desk, splashed a large quantity into a tumbler, and thrust it at Ritchie. "Here. Drink this. I gotta have somebody to celebrate with, don't I?" His face looked lopsided and Ritchie wondered how long he'd been sitting back there, drinking all by himself.

"Okay. But just a short one. I told Vinnie I'd be right back."

"*Fuck* Vinnie. Great big sombitch like him—he can handle it. Let's you and me have some fun. I know these Swedish girls. Heidi and Dagmar, something like that. The Masseuse Sisters—they'll do stuff to your muscles you won't believe." He began rummaging through little bits of paper and torn matchbook covers scattered across the desk. "I got their number here somewhere. I'll give 'em a call. Tell 'em to come over and bring their rubs."

Ritchie said he really wasn't interested.

"From *Sweden*, Kohler. The land that brought us lust. Those people practically *invented* screwing." He kept picking up pieces of paper and throwing them to the floor. "What do you say, roomie? Let's get hairy, just like the old days."

"I can't, Mars. Maybe some other time."

"Goddammit. I know I got it here somewhere."

"Hey, forget about Sweden for a minute. I got a favor to ask."

Mars leaned back in the chair again. His head wobbled slightly, like one of those little football dolls. "A favor? For you, roomie, anything. Your wish is my command."

"It's about that little problem that's developed in the lounge."

"What problem?"

"Getting a replacement for Teddy."

"*That* schmuck." Mars stuck a finger into one side of his head and rapidly popped an ear. "He picked the wrong day to get huffy with me, Kohler. He comes in here with this song and dance about being a second-class citizen and how nobody appreciates him blah blah blah. Zap! Did I tell you? I fired his ass."

"Yeah, I know. That's what—"

"No more Mister Nice Guy, Kohler. All new terms, that's what he tells me. Bigger dressing room. I gave him a bigger dressing room. I told him to change outside."

Ritchie went right to the point. "Listen. What if I told you I knew someone you could get to replace him?"

"Black or white?"

"White."

"Not interested. If I can't dance to it, I got no use for it."

"But she sings black," Ritchie quickly added. "Very funky. Extremely soulful. You hear her sing "Stormy Weather," it'll break your heart."

"Just what the world needs," Mars said, "another torch singer. Now if you were talking some foxy black chicks I might be interested. I been thinking about adding a trio of chicks to sing backup for the band. Call 'em the Funkettes, throw 'em into slinky outfits—can't you see it, Kohler? You wouldn't happen to know any black chicks I can use in my act?"

Ritchie sipped his drink. "This vocalist I'm telling you about? She's a pro, Mars. She's highly experienced. I really think I'd be doing *you* a favor if you gave her a shot."

Mars was looking at him quizzically, as though there was something unfamiliar about his face. "This new Lena Horne—her name wouldn't happen to be Gallenko, would it?"

"Professionally, she just goes by Louise."

Mars reached up and popped his other ear. "I can't believe you, Kohler. Give it a rest. What are you—in *love* with this woman?"

Ritchie stared into his drink. In love with Louise? The question had never occurred to him. But now, just thinking about it made his heart start beating fast.

"Look, leave my personal life out of this. I'm talking business here. Dollars and cents. You need a singer and I happen to know one that's available. You should hear her, Mars. She's good. She's better than anyone you could book back there. For that matter, she's better than half your main attractions—and that includes your Juice Newtons, your Wayne Newtons, your Fig Newtons, your Olivia Newton-Johns."

"So?"

"So why don't you give her a chance? Put her back there a couple of nights a week and see what happens."

Mars had relit his cigar and was blowing tentative ovals up toward the ceiling. "It's against my principles, Kohler. You know my rule on firing people—once they're gone, they're gone."

"I know it. But you can always make an exception, can't you?"

"Sure—but what will people think?"

"They'll think better of you for it. They'll think you're swell. They'll have to rewrite the old saying: To err is human, to forgive is Mars."

Mars was now examining his fingernails. Ritchie could almost hear his irritation, crackling like static on a cheap radio. "This is bringing me down, Kohler, I gotta tell you, man. I'm celebrating here. I'm thinking Swedish meatballs—and you're hassling me about this woman again."

"Hey, it's very simple. Just make the deal with me and then call the girls."

Mars studied Ritchie's face again, squinting through the smoke. "Okay," he finally said. "I'll talk to contracts and we'll work out the details. But remember, Kohler: I'm only doing this as a personal favor."

"It's a smart business decision, Mars. You won't regret it."

"Sure I will. All this success must be making me stupid. I'm getting soft. My heart's as big as the great outdoors." He kept staring at Ritchie and suddenly he brought his hand down on the desk top. "I knew it!"

"Knew what?"

"I knew it was something. You shaved off your mustache. How come?"

Ritchie ran a finger across his naked lip. "I don't know—I just felt like it." It was something he'd been thinking about doing for quite a while. As far as he was concerned, the hair had outlived its usefulness. More and more it had begun to feel like a disguise.

"Bad move, Kohler." Mars wagged his head. "You're looking like a muppet again. I don't like it—and the chicks aren't going to like it either. Gertrude and Wanda. Licensed to serve. Trained for pleasure. I think they even might be twins."

He was still muttering to himself and rooting for the number as Ritchie eased out the door.

———

At first Louise thought he could use the hair; without it his face seemed bland, nearly insipid. When she saw him walk in he was once again the young sailor boy she'd seen for the first time in the Oasis, a little puppy dog right off the boat.

"I don't know, Kohler," she'd said, studying his birthday features. "I think it was a mistake."

"Forget the hair," Ritchie had told her. "This is the real me."

Now she thought he was probably right. She kept looking at his face and seeing things there, a certain hidden character, a kind of nobility. There was something strong and all-American in the determined set of his mouth.

They were sitting on the cinderblock sofa planning a private celebration. Ritchie had brought some bubbly and Louise lit a candle and put on the Duke. Then Ritchie fired up the enormous stogie and they leaned back and looked out the window at the luxury high-rises that stretched above rooftops into the cold black downtown Chicago sky.

"I think we should go to that steakhouse on Wabash," he was saying. "You can get a T-bone there bigger than your head."

Louise made a face. "Why don't we go to that fancy French place in Wheaton? Blow a bundle on cheesecake and snails."

"Snails? What do they do, Louise—bring them out in a big bowl, like Cheerios?"

"Or we can hit that place at the top of the Hancock Building. You know—the one that spins around?"

"The Top of the World?"

"Sure. That's it." She was sitting close to him and he could smell the lemony fragrance coming from her shoulders, see candlelight shining in the wave of her hair. "They say up there you can see all the way to Indiana. They say you can see everything up there."

At first, when he'd sprung his big surprise on her, she hadn't known how to take it. She didn't know if she really wanted to go back to the Oasis; it seemed like just another unlucky stop along the way. Plus there was Joey to consider. He needed a stable home, a regular routine, a mom who was there at night if he needed her. She knew she could count on Jessie, but she didn't know if she really wanted to start that up again. She'd been thinking about giving the clubs up entirely and getting some ordinary daytime job.

Sales clerk, cashier, something like that. She'd been checking out the want ads. And in the meantime, Walgreen's wasn't so bad. It was a living. What kind of mom stayed out all night like an owl?

She sat there, thinking it over, while he pried open the champagne. Joey was asleep, the TV was off, and nobody was talking, but the apartment was still full of noise. A faucet was dripping in the kitchen, heavy metal pounded down on her from overhead. The baby across the hall was crying again. Outside, in the alley, cats were knocking over garbage cans. The heat clanked on. The apartment seemed to be shrinking even as she sat there, the walls closing in. It was like all the bad luck of her past was suddenly ganging up on her, coming to life in the form of cheap theatrics in a second-rate horror flick. She looked around, disgusted with everything about the place—the cramped rooms, the tissue-paper walls, the trashcan view outside the window and the chain-gang noises the heat made whenever it came on. They had cells in medium-security prisons nicer than this. She was sick and tired of living like an inmate. She *deserved* this break; more important, Joey did.

At that moment she heard the cork pop and Ritchie came back with the still-foaming bottle, a couple of glasses, and a towel draped over his arm. He filled the glasses and then held his up for a toast.

"To success."

They clinked glasses, drank. Then Louise proposed another toast. "To you and me, Kohler. To us."

They sat there and listened to the Duke and kept filling the glasses. After a while they dispensed with the glasses altogether and just started passing the bottle back and forth. They toasted Mars and they toasted Teddy. They toasted the Mighty Funkateers. They toasted all the things in the past that had brought them together, even Gordon, the poor bus station soul. Every so often Louise would sit back and reflect on her new good fortune.

"I still can't get over it, Kohler. Me. Louise Gallenko. A nobody, from Nowhere, Indiana. Now appearing at the Oasis, live and in person—who would've thunk it?"

She laughed. Ritchie laughed too. He had a hard time believing it himself. Mostly he was surprised at how easy it'd been. It was supposed to be a cut-throat business, right? Dog-eat-dog. But this had been so simple it was almost a crime.

"I'm thinking, Louise. Maybe I have a talent for this. Maybe I oughta be your agent."

"Absolutely. You talk, I sing. We could have cards made up that say it."

They kept passing the bottle and toasting everything. They toasted Joey and Jessie and Vince the God. They toasted the Duke and Billie Holiday. They even toasted the moon.

Pretty soon the candle had burned all the way down and the Duke was silent. Ritchie lifted the bottle to his mouth and blew mournfully into the top.

"All gone."

She turned her head and looked at him. He was leaning forward with the empty bottle in his lap. She kept watching him, studying his profile, and she couldn't get over how familiar it looked, as if she'd known it all her life. She stared at the clean open planes of his face and wondered if he was the one she'd been waiting for, the one she used to sit by the trailer window and watch for all those hours back in Indiana, a long time ago.

He glanced at her once and then quickly looked away. His heart was pounding and he felt like a fool. He was afraid to touch her, but he was even more afraid of that look she was giving him, as if maybe she was seeing something in him that wasn't really there.

He broke the awkwardness of the moment by putting the bottle down on the trunk and rubbing his eyes. "It's late. I guess I should be going."

"What's your hurry?" She smiled, moved even closer to him, and then fell lightly into his arms. "The night's just beginning. Take me places, cowboy. Carry me away."

11

She wanted to go out early. She wanted to rush out and see the city, take a cab to the Loop and strut down Michigan Avenue and look in all the stores. She remembered how when she first came to town—eighteen, just a hick from Indiana with nothing in her jeans— she used to walk by those fancy shops and stare in all the windows, gazing at the scarves and shoes and sleek elegant dresses like they were figments of her imagination, a Windy City mirage. Sometimes she'd go in and actually touch the merchandise, run her fingers over silk and tweed and one-hundred-percent virgin wool, conscious of the salesgirl's wary glances, the hard-edged eyes staring from behind the counter, aware she was being pegged as a thief.

That seemed like another lifetime, something that had happened a thousand years ago. She could go into those places now and nobody would say boo to her. Just the way she carried herself would tell everyone she belonged.

She was in her apartment, standing in front of the bathroom mirror, listening to the radio and applying mascara with a tiny wand. She wanted to look nice for him. She wanted to look better than she ever had in her life. Every so often she'd lean back and study herself, wondering if she really was different, if she actually had changed. She wondered how it was possible. Could it be that one night, one lucky development, could even transform a person's face?

Jessie seemed to think so. A little while ago, when Louise dropped Joey off at her place, Jessie had taken one look at her and seen it right away.

"Okay," she'd said, coming over, rolling up her sleeves. "Out with it, girl. I want to know his name."

"What are you talking about?"

Jessie stood there staring at her, a smile spreading over her big horsey features. "You know what I'm talking about. First you ask if Joey can sleep over and now you float in here with that look on your face."

Embarrassed, Louise ran a hand through her hair. "Is it that obvious?"

"Of course." She came up and, grabbing Louise's elbow, adopted a hushed conspiratorial tone. "All I want to know is who is it. Do I know him? Would I recognize his name?"

"Yeah—but you won't believe it if I tell you."

"Try me."

Louise hesitated, then leaned over and whispered it.

"No!"

"Yes."

"Him?"

"I told you you wouldn't believe it."

Jessie gave her a cagey look. "Wait a minute. Are you telling me what I think you're telling me?"

Louise nodded.

Jessie rolled her eyes. She bammed Louise's shoulder and they both started laughing. "You and Mister Rogers, huh?"

"Tell me about it," Louise said. She remembered how he'd been that first night together, not frantic and ugly like the railroad man in the trailer, and not like the genius either, who prided himself on all his secret tricky ways and used to twist her around like a pretzel, but patient and sweet and gentle—and the *most* amazing thing about it was that she didn't have to pretend or transport herself elsewhere. She'd been with him the whole time. She beamed at Jessie, remembering it, and said, "I don't believe it myself."

Ritchie was having a hard time remembering his orders. That black guy at the bar, for instance, the one who kept asking about Mars— he was drinking stingers but Ritchie couldn't get it straight. The black guy would signal with his hand and Ritchie would nod and bring him a volcano, or a candy drink with lots of fruit in it, and the black guy would just look at it and shake his head. He was a short, compactly built man with the sloping well-muscled shoulders of a fighter or a cornerback wedged snugly into a pink satin shirt. He had eight or nine chains coiled around his neck and mucho flash and glitter on his fingers. Ritchie kept thinking he knew him from somewhere, but he couldn't place him. Maybe he was a Mighty Funkateer. Mars would know. If Mars were there Ritchie would ask him, but the acting boss seemed to have vanished down a manhole. Nobody had seen him for a couple of days.

"What time you got, Vinnie?"

The God dunked about seven glasses at once and stacked them upside down on a ledge behind the counter. "Five minutes after you asked me the last time."

That would make it about ten. He was meeting Louise in an hour. Top of the city. Top of the World.

"You sure it's only been five minutes? I don't want to be late, Vinnie. I got a big date tonight."

"Yeah, I'm sure." Vince glanced at Ritchie in irritation. "What happened—you lose your watch?"

Ritchie nodded, but it wasn't true. Actually he'd stopped wearing his old watch and hadn't yet gotten another. The old watch was the sleek Bulova Mars had given him, a long time ago. Ritchie had stashed it in a drawer. He'd started feeling funny every time he looked at it. It didn't seem right to be wearing someone else's initials, to have someone else's leather wrapped around your arm.

As usual, on Tuesday, it was pretty slow. There were only a handful of couples scattered at the tables, and Babs and Karen, the new harem girl, didn't have much to do. The stews and the stockbrokers wouldn't be in until tomorrow, and there were even some empty stools along the bar.

There was nothing happening at the piano either, but Ritchie still found himself gazing at it often, at its clean black lines and the pleasant canopy of leafy branches that stretched above it, shining emerald green in the light. He kept hearing music inside his head. It wasn't the harsh jangling discordant music he usually heard at work—that fandango of laughter and shrieking voices that called to one another across the bar like jungle birds—and it wasn't the lame melodies of Teddy Drake. This was his own private music, lush, throaty, soft as a whisper and yet strong enough to lift him off the floor. He realized for the first time in months he wasn't hungry. His insides felt solid, humming with sound. He couldn't get over how strange it was. He'd thought he was just doing her a favor and instead he found himself with a brand-new heart.

"Hey, Kohler."

Ritchie glanced up and saw that the God was gesturing at him: the black guy at the end of the bar wanted another drink. Ritchie remembered this time and brought the stinger over, and the man acknowledged it with a barely perceptible nod. There was an air of permanence about him, something stolid and inevitable in the way he was sitting there, his shoulders hunched over his drink. His face was like something printed on a coin. He looked like a man who was not only waiting for something, but was prepared to wait forever to get it.

Ritchie, however, was not. He was eager to get going. The music was getting stronger, pulling him away.

"Hey, Vinnie . . ."

"Kohler. Gimme a break, will you? You're driving me nuts tonight."

"Yeah, I know. Listen, you think you can handle it now? I want to take off."

"Go ahead. You might as well." Vinnie went to pour a round for the regulars at the bar, the wet-sleeve guys who were in there every night. It was a standing arrangement: about every twenty minutes he'd get out the bottle and fill their tanks again.

"Thanks, Vinnie. I owe you one, man."

Ritchie threw down his bar rag and edged past his partner to the little hatch at the end of the counter. He had his best suit hanging in the employees' room just off the lobby, looking sharp inside the dry cleaner's plastic bag. A quick change and then hop on the Kennedy, express lane all the way. Straight downtown to the big building off Michigan Avenue. Up the elevator. She'd be sitting there just like in a movie, waiting for him at the top of the world.

He was halfway to the lobby when he heard the God shouting, calling him back. Ritchie turned and saw he had the bar phone in his fist.

"What's the matter?"

"Telephone call. For you."

The city looked like it was lit up with candles. It reminded Louise of a gigantic birthday cake. She was sitting in the restaurant lounge, ninety floors up, watching the world revolve slowly beneath her and waiting for a waiter in a tuxedo to bring her another rosé. A candle flickered on the table and baskets of carnations lined the windowsill. In the dining room reservations awaited, but Louise didn't mind sitting there alone. It had taken her whole life to get there, and she wanted to savor the moment. She didn't want to rush things along.

The lounge was dark and nearly empty. A young couple sat at a secluded table, near the piano, and a handful of middle-aged gentlemen were clustered together talking to a young woman at the far end of the bar. They were tan and prosperous-looking in their three-hundred-dollar cordovans, their custom-tailored suits. The rich dark fabrics they wore gleamed in the polished wood of the bar, which was as smooth and glassy as a mirror. A little while ago one of those gentlemen—he had a watch chain on his vest and a flower in his lapel—had eased over and politely inquired if he could buy Louise a drink, and she had smiled and politely declined the offer.

"I'm waiting for someone," she'd said, and the gentleman had smiled back and nodded, as though this were obvious, as though it were impossible that a woman as stylishly dressed and attractive as she would be unaccompanied for long.

When the gentleman went away Louise turned and glanced at herself in the window. She looked wonderful. Never in her whole life had she considered herself elegant but there was no other word to describe the person she saw—a tall elegant woman wearing a simple black dress and pearls. True, the image in the glass was faint and seemed to hover above the city like a phantom, but it was all the reassurance she needed at the moment. She looked like she belonged.

The woman at the end of the bar had gotten up and gone over to the piano. She began to play, warming into it with some soft tentative chords. The piano had a rich shimmering sound. She was slim, almost anorexic-looking, with a dark spider web of hair, and when she sang her voice was thin and reedy too, barely above a whisper. Hard lines edged the corners of her eyes. Louise wondered how long she'd knocked around before landing a spot like this, how many dues she'd paid and losers she'd encountered, how many ill-starred nights she'd suffered through to put that dry and brittle sound in her throat. To sing well you had to be blue—that's what they always said—but Louise didn't believe it. You sang better when you were in love.

She turned and looked out the window again. The moon was like a big spotlight on the city, which lay spread out beneath her like a personal gift. If she looked in the distance she could see all the way to Indiana, but she wasn't interested in looking back there. She waited for the room to turn and give her a view in the other direction—to the airport and the lights that glittered along the strip. It wasn't exactly the wide-open spaces, but now it was all the farther west she wanted to be.

She glanced at her watch; almost eleven. Suddenly she felt a quick surge of panic, but she lit a cigarette and put the thought out of her mind. He'd probably just gotten tied up at work. He'd be here, she wasn't worried. He wasn't like the others. Her luck was different now. Things were breaking her way. Any minute he'd be coming around the corner with unruly hair and a sheepish smile on his face, a Windy City Romeo who would wave and hurry over to sit in the moonlight with the new Louise.

"Take another look, Kohler. Are they still out there?"

Ritchie edged over to the window. A tall rubber tree had been dragged in front of it, and he peered through its tongue-shaped leaves at the sleek gray auto that was parked in front of a dumpster. It had two sharp fins sticking up in back and grillwork like teeth. Three black men were sitting inside it and another stood leaning against a door. Ritchie could see the small red points of their cigarettes glowing in the darkness.

"Yep. They're still there."

"How many?"

"I already told you—four."

"Any of 'em got a hat on?"

Ritchie looked again. "Nope. No hats."

They'd been hiding in the office for quite a while, Ritchie sitting in the swivel chair and Mars down on the floor way over in the corner, his back pressed tight against the wall. The room was dark, wreathed in shadow. The only light came from outside, where the four men waited—a thin silvery column of lamplight that slanted in and fell at Mars's feet, faintly illuminating the cigarette butts that littered the floor around him like a swarm of squashed amber bugs. The air was stale and smoky, but a certain other smell, a pungent animal scent, was coming from the corner where Mars slouched, his legs drawn up, a bottle of Scotch in one hand and a gun in the other, the barrel resting against his knee.

Ritchie reached over and grabbed something out of the liquor cabinet, he didn't care what it was. Mars put the bottle down and lit another Kool. The remnants of a meal were on a tray in the corner, bones and skin in a bloody-looking sauce. Similar trays were piled up near the door. He'd been cooped up back there for a couple of days, he'd told Ritchie, paying a busboy to slip food to him, squatting in the corner with the lights out and sucking on those meals like a ghoul.

"Are they still out there?" Mars asked again.

Ritchie told him not to ask that anymore. He'd been asking that constantly, ever since Ritchie had come back to see what he wanted. He'd walked through the reception room and gone to that little back office and stood uncertainly in the doorway. The room was dark. Nobody home. Annoyed, wondering what kind of stunt the soul man was pulling on him, Ritchie had been about to turn around and head back when he heard a low poisonous voice beckoning him from the floor.

"C'mon, Kohler," Mars was now saying. "Take another look. Tell me what you see."

"Cars. I see cars."

"A gray one?"

"Yes, a gray one."

"Jesus." Mars swallowed. "Listen. Did you happen to see . . . was there another brother in the lounge? Muscular motherfucker. Five-seven. Wearing a hat?"

Ritchie hadn't caught the hat, but he remembered the man. "Yeah. As a matter of fact he's been asking for you."

"Sure. Of course he was."

Ritchie fidgeted in the swivel chair, making it squeak. He pictured her sitting alone in the restaurant, waiting, a worried look clouding her face. He could still get there a few minutes late if he hurried, but time was evaporating and he sensed the night slipping away. Mars, meanwhile, had temporarily lapsed into stoic silence, like a soldier trapped behind enemy lines.

"Hey. Wake up over there." Ritchie threw a ballpoint at him. "Tell me what's going on."

"I already told you—I can't."

"I'm leaving then." Ritchie leaned forward, putting his hands on the desk. "I'd like to help you, man, but I can't wait around here all night."

"You *can't* leave, Kohler. You gotta help me." His voice came out of the shadows in low choking tones, as if someone's hands were already wrapped around his throat. Ritchie smelled that smell again. He'd never smelled anything like it before; it was the sweat of desperation, the odor of pure fear.

"Look. How do you expect me to help you if you won't tell me what it's all about?"

"All right," Mars said. "I'll tell you." He hesitated, looked around. "But you got to promise not to say anything about this to anyone else, Kohler. You got to swear it."

"Okay," Ritchie said.

"Swear it."

Ritchie sighed. "I swear not to tell anyone. Now please tell me what the hell is going on."

Mars reached for the bottle between his legs and told him. It all began, he said, with the Mighty Funkateers. The big night at the Imperial. He asked Ritchie if he remembered about the big night at the Imperial. Ritchie said sure, how did it go? Mars said don't ask how it went. It went terrible. It went straight down in flames. It was all his fault too, he admitted. He'd miscalculated. By pairing the Mighty Funkateers with that perennial fave at the Imperial, XX, a certain visionary figure on the local music scene had fucked up.

"How so?" Ritchie said.

Mars continued. It seemed that the soul band went on first and they did not go over all that well with XX's loyal following, who'd come to worship their nihilistic heroes and blow off some steam; in other words, they didn't have a lot of patience for love funk in capes and hats. As soon as the brothers came out, the crowd turned hostile. They started booing and stamping their feet and demanding that the Funkateers get their asses off the stage. The soul men had drawn some South Side followers of their own, who weren't about to sit still for this rudeness. The situation grew ugly. There was name-calling, threats, put-downs of musical taste. Punches were thrown. Weapons were whipped out. Someone fired a beer bottle at the stage. The Funkateers hastily unplugged their instruments and exited, but it was too late, the fighting had started, ill will reigned inside the Imperial with punkers and funkers beating on each others' heads.

"Jesus," Ritchie said. "Where were you when all this happened?"

"Backstage with Tommy T. Dig this: we were congratulating each other, how about that for a laugh? We're giving each other fives and tens for our unique vision of the future. Black and white—that was the idea. Punk and funk, together for the first time, for the edification of America and our mutual gain. We're at the dawn of a new age in the industry." He hit the bottle again and wiped his mouth on his sleeve. "What a joke."

"Don't blame yourself," Ritchie said. "You had an idea. It wasn't your fault that it didn't work out."

Mars leaned his chin on the bottle, considering this. "Yeah, but I should've known better. I should've used my head. Tommy tried to warn me. He told me it might not work. He said the mix wasn't right. It was, like, too extreme. You've got to see this XX following, Kohler. These people are total animals. They live in caves. Tommy said he had serious qualms about it, but I won't take no for an answer, see? I'm getting antsy. I can't wait. I've got a tremendous investment in these jungle bunnies and so I strongly suggested to my queasy friend that it would be better for him all the way around if he went ahead and made the booking."

He was silent for a moment. Ritchie was leaning back in the swivel chair. He had no idea what all this had to do with the gun in Mars's lap and the four men in the parking lot—or, for that matter, with him. All he knew was that he had reservations with Louise at eleven: he wished Mars would get to the point.

"Listen," he blurted. "I've got another commitment here, Mars. I got to get going. I can't—"

"When the bottles started flying," Mars continued, "I knew we were in big trouble. Boom—I see this fucker hit the back wall and I knew I had to act fast. I run out and hustle the Funkateers off the stage and then I try to be a hero, dig? I've got a deal for two more nights in this hell hole, so I grab a mike and start telling everyone to calm down. Tommy's out there with me. We're waving our arms and begging everyone to be nice and knock off with the stomping. No way. It was unstoppable, Kohler. It was strictly punch and kick. We're up there, two cooler heads trying to prevail, and pretty soon people are throwing shit at *us!*"

"Christ. What happened then? Did you get out of there in time?"

"Believe me, I tried. But they came after me, Kohler. A whole bunch of these burnouts got together and all of a sudden, like, rushed the stage. *Chicks,* Kohler! The chicks were the worst. They were all over me, man. This one chick in a mohawk is coming at me with a nail file. This other chick with orange hair has got her knuckles in my eye . . ."

He'd been wearing dark glasses, and suddenly he lifted them off and turned his head around, showing Ritchie the damage. The area surrounding his left eye was a hideous magenta color, and the eye itself was swollen nearly shut. Even in the darkness Ritchie could see he had one prize-winning booboo there—it looked like something that had burst out of a cocoon.

"The human hand, Kohler," Mars went on. "Don't tell me the human hand can do this kind of destruction. Not without help. Take a look at this mutha, will you. Hurt? I think the slit must've used a weapon on me. A bottle opener or something. Maybe she had fangs on her ring. I'm talking orange hair, Kohler, all teased up and frizzy, like she'd crawled out of the atomic rubble somewhere. You ever have your eye gouged out by a chick with orange hair? It's humiliating, Kohler. It's no fun at all. And you know what else? They stole my mink. I'm serious. These vicious twats, like, all ganged up on me and tore it right off my back—do you believe it? Right now, right this very minute, some chick in a mohawk is bouncing off the walls wearing *my* mink coat."

Ritchie was still staring at the eye. "You ought to stick some ice on that, Mars. Put a couple of cubes on it to get the swelling down." He reached for the small ice bucket in the liquor hutch but it was only full of lukewarm water. "You want me to get some? No problem. Wait here and I'll go get ice."

Ritchie got up off the chair but Mars waved the Turk at him, motioning for him to sit back down. It wasn't a particularly threatening gesture, but Ritchie respected it nonetheless.

"Forget the ice. The ice doesn't matter." Mars now folded his arms across his chest, imitating a stiff. "Those chicks, they should've just finished me off back there. They would've been doing me a favor if they'd like church-keyed me to death. I'm ruined, Kohler. It's all over for the kid. My boogaloos are history. My master plan is down the drain." He bumped his head against the wall and then sat up and looked at Ritchie, his bad eye shining like a patch of rust in the lamplight. "You're my last hope, Kohler. You got to help me find a way out."

"I still don't understand."

"You see those bros out there? The guys in the car?"

"What about them?"

"They want me, Kohler. Them and their boss man, Brim."

"What for?"

"Money," Mars said. "I owe them some money."

"How much?"

Mars shrugged. "About twenty grand."

"Twenty grand!" Ritchie said. "Let me get this straight: you owe that guy in the lounge twenty thousand dollars?"

"That's right."

"Jesus." Ritchie whistled, thinking about it.

"It was so simple." Mars's voice had taken on a ghostly, wistful tone. "We were partners, right? We'd done business before. International transactions, if you know what I'm saying. Air freight. Colombia to Miami to O'Hare. A regular circuit, the right people bought—I pick it up in the limo and drive it over to Congoland. No muss, no fuss. Everyone's happy. And then these fucking jocks start croaking, the President gets on TV, everyone gets hysterical, and the party's over—my guy in the sky won't come near me anymore."

"So?"

"So I've got to come up with a new connection. Low risk. I tell my partner twenty large and we'll see what develops. I tell him I've got a new guy who's shopping around. If a deal's there, he'll come back with the product—if not, everyone gets their money back. No sweat. It's a fishing expedition. There was only one problem. I made it all up."

Ritchie squinted at him. "You made it up? What for?"

"For *hats*—that's what for. For capes and brand new glitter. Better equipment for my bros. Amps, Kohler. Fucking pianos. Drums. Do you have any idea, roomie? You got the slightest notion what that shit runs?" Mars wagged his nose and hit the bottle again. "*Image*, Kohler—that's what I'm talking about. To make it big you can't nickel-and-dime it. You got to go first class. It was a sound business decision. I divert Brim's capital, I finally get a shot at the Imperial which leads to other more lucrative opportunities, I get a good yield on my investment and then I go back to Brim and tell him my guy came up empty and give him his money back. Perfect! My plan was slick, my reasoning flawless—and then these mutants crawl out of the woodwork and Brim starts asking questions and now I can't even leave the building. You gotta help me, roomie. What am I gonna do?"

"Talk to them," Ritchie said. He could see her again, a lone figure sitting in candlelight, waiting at a table by the door. It was dim where she was sitting. He could barely see her face. "Just wave 'em all in here and tell 'em you want to chat."

Mars's voice came out of the darkness, a shrill whine. "I can't do that. What am I gonna say?"

"Anything. Tell 'em your guy got robbed or something. Make something else up."

Mars waved the gun. "Don't like it. Think of something else."

"Call Nicky. Get on the horn and explain the situation to him. He's your cousin, right? He's gotta help you out."

There was a brief silence; for a moment Ritchie thought he'd hit the jackpot, but then Mars spoke again, this time with a note of embarrassment in his voice. "I can't call Nicky."

"Why not?"

"Because I've been stealing from him, too."

Ritchie nearly jumped out of the chair. "You've been stealing from the *company*?"

"Publicity, Kohler. Brochures. Demos. You think it's cheap renting a studio? This is a highly competitive industry, roomie. How do you expect to get anywhere if your act isn't known?"

Ritchie rubbed his palms together, washing his hands of the reprobate. "You fucked up, Mars—that's my opinion. Lying, scheming, stealing from your own relative . . ." He got to his feet. "Sorry, man—there's nothing I can do."

"But you've *got* to help me, Kohler!"

"Why?" He stood there a moment, looking down at the soul man. Mars's eyes were sullen and his jaw hung down to his chest. More and more his face seemed to be taking on the dull glazed appearance of a victim. "You called this tune, Mars—give me one good reason why I should help you out."

That hangdog expression suddenly left Mars's face and he, too, snapped to his feet. "Because you *owe* me, friend—that's why."

"I owe you?" Ritchie said. He was looking up at him now. "How do you figure that?"

"C'mon, Kohler. Think a minute. Where do you want me to start?" He extended his bony fingers, one by one. "I gave you a place to live. I got you a job. *Women*, Kohler. What about all the women I lined you up with? You think any of those bimbos you diddled would've even *talked* to you if it wasn't for me?"

Ritchie moved his shoulders around. His hands were jammed deep into the pockets of his shiny red knicks. "Yeah—but I'm not interested in that anymore."

"You were then. Then you were extremely interested. But now you're above all that, right? You're in *love*." Mars chuckled and moved in a little closer, his shadow looming large against the wall. "You owe me for that too, roomie. Who the hell brought you here? Who got you out of that little grinder shop you were working in?" Mars drew all his fingers together and then poked one into Ritchie's chest. "Face it, Kohler. You owe me for everything. You'd still be back there selling your daddy's Ding Dongs if it wasn't for me."

He poked him again and Ritchie fell back into the chair, as though bitten by a snake. He looked for a way out, but there wasn't any.

Mars was right in front of him, and the walls seemed to be closing in.

"All right," he finally said. "What do you want me to do?"

"Get my ass out of here."

"How?"

"Stuff me into a garbage bag, how do I know? Go out into the kitchen and get a big cardboard box."

"Then what?"

"Load me in your car and drive me to the airport."

Ritchie thought a minute, rubbing his chest. Maybe he could get her a message. He'd leave word at the desk that he'd be a little late.

"Okay. I'll find something and drive you to O'Hare."

"No. Not O'Hare."

"Why not O'Hare?"

"Because he'll have guys at O'Hare. I know him, Kohler. His primitives will be all over the place, watching for me. Think of someplace else."

They hunkered together, sweating, and thought about the sky.

"Where's the next closest airport?" Mars was saying. "Out of the city."

"I don't know," Ritchie said. "Milwaukee?"

"Fuck Milwaukee. Indiana—that's it. We're going to Indiana, roomie. It's a state, isn't it? They gotta have an airport there."

12

Teddy Drake's dressing room was surprisingly big, bigger than her living room. It had nicer furniture, too—she especially liked the love seat occupying the far corner of the room. It was violet and had a pattern of pale yellow roses woven into the material. The vanity she sat in front of was equipped with a big mirror with bright golden bulbs running along the edges of it, just like in the movies. The narrow bathroom in back had a shower stall. She reached for the bottle of vodka she'd taken from Mars's office and thought how pleasant this room was, how a person could practically live here if she wanted to; unfortunately, this room, too, was a lie.

When she'd gotten to the club Vinnie had tried to explain that they'd already left—he'd even buzzed the office for her a couple of times—but she'd had to go back and see for herself. She was still angry, but she felt something else, a flicker of hope, the tiniest belief that it was just a misunderstanding, that he'd be back there somewhere with a good explanation why he'd left her in the cold. So she went back with Vinnie's key and opened the office, walked through the reception area to that small inner sanctum still believing she'd find them there—the lowlife suffering maybe from some terrible affliction, a severe case of inner rot, and Ritchie ministering to him, spooning him sips of ice water and wiping his head with a cloth.

But they weren't, of course. *Somebody* had been there recently—the room was in total chaos and had that lived-in appearance, if it were being lived in, that is, by Goths—but Vinnie was right: they were gone. Still, even then she felt that tiny flame burning inside her, and she rushed to the window to see if his car was there, parked in its usual spot. The lowlife's van was there, hogging up two spaces as usual, but there was no sign of Ritchie's meek little car. She scanned the whole lot, looking for it, looking for any sign of life out there, but all she saw were four black men sitting inside a long gray auto and staring back at her with sullen unflinching eyes.

Vinnie said he hadn't left a message either, but she searched for one anyway, her hands sweeping across the desk. She knocked over a bottle of stomach medicine; the cap was loose and a little bit of pink fluid leaked out and collected at the base of the Rolodex. She ran across all kinds of stuff—inventories and ledger sheets and bills from a State Street funk shop—but no message, nothing, not a fucking word. She felt the anger flare inside her then and thought, Why should he leave a message? Why should he be any different? She could see him, cruising the strip with his buddy, el demento, some 747 airhead hanging on to his arm. Just like old times. She stopped looking. No, there wouldn't be a message. There never was.

She'd had four or five drinks at the restaurant and was already pretty loaded, but she reached for a half-full bottle of vodka in the liquor cabinet and took a giant glug. She took another. Might as well get good and shit-faced. Might as well get bombed. When she got up and left the office she took the bottle with her, passing through the empty reception area where, above her, on the walls, a constellation of stars gazed down, beaming their toothy show-biz smiles.

She saw more pictures in Teddy's dressing room: Ella, Della, Peggy Lee and Sara Vaughan. He'd had the glossies taped to the mirror for inspiration; she was surprised he'd left them behind. They were the first things she'd noticed when she'd wandered in, more out of curiosity than anything else. The door had been open and she'd wanted to see what the room was like. For a brief moment she wanted to sit in there, in front of those pictures, and pretend she really was somebody instead of a sorry Hoosier, just like her mother, with that sorry Hoosier luck. The thing was, she hadn't even asked for this. She'd thought she was immune. All she wanted was to make a few bucks and take care of Joey—and then out of nowhere this goofy crusader rides up, Kohler the Just, Sir Ritchie the Lionhearted, doing her favors and being Daddy to her kid and asking nothing in return. He'd messed up her head, punched new keys in her program. And then, just when she'd started trusting again, he'd made like a Davis and hit the road.

Well, at least she'd finally learned her lesson. And she wasn't angry anymore. Just numb. She looked at the bottle; it was nearly empty. She looked at herself in the brightly lit, unforgiving mirror and the old Louise looked back, an ordinary woman who seemed older than she was, the hard-edged lines of experience settling deep about her eyes.

She got up to go to the bathroom, reeling across the floor. She was a lot drunker than she'd thought she was. She was good and skunked. The vodka in her mouth tasted like kerosene and the carpet had a sharp synthetic smell. She found herself sitting a long time in the bathroom, and when she finally got up she stumbled against the sink. Nice going, girl, she said to herself—now you can't even leave. The room started spinning and she pitched herself onto the love seat and decided to rest there a moment, to see if her head would clear. Just a few seconds, that's all she needed, and then she'd hop a cab over to Jessie's place, wake up her baby, and take him home.

The road was dark and slippery. A light powdery snow was falling, icing the pavement so that it seemed to slither under Ritchie's wheels. They'd taken the Congo Express out of the city and now were darting through the flat Indiana countryside, passing empty fields which lay cold and dead under the moon. Sometimes a stand of trees rose up, the bare branches stretching toward the sky like skeletal arms.

Ever since they'd gotten past Gary, the signs were fewer, and farther apart. The last one had been for Michigan City, Ritchie seemed to recall. There was very little traffic. Except for an occasional semi that came bearing down, only to veer sharply at the last moment and shriek by on the left, Ritchie had the road to himself. There were no lights to mark where he was going and the snow kept swirling in his beams. The black road seemed endless, rushing up a few yards at a time.

"Jesus, Kohler—slow down a little. What are you trying to do—get us killed?"

Mars was right. There was no need to hurry. Ritchie eased up on the gas.

Ever since they'd left the city, the soul man had been in an up-tempo mood. For the first few miles he'd remained hidden in the garbage bag wedged into a cardboard box back in the hatch, bleating at Ritchie from time to time through the dark green plastic of the oversized Hefty. "Take a look, Kohler. You see anything? Are they back there?" Ritchie would glance in his rearview mirror and then turn slightly and address the bag. "How many times do I have to tell you? They're not there."

Finally, when they pulled off the Congo onto the Skyway, Mars climbed out of the bag, tearing at the plastic and breaking free like some enormous reptile emerging from its shell. Even then, he stayed back in the hatch for a while and kept his head down, wriggling around on his belly to see if any of Brim's men had suddenly picked up his scent. He seemed to have ascribed miraculous numbers and powers to his enemy. They could be anywhere, which was why he had nixed the idea of stopping at Gary. Ritchie was pretty sure they had an airport there, but Mars immediately vetoed the plan.

"Are you crazy? We can't stop at Gary." He was gazing out the window at the hellish landscape, at the innumerable towers belching thick sulphurous smoke into the sky.

"Why not?"

"Use your noodle, Kohler. Too many spades."

He laid low a little while longer back in the hatch; then, when they got beyond Michigan City, he felt safe enough to join Ritchie up front. He signaled this move with a sudden burst of laughter, a low primeval noise like something bubbling in a swamp, and then he jumped into the front seat and immediately threw back his head and roared.

"We did it, roomie! We made it! We tricked the primitive!" He bounced up and down on the seat, waved his arms. It did not seem possible that the car could contain his elation, and, for a moment, Ritchie thought he might crank down the window, vault out, and start dancing across the hood.

Suddenly he grabbed Ritchie's arm. "Tell me about it, Kohler. What happened? I couldn't see shit in that bag."

"Nothing happened. I just loaded you in the car and drove away."

"Yeah—but didn't they even look at you?" At that point, fifty miles from danger, Mars seemed genuinely disappointed he hadn't made a hairier escape. "Didn't any of 'em even get out of the car?"

"Nope." The truth was, Ritchie didn't know. He hadn't been looking. All he remembered were the glances he got, first from a couple of waiters and then from the cooks, as he wheeled the big dolly through the restaurant, into the kitchen, and then out back to the loading dock—that and how heavy his burden was. It wasn't easy moving a human being on a dolly, even if he was fitted snugly inside a cardboard box: a couple of times Ritchie had lost the equilibrium, the momentum shifted sharply downward, and the box spilled off onto the floor, producing squawks of protest from inside the Hefty.

"You had me going back there," Mars was now saying. He'd lost that sharp adrenaline edge and was leaning back in a mellow, more quietly expansive mood. "You gave me a pretty rough ride. I didn't know what the fuck was going on, especially those times I hit the floor."

"Sorry about that." Ritchie reached around and grabbed at his shoulder. He had an ache there and a dull pain in his groin. He believed he'd severely strained several muscles, particularly when he'd loaded Mars into the car.

"That's okay. Forget it. We made it—that's the important thing. We're going down in history, Kohler. We pulled the great white escape, just like Redford and Newman. Hey"—he abruptly sat up—"maybe we can get those guys to make the movie. I see Newman as you and me as Big Bob—or maybe it ought to be the other way around."

"I don't know, Mars," Ritchie said. "You decide."

He didn't feel like talking. A deep gloom had settled over him right around Michigan City and he just sat there, one hand on the wheel, staring at the snow. What bothered him most was that he hadn't even been able to leave her a message. He'd tried, but when he called the restaurant and described what she looked like, the person said sorry, she was already gone.

"I can't believe it, Kohler." Mars had settled back in the seat again. He was breathing easy, both hands behind his neck and his feet up on the dash, like a man leaning back on the deck of a yacht.

The bruise around his eye looked like a holiday decoration. Ritchie was the one who was all hunched over now, squinting through the fog on his windshield like an escaped con. "One minute I'm in it up to my eyeballs and the next I'm cruising down the highway—a free man. This is a great country, Kohler. You know why this is a great country?"

"No. Why?"

"Because you can get away with stuff. If you've got the balls and the right know-how, you can get away with anything you want."

Ritchie checked his gas gauge. He was starting to run a bit low. "Where are you going, incidentally? You given any thought to that?"

"Who cares? I'm outta here, Kohler. I'm free as a bird." He'd reached into his pocket and produced a thick roll of petty cash, no doubt lifted from the safe Nicky kept in the office. "What I was thinking of doing was heading for the islands. Plant my butt on the beach for a while and work on my tan. Drink rum and check out the native girls. Get me one of those itty bitty island suits that shows off your wang. Hey, you want to come with me?"

Ritchie shook his head.

"Why not? You and me, roomie. Paul and Big Bob—just like old times. They got some places down there haven't even been discovered. Tropical paradises, Kohler. Bananas everywhere. The bimbos wear no tops. You follow me? You see what I'm saying? We go down there, a couple of hot-shot Yankee bwanas like us, get ourselves big white suits with lots of medals on them and completely take over the joint."

A sign suddenly loomed out of the darkness: South Bend. Ritchie slowed and put his turn signal on.

"What are you doing?"

"Getting off."

"Here?" Mars looked around. They were on a slope and hints of civilization could be seen below them: a traffic light, Golden Arches, the caterpillarlike sprawl of a Holiday Inn. "You think they got an airport?"

"Sure. On account of the university."

"Which one?"

"Notre Dame."

Mars grinned. "You kidding me, man? Notre Dame, huh. The

Gipper. Knute Fucking Rockne. Rah rah rah. Gotta love it." He
leaned over and looked at Ritchie again. "You sure you don't want
to come with me? Think it over, friend—we'll live like princes."

Ritchie told him he wasn't interested. He didn't happen to feel
like a prince at that moment. He wasn't sure he could even make
it home.

"Well, at least take some money, then." Mars pressed a couple
of bills on him. "For gas."

Ritchie tried to give it back, but the money stuck to his hand.

Once they were all inside the building, the black men worked fast.
They each had a can of gasoline and went silently through the
deserted restaurant, like shadows, splashing the drapes, the tables
and chairs, dousing everything in sight. Painted camels gazed down
from the walls. The fig trees dripped like candles. Vapors rose to
the ceiling where, through large glass panels, the moon glowed
faintly behind a curtain of clouds.

When they were finished with the dining room, the men split up.
One headed for the kitchen, one went into the lounge, and two more
ducked into the corridor to take care of the office. The man with
the gold chains, Brim, sat on the stage and directed the operation
with a series of curt nods; other than that, he remained motionless
with his hands folded across his chest, like a Buddha, a stone authority, a monument to justice in another part of the world.

He was disappointed, naturally, that the rabbit had temporarily
escaped, but other than that the operation was going well. They'd
had no trouble gaining access to the building. All he'd done was
wait until closing and then hide in the men's room until everyone
had had a chance to clear out. He knew they'd send somebody in
there, but he wasn't worried about that, not even when it turned
out to be the bartender from the lounge, the big motherfucker with
the scar by his eye. He came in and poked his head into all the
stalls; when he got to the one at the end, near the towel machine,
Brim, who was sitting in there reading a *Trib*, pointed a gun at his
head and shushed him with a finger. The bartender turned as white
as the porcelain and didn't say a word.

"You didn't see us and you didn't hear us," Brim said later, after
they all were in. "It was just a dream, understand?"

The big bartender, the one called Vince the God, stared at the gun and nodded. "I didn't see nothing."

"Smart cookie."

"Now what?" The God licked his lips.

Brim opened his eyes wide and stretched up on his tiptoes, so that their faces were only a few inches apart. "Poof," he whispered. "Disappear."

The men came back out of the shadows, carrying their empty cans. Already the Oasis was burning. Fire crackled in the lobby and the kitchen was filling with smoke. There was a big pile of table-cloths in a corner of the dining room and the men lit them and hurled them about like flaming flags. Brim watched from the stage. It would be a fine show, a righteous blaze indeed—and a nice surprise for the rabbit, something for him to think about until he was finally tracked down and skinned.

Brim hopped off the stage, motioned with his head, and the men pitched their empty cans and followed him out a side exit, the fire shining in their jackets, glowing in their eyes. Fire danced in the lounge and raced through the lobby, snapping up the drapes and blackening the photos, the glossy faces of the stars. Alarms went off and the ceiling began to drizzle, but by then the whole restaurant was burning and a thick black smoke belched up toward the ceiling, obliterating the moon.

Smoke poured from the back office, too, filling the corridor with a dense choking fog that seeped into the dressing rooms, including the one where an unlucky woman lay sleeping, dreaming of the mountains and the wide open spaces, a more honorable place where the air was pure and people kept their word.

13

"You know what's wrong with human beings, friend?" the little man with the eye patch was saying. "Our personal habits. Smoking. Drinking to excess. Putting all kinds of trashy food in our systems. You take a real close look at a Whopper lately?" The man shuddered and covered his good eye.

He lifted his glass and Ritchie poured some orange juice in it. He was perched on a stool right in front of the cash register with his own bag of nuts, which he cracked open one by one with the fastidiousness of a monkey picking bugs off itself. Ritchie wasn't sure if he was an extremely short man or a tall midget: he didn't appear to be even five feet tall. On the other side of the bar, a couple of skinny guys with big noses were hunched on their stools like buzzards, drinking Pabst Blue Ribbons and staring at the naked woman who danced on a platform in a corner of the lounge. She wasn't completely naked, nor was she young. She wore high heels and a G-string, and moved lethargically, with practiced aloofness, bumping and thrusting mechanically in the spotlight, her big yams swaying and a look of complete detachment on her mannequin face. Another woman, also in high heels and a G-string, carried drinks to the men at the tables, sitting in pairs or alone in the dark and watching the woman who danced on the stage. The music droned on endlessly. Occasionally the woman would walk out onto the runway and squat, or lean over and dangle her breasts above a table; a hand would reach out with a dollar bill in it and the woman would take it with that same air of indifference and jam it into her string.

"You follow me, friend? You know what I'm saying? Take yourself, for example." The man cracked open another nut and tossed the shell into an ashtray. His eye patch was a piece of yellowish gauze tied to his head with a shoelace. "Be honest. Ask yourself a question: How much red meat do you consume in an average week?"

Ritchie pried the tops off a couple of Budweisers and put the bottles on a tray. "I really wouldn't know."

"You should, friend. You should keep track of stuff like that. It's a basic scientific principle: You are what you eat—nothing less, nothing more."

The music stopped. The woman walked back to the record player that stood behind her on the platform and turned the record over. Then she started dancing again. Ritchie didn't know her name. She'd dance both sides of the record and then she'd get down off the platform and start waiting tables while the other woman in the G-string got up there and took her place. Her body was about the same as the first dancer's, only a little heavier, and she danced the same way. Ritchie didn't know her name either. Nor did he know the name of the lounge he'd been working in the past few weeks—a dive just off Wabash, under the tracks. As far as he knew, it didn't have a name, just a purple sign—GIRLS—flashing in the window and a couple of numbers above the door.

This was the third or fourth place he'd worked at in a couple of months—he couldn't remember exactly how many. All he knew was that each place was sleazier than the one before. He'd started on Rush Street and moved progressively south, into the flesh district; the farther south he went, the seedier the clientele and the less the dancers wore. The women here were supposed to wear their strings at all times, but sometimes on a Friday or Saturday they'd take them off and dance in the altogether, and that's when Ritchie was supposed to keep a sharp eye out. The lounge had a strict no-groping rule, and it was one of Ritchie's duties to make sure none of the customers got out of line. So far, nobody had, but he kept hoping. He longed for conflict. He kept looking at those anonymous figures sitting in the shadows and hoping that one would reach out for a dancer, or spring up onto the stage, and he'd have to come out from behind the bar and rescue her. Maybe it would be some big drunken meatball who'd take offense, and they'd have to go outside, in the alley, and settle it. Cut each other with broken bottles.

Make each other bleed. That's what he wanted, but so far all the customers did was sit in the darkness and stare, motionless, like cardboard outlines of men, one hand under the table and the other clutching a greasy dollar bill.

"It's all in the diet," the little man with the eye patch was saying. The music kept beating like an artificial heart. "Take your great apes, for example. You don't see them clogging up their systems with a lot of that trashy red meat, do you? Hell no. They stick with your basic fruits and vegetables, and they live healthier and happier lives than we humans do. It's a fact. They get along with each other, too. None of this fighting and warlike shit we're always into—and where do you think we get that from? From *meat*, that's where. We live on the flesh of other creatures, friend—what do you expect?"

On the way home that night, Ritchie thought about the naked dancers and the repulsive little man with the patch on his face and decided not to go back there anymore. About a week in one place was all he could seem to stand lately, but that wasn't a problem. There were lots of places to hide in the city, places every bit as bad as that one, or worse. You didn't have to look very hard to find them either—just watch for the night crawlers and you'd know where to go.

It was the end of February, but the weather was freakishly warm. Strange. Ordinarily you drive home this time of year you see ice floes on the lake and a tundra of snow-covered beaches, but tonight was so mild and breezy Ritchie could see people walking along the sand in their shirtsleeves like it was the Fourth of July. Cabbies drove by with bare arms dangling out of windows. Ritchie, on the other hand, splashed through the city with his heater going full blast, and still he felt chilled to the bone.

An old sitcom was playing on the television when Ritchie got back to the apartment. He could hear that phony canned laughter as soon as he opened the door. It was a habit he'd gotten into recently—leaving the television on. He couldn't stand silence, even for one second, so he just kept the TV on at all times.

He threw his keys on the kitchen table and then got a bottle of wine and a Flintstones glass out of a cabinet and carried them out to the set. He went rapidly through the channels to see what was on. Besides the sitcom there was a cooking show, a war movie, and a *Big Valley* rerun—Barbara Stanwyck with the whip and the leather pants. He decided on the war movie and then sat back on the cinderblock sofa and filled up his glass. Heavy metal hammered down from the ceiling; across the hall, the baby cried. He checked the level in the wine bottle. It was about half full, just enough to get him to sleep.

He awoke at daybreak, shivering, his whole body clammy with sweat. He'd been having that dream again, the one he'd had almost every night for the past two months. The dream seemed real and never changed. It always started at the Oasis—the fire, the smoke, the murky weblike membrane that confined him and resisted the frantic tearing motions of his hands. That was the scariest part. Then it switched to the attendant with the clipboard and the thick brillo pad of hair leading him into a big chilly high-ceilinged room that reminded Ritchie of the bus station. It had that impersonal quality of a bus station, the sense that everyone in there was on his way to someplace else. The back wall was lined with lockers, just like in a bus station, only these were bigger. The attendant was dressed all in white, like the Good Humor man, and before he unzipped the bag he warned Ritchie to do this quickly and to stand on the side of her face that hadn't been burned so bad.

   That was the most vivid part, the one he remembered best. The haziest part of the dream was at the graveyard, probably because it had so little to work with; it was as though what happened there was buried so deep in his mind not even a nightmare could unearth it. All he remembered of the actual event was his determination to handle the arrangements—under the circumstances he felt it was the least he could do—and the small procession that left the cemetery, the same one where his mother was buried, just a handful of friends and a few people from Indiana packed into four or five cars, not even enough to cause a minor traffic jam. He remembered that and how, on the long ride home, the boy sat beside him in the back seat of the limo and looked out the window with those big dark eyes. His mother was dead and he was soon on his way to live in Indiana, and Ritchie had wondered what he was thinking, how the world must have looked to him then. Snow was falling, coating the

bare trees and smothering the frozen ground. Ritchie had the feeling
he was screwing up, that he ought to talk to him and comfort him
in some way, but he couldn't do it. He didn't know how. It also
occurred to him that there were a lot of places he hadn't taken him
yet. He hadn't taken him to Great America yet, or to the top of the
Sears Building. He hadn't even taken him back to the museum to
see Bushman the gorilla again, like he'd promised him he would.

He tried to go back to sleep, but bright sunshine was already pouring
in through the window and his neck was sore from passing out on
the couch again. One of those chatty morning shows was playing
on the television. Ritchie sat back and rubbed his neck while a bald
weatherman with a joking manner came on and explained the freakishly warm weather that was happening all over the country. Behind
him, there were big smiling suns all over the map. They looked just
like the weatherman.

Somebody in Kansas that was over a hundred had knitted the
weatherman a pair of wool mittens. Ritchie watched him try them
on. After a while he got up and went into the kitchen. Cups and
glasses were stacked on the counter, but no dishes; he ate very little
now and what he did eat he put on a paper plate.

For breakfast he pried a Fudgesicle out of the freezer, and then
he put the teakettle on. While he waited for the water to boil he
found himself staring at the telephone. Suddenly he had an impulse
to call someone. But who? He could call the police again and see
if they were getting anywhere on the case, if they'd followed up on
all the leads he'd given them, but he was pretty sure they'd just tell
him the same thing. It was still under investigation. Manpower was
limited. They were doing the best they could. For a while he'd been
calling almost daily, and finally one of the detectives on the case—
a man named Hamilton—had told him to please not call anymore,
they'd notify him as soon as something broke. There had been a
distinct note of weariness in the detective's voice, and Ritchie realized the policeman had begun to consider him an annoyance,
possibly even a crackpot, a deeply troubled man. Ritchie couldn't
blame him for that.

No, he couldn't call the police again. Still, he felt the need to talk
to someone and he wondered who else he could call. He could call

Big Joe, or even Margie. He could chat with them a while and see how they were doing and maybe even make plans to drop in for a visit pretty soon. Hardly a day went by when he didn't think of doing that; sometimes he even picked up the phone. But then he always put it down again. They'd have nothing to say to him. He'd burned all those bridges a long time ago and there was no going back.

He poured himself a cup of instant coffee and carried it over to the window. The big thaw continued. Snow and ice dripped off buildings, and the piles of slush along the curbs and sidewalks were softening and turning gray in the lunatic heat. That crazy hot sun had only been out a few moments but already the city was melting, dissolving in front of his face. No, there wasn't anyone to call, not even Hilda. Why should she want to hear from him?

He also knew it was time to start moving. He'd kept paying the rent and living in the apartment, but now he knew there was nothing to keep him there, nobody to pin him down. He was finally free, truly anonymous. He also was having a problem with his eyes. He didn't know where to look, that was the problem. The candle, the sketches on the walls, the Ellington record leaning against the stereo— her things were everywhere. Everywhere he looked reminded him of Louise.

He glanced at these things and then he shut his eyes, but he could still see them. He could see everything. Eyes open, eyes closed— it didn't make any difference: what he was seeing was exactly the same.

14

Ritchie was zonked out again on the sofa when the telephone rang. He bolted up and looked around in confusion. Outside the street lights were on. The apartment was as dark as a tomb.

The phone kept ringing in the kitchen, a harsh insistent noise that jangled his nerves like a fire alarm. It had been so long since anyone had called him that at first he'd hardly recognized the sound. Now he wondered who it could be. The only person he could think of was the club manager. Ritchie was due at work at seven, but he'd slept all day and well into the night, and now he supposed the guy was calling to find out where the hell his bartender was. Well, he could just forget it. That place was history. Ritchie had made up his mind not to go back.

He sat on the edge of the sofa until the telephone finally stopped ringing and then he slipped under the blanket again. He stared at the television. Some time during the day the picture had shrunk, telescoping into a small square in the center of the set; he could barely see what was on. A warm breeze blew in through the window and he could hear water dripping off the building, hear the drainpipes gush.

He was about ready to get up and give the TV a couple of whacks when the telephone rang again. Ritchie froze. Why did it have to keep bothering him? Why couldn't it leave him alone? He picked up his pillow and wrapped it over his ears but he could still hear the phone, jangling interminably, loud enough to awaken the dead.

Finally he got up and stalked into the kitchen and wrenched the receiver off the hook.

"What do you want?"

There was a brief pause and then a small, childlike voice came over the wire. "Kohler?"

"I don't know any Kohlers." Ritchie tried to make out the voice. It was vaguely familiar but he couldn't quite identify it. His memory was boarded up.

"Come on, Kohler. Don't joke around." There was another pause and then the voice grew louder. "Don't you know who this is?"

"No," Ritchie said.

"It's me. Joey."

"Joey?" Ritchie's heart started beating. He began to feel warm. "Joey Gallenko?"

"Who else?"

His heart was racing now and he felt warm all over; he even felt a tingle in his toes. "Are you still in Indiana? Listen, where are you calling from?"

"I'm at the bus station."

"The bus station! You mean here? The one downtown?"

"Where else? Hurry up and get over here, Kohler. The cops are giving me the eye."

He was sitting on a long wooden bench in front of the lockers, flipping a penny from hand to hand. On the floor beneath him was the hard little suitcase he'd taken to Indiana. It was boxlike in shape and resembled the sort of thing a ventriloquist would keep his dummy in. He had it tilted on end, his legs dangling over the side.

Ritchie bounded down the escalator and hit the floor running. Joey saw him coming, scrambled off the bench and picked up the suitcase and hurried toward him, lugging it with both hands. They met in the center of the lobby, under the big No Loitering sign.

Ritchie picked him up and hugged him; then he put him down and squatted so he could look at him eye to eye. The boy was getting bigger, there was no doubt about it. He was growing up fast.

Joey sniffed his breath. "You drunk?"

"No. Yeah. Maybe a little." He hadn't had anything to drink since morning, but lately it wasn't that unusual for him to wake up from his afternoon naps still sloshed. "I can't believe it. I mean, what are you *doing* here?"

"I came for a visit. Aren't you glad to see me?"

"Are you kidding?" It'd been two months since Joey had gone to
live with his Aunt Lucille in Indiana, but it seemed to Ritchie a lot
longer. It seemed like he'd been gone for years. "C'mon." He stood
and looked around, and then he picked up Joey's suitcase. "Let's
get out of here. This place gives me the creeps."

He took him around the corner to a twenty-four-hour Walgreen's,
bought him a cheeseburger and a Coke. The place was just like its
name—green walls, green light, even the men standing at the magazine rack had a greenish cast about them.

"So," Ritchie said, picking up a soggy french fry, "how are you
and your aunt getting along?"

"Okay." Joey hunched his shoulders in a noncommittal fashion.
He'd seemed unusually quiet and subdued ever since they sat down.
He drew his arms together and sipped his Coke and stared at the
door with cagey eyes, like an illegal alien.

"It was pretty nice of her to let you come for a visit," Ritchie said.
He examined the french fry and dropped it back onto the plate. It
had occurred to him that there was something very odd about this
whole situation. "What I can't get over is that she'd let you ride in
all by yourself like this—don't you think that's strange?"

Joey didn't answer. He hid his hands under the table and began
fidgeting on the seat.

"Whatsa matter? You need to go to the rest room?"

"Uh-uh."

"You sure?"

"Of course I'm sure. What do you think I am—a baby?"

Ritchie pursued his train of thought. "You didn't answer my
question. Don't you think that's odd—to let a little kid ride into a
big city, all by himself, late at night, on a bus?"

Joey blew into the straw and made the cola bubble. "She didn't
have nothing to do with it."

"Huh?" Ritchie leaned forward. "You want to run that by me
again?"

"She doesn't know. I waited until she fell asleep and then I stole
money out of her purse." He blew into his Coke again and then he,
too, leaned over the table, his eyes even bigger than usual and a

look of pure astonishment lighting up his face. "You want to hear something, Kohler? I ran away."

Two Cokes later the kid was still showing him the money. He had a big wad of bills in his fist and waved it under those green fluorescent lights as though it were plunder, or a captured flag. Ever since he'd told Ritchie the story of his escape—Ritchie had made him repeat the part about the sleeping pills—he'd been bobbing around in the booth like one of those little balloons you could buy in aisle five. He was so proud of what he'd done, so delighted by his own audacity, Ritchie had the feeling he might break free of his moorings entirely and float away. Ritchie, on the other hand, was hunched over the table like a turtle, his head low and his elbows at his sides. He felt an oppressively heavy, shell-like weight on his back, pressing down on him, pinning him to the seat.

"I'm not gonna count that money," he was saying. "Put it away."

Joey spread out the bills in both hands, like playing cards. He had a twenty in there, Ritchie could see, and a couple of tens. "Check it out, Kohler. There's over sixty dollars here. We could go *anyplace* with all this."

Ritchie snatched the money away from him and put it in his pocket, for safekeeping. "How many times do I have to tell you? *We're* not going anywhere."

"Why not?"

"Because I say so, that's why. Look, you shouldn't even be here in the first place. Your aunt is probably worried sick. She's probably got every cop in Indiana out looking for you already." He wondered what the rap was for harboring a runaway.

"No, she doesn't. I already told you, I put sleeping pills in her tea."

"How many?"

"Just three."

"You're sure?"

"Positive. What do you think I wanted to do—kill her?" He said this as though it had been a possibility. "The old bat is probably still snoring on the couch. She doesn't even know I'm gone."

Ritchie laid his head on the table. Drugging her tea, stealing her money . . . Jesus, what next? "Okay." With great effort he drew himself erect. "It's too late to straighten this out now, but first thing tomorrow I'm putting you back on a bus."

"Go ahead." Joey stuck out his jaw. "Put me on a bus if you want to—just don't send me back there."

"Why not?"

"Because I'm never going back there, Kohler. Never in a million years."

"But you have to," Ritchie said.

"How come? Why can't I just stay with you?"

"You can't, that's why. It's completely out of the question."

Joey squinched up his face. "Why are you being like this, Kohler? I don't understand."

Ritchie let out a long weary breath and glanced off into the toothpaste aisle. He didn't know how to explain it to him. He didn't know how to tell him that he had to start moving, the sooner the better, and that he couldn't drag along a little kid. *Especially* him. He drummed his fingers on the table, fidgeted his legs. He felt like jumping up, rushing back into the station and hopping on a bus himself, but that weight was still there, on his back, heavier than ever, and the boy was looking at him with pleading eyes. Why was it that every time he looked into them he, too, felt like a runaway?

"The answer is no," he finally said. "And don't ask me any more questions. Tomorrow morning you're back on the bus."

Joey's lip quivered. For an instant it seemed like he might start to cry, but he fought back the impulse and instead glared at Ritchie with that fiercely stubborn look, his jaw jutting and his dark eyes flashing defiantly. Ritchie recognized the expression, could see Louise's fistlike determination all over again.

"Go ahead," the boy was saying. "Put me on a bus. Put me on a thousand buses—I'll just keep running away."

Ritchie decided on a different approach. "Listen," he began. "I know how hard it is to adjust. I know what it must be like for a kid your age to go and live with a stranger. You've just got to give it time, that's all." He stroked the hair on his face; it was long and silky, well past the stubble stage. He wondered when was the last time he shaved. "Believe me," he continued, his voice taking on the lofty self-important tone of a TV aspirin salesman, "all you've got to do is hang in there a little longer and everything'll be okay."

Joey was picking at a thread on his sleeve. "She puts me in a closet," he said.

"What?"

The boy nodded solemnly. "She locks me in a closet, Kohler. With all her funny-smelling coats. It's dark in there. I can't breathe. I feel like I'm suffocating to death."

Ritchie stared in disbelief. "She locks you in a closet? For what?"

Joey shrugged. "It depends. For getting her stupid floor dirty, or for not cleaning my plate. Sometimes she puts me in there just for what I'm thinking."

"For what you're *thinking*?"

"Uh-huh. She says she can see right through me. She says she can look right inside my head and see all the nasty thoughts I have. 'Muling her'—that's what she calls it. 'You're muling me, boy—back in the closet again.' "

Ritchie leaned across the table and looked directly into Joey's face. "You're not making this up, are you? You're telling me she actually locks you in a goddamn closet—just for what's inside your head?"

"Yeah—and that's not all she does." His face was now narrowed into an angry squint. "She pinches me, Kohler, pulls my hair. Once, I said the F word to her and she stuffed my mouth with soap." He abruptly made a gagging expression. "You know what that's like, Kohler? You know what it tastes like to eat a whole bar of soap?"

Ritchie didn't answer. Anger choked him. He breathed fiercely through his nose.

"She never leaves me alone. She won't let me play with any of my stuff. She took away my GI Joes. 'You won't be needing these nasty things,' she said and threw them in the garbage. She reads the Bible at me, Kohler. For hours and hours. The same stupid stuff. She makes me get down on my knees and pray. 'You're muling Him,' she tells me. 'Get back down there, boy. You think you can mule the Lord?' "

Ritchie suddenly felt lighter, as though his anger were a rocket lifting him off the floor. "Listen, haven't you told anyone about this? Haven't you mentioned it to your friends?"

"What friends? I don't have any friends. She won't let me out of the trailer. Once, when she was taking a nap, I snuck away to pitch pennies by the playground and she caught me out there and locked me in the closet the whole rest of the day."

His nose was running and his eyes were red, but still he refused to cry. His fists were clenched tight. Seeing the strength stored deep inside that little body filled Ritchie with a kind of grace, that sense of being uplifted he hadn't felt for a long time: here the kid had been orphaned, locked up, abused, put through eighty kinds of hell—and still he hadn't lost his spirit.

"Now do you understand, Kohler? Now do you see what I'm saying? Go ahead, put me on a million buses—I'm not going back. Not ever. I wish she was dead. I wish she was almost dead and birds were all over her, pecking out her eyes."

Ritchie stared at Joey's suitcase, which sat in the booth beside him. Birds were too good for her—that's what he was thinking. Rats would be better. Or maybe those vicious South American bees. Put a swarm of those fuckers on her and see how she liked it.

"Where are we going, Kohler?" Joey said. Ritchie had suddenly bolted out of the booth, seized the suitcase, and begun heading for the door, pushing past the green men with their heads buried in dirty magazines. "You're not taking me back to the bus station, are you?"

"No." He was outside now, on the sidewalk, the boy standing right behind him. The street was deserted and tall buildings rose up all around them like an impenetrable mountain range. It was raining and the wind blew wet rags and bits of paper at them, hurled grit at their eyes. Ritchie stood there with the suitcase, glancing in one direction and then another, looking for a sign.

He felt Joey tugging at his coat sleeve. "Where, then? Where are you taking me, Kohler?"

He didn't answer. At that moment, he didn't have a clue.

15

Big Joe was underwater. He lay submerged in the tub like a whale, with just his eyes and nose sticking up above the surface, and also his knees. The water, hot and soothing, seemed to mingle in his system with the whiskey he'd drunk; the combined effect put him in a pleasant stupor and gave him the feeling he was suspended in a liquid cocoon.

A bottle of Hamms sat on the edge of the tub, and every so often Big Joe would reach up and take a sip; then he'd sink back under the water again. Next to the tub, on the soggy green bath mat, lay one of his pictorial histories of war, but Big Joe didn't bother looking at it. The book was just for show. Hilda was the one who insisted he bring a book in there with him. She didn't like him taking a bath after he came home from drinking; she was afraid he'd fall asleep and drown.

One time he'd forgotten his book and Hilda had barged in there with it and come right over to the tub to give it to him, and Big Joe had had to cover himself with a cloth.

"You forgot your book," she said.

"For Christ's sake," Big Joe said. "Can't you even knock?"

"I did." She stood there a moment, staring down at him, at the great white nearly hairless mass of him curled up in there like an enormous baby, and she'd compressed her lips and given him the withering look he'd seen her give him only two times before: once, when he refused to come up with a name for Ritchie, and the other time, a few months after Milly died, when she'd found him passed out in the bushes in the back of the house.

"What?" Big Joe said. He was unaccustomed to being seen naked by any woman now, especially his own sister, and, respecting taboo, he twisted his body to the wall. "I'm taking a bath in here—do you mind?"

"Look at you," Hilda had said. There was something about him that seemed to provoke a powerful disgust in her, as though he were a big ugly mess she kept finding in her bathroom and couldn't scrub away. "Why don't you get up out of there and go to bed?"

"I can't sleep in bed. You know that."

"Then help me out around here. Do something."

"Like what?"

"Fix the faucet." She pointed behind her, to the bathroom sink, into which leaked a steady stream of cold water. "Fix the toilet." The chain was broken. "The whole house is falling apart. Here, you can start with this." She went over to the hamper and picked up an aluminum towel bar that had fallen off the wall and shook it at him like a weapon. "Get to work around here—instead of lying in that tub all night."

"I don't feel good," Big Joe said. "Leave me alone."

"You don't feel good." Her face was a caricature of sympathy. "You don't eat right. You drink too much. You smoke." She pointed the towel rack at him and added, "You know what the doctor said."

"The doctor," Big Joe said. "The doctor can't do anything for me. The doctor can go to hell."

Hilda stood there looking at him a moment longer, then she finally let go of his war book which thudded like a mortar round onto the mat. "I give up. You're hopeless. Just don't fall asleep in here and drown on me," she warned him. "I'll have to call the circus to get you out."

She'd stalked from the room and Big Joe had picked up the washcloth and draped it over his eyes. She was right, of course—the house *was* falling apart. So was the store. It was dirty, one of the freezers had quit working, the meat slicer needed to be oiled. Produce moldered in the storage room and there were great empty spaces on the shelves. It looked like a store that was going out of business, which wasn't far from the truth. Every month Big Joe was losing money. Even his regulars, his most faithful customers, were going elsewhere and Big Joe couldn't blame them—his food was spoiled and his temperament was rotten; some days he didn't even bother to shave. The whole place was a disgrace to Big Hans, his father—which was why, one night, when the wind blew the sign off the store, Big Joe had just let it lie where it had fallen, in the alley by the dumpster. He didn't want his name up there anymore. He was too ashamed.

She was right about his drinking, too. He was drinking every day. He'd start with a six-pack, while he was working in the store, and then he'd close up early and walk down to the lodge and drink whiskey until his eyes got fuzzy and his head started to roar and he knew if he had another he wouldn't be able to make it home. Occasionally he drank with Frankie the cop or Louie the mailman, but mostly he drank alone. That was fine with him. The lodge had changed. Some of the older vets had died and others had stopped coming; new younger vets had taken their place. Big Joe didn't like them. He didn't like the way they looked—they all wore beads and one of them even had a pony tail—and he didn't like their attitude, the way they walked around in khaki jackets, with little flags stitched on the pockets of their jeans. They seemed to have a chip on their shoulders and their own style of doing things, their own personal way of showing respect. Big Joe would sit off by himself, near the television, and observe them, watch how, even in a simple card game, they seemed to project that cynical attitude, like they were all holding a grudge. Fuck 'em, Big Joe would say to himself; no one gave *me* applause either. He listened to them, but he could not understand their language. He didn't even know how to shake their hands.

One night he exchanged words with one of these new vets—he couldn't remember what about—and later Frankie came up to him and told him he was drinking too much. From then on, Big Joe stopped going to the lodge and instead did his drinking at a tavern on the other side of the street.

He didn't talk to anyone there, either, although everybody knew him. He didn't talk at all, not even to Hilda. She kept after him, asking what was the matter with him and suggesting things for him to do, as if what ailed him could be fixed as easily as a leaky faucet. The truth was, he couldn't tell her what was the matter with him because he didn't know himself. And then, that night she let him have it in the bathroom, he finally realized what it was. She was right about that, too: he was hopeless. He had nothing to live for, that was exactly what was wrong with him. Joe Junior had moved to Florida and his other son had disappeared. For all he knew, the kid could be in jail somewhere or bumming quarters on the street, one of the displaced people who ride the trains all day and sleep at night underground. What ate at him the most was that a couple of times he'd wanted to contact him, to find out how he was doing, to make the first move. He'd even had the phone in his hand, but he couldn't go through with it. He couldn't make the call. Now he couldn't reach him even if he wanted to. The goddamn joint he'd been working at had burned down and now Big Joe didn't even have a number, a place to start. The kid could be anywhere. He could be on the other side of the moon.

It was probably just as well, Big Joe thought. He'd lost that one a long time ago. In a way, he'd lost them both. The smart one, the success, didn't need him anymore, and the one who did need him didn't want what he had. He still got up every morning and opened up the store, like he'd been doing his whole life, but more and more his heart wasn't in it. Sometimes, hung over, he could barely drag himself out of bed. A dad ought to be needed, he'd think to himself bitterly—or what the hell was the point?

Maybe Joe Junior was right. Maybe he ought to sell everything and move to Florida. Everyone else was down there. He could die down there just as easily as here. Easier. Down there they dropped on the beach every day like flies. But he didn't want to be buried down there. No sir, not him. He already had his place reserved, in the boneyard, right next to Milly. If he moved to Florida he'd have to make them swear in writing to ship him back up, air freight if they had to. Put him on ice, like a mackerel. Be buried in Florida? It was out of the question. He'd never rest in peace.

He took another glug of beer and thought about the little man from the travel agency who'd come into the store the other day and asked him what he wanted for the property. It was a good spot, he admitted, a choice location, right on the corner in a residential area—they wanted to diversify, go where the people lived, they'd been putting too many outlets in malls. "I'm prepared to make you a very nice offer," the man had said. He'd looked around, as if he didn't think much of the present establishment, as if any offer at all would be doing Big Joe a favor, and Big Joe had told him it wasn't for sale. How could you put a price on everything you'd worked for? How could you sell your life?

He probably should've at least considered it though. A travel agency wasn't so bad. It was better than chicken, better than a taco stand. Still, every time he thought about it, his heart started to shrivel and all his insides revolted, disturbing that pleasant liquid world he was floating in. So he didn't think about it but just settled deeper into the water and lay there motionless, his eyes closed and his skin puckering, suspended, like something waiting to die—or waiting to be born.

He was still in the tub, half asleep, his nose barely sticking up above the water, when the bamming started. His ears were waterlogged and at first he could hardly hear it; the sound was faint, muffled, like something you might hear in a dream. Then he heard it again, louder, and he lifted up his head: someone was at the front door. The bell didn't work—that was another thing he hadn't gotten around to fixing—and someone was out there, pounding on the door with a fist.

He sat up a moment, dripping, and then eased back down into the tub again. It was probably just Henry Glotz complaining about the dog. He lay there, trying to become amphibian, but the bamming continued and he realized that if he wanted any peace he'd just have to get up and deal with the man. Hilda was probably down in the basement, doing the wash and listening to the radio—she seemed to be spending more and more time down there, as if she wanted to get as far away from him as possible. His mother was deaf. No one could hear the pounding but him.

He got up, cursing, great streams of water trailing from his body, and threw on a robe. Then he tromped down the stairs to the front door, flicked on the porch light, and peered through the diamond-shaped window, expecting to see the sour indignant puss of Glotz.

But it wasn't Henry. It was a small hairy stranger who was standing out there, his hands jammed deep into his pants pockets and the collar of his jacket turned up to keep the rain off his neck. Next to him, on the porch, was a nicked-up little suitcase, and next to the suitcase was a boy. He was about eight, Big Joe guessed, and stood in exactly the same posture as his older companion, his hands in his pockets and his back to the rain. Rumpled, exhausted-looking, their hair wet and plastered to their foreheads, they seemed like orphans who had endured a long and arduous journey, a pair of ragamuffins whom the wind had gathered up and for some reason deposited at Big Joe's door.

Well, he was no Salvation Army. Nor was he inclined to be the mark in some criminal game. He reached for the Louisville Slugger he kept by the door for just such situations and was about to open up and shoo these vagrants off his property when the older one suddenly reached out and mopped the boy's hair with his coat sleeves; then he put his hands in his pockets again. That gesture, the hands in the pockets, awakened something in Big Joe. It was as familiar to him as the smell of cold cuts that greeted him every morning. How many times had he told that kid: Keep your hands out of your pants.

Big Joe was not an emotional person, nor was he devout, but at that moment he felt like the old man in the Bible story, the one who rejoiced when his prodigal son returned. If he'd had an ox he would've slaughtered it, but instead he flung open the door and hollered, "Get in here before you catch cold."

That night they didn't do much talking. Hilda got dry clothes for them—she still had some of Ritchie's boyhood stuff in a trunk up in the attic—and warmed some soup, and they all sat around the kitchen table—Big Joe, Hilda, Ritchie and the boy, even Grammy Kohler got her old bones up off the davenport—and looked at each other with big sheepish smiles.

At one point Cha Cha slunk out of the closet to sniff out the new arrival, sidling up with his teeth bared and a typical suspicious growl. Undaunted, Joey reached down to pet his head, whereupon Cha Cha stopped growling and immediately fell onto his back, his little tail wagging and his legs sticking up in the air. Everyone laughed in amazement—everyone, that is, but Big Joe, who fixed his gaze on Joey and scratched his head, as if the boy were endowed with some strange magical presence the purpose of which was impossible to divine. Ritchie hadn't yet fully explained who the boy was or what he was doing there, but Big Joe wasn't surprised he'd brought him: it was just like Ritchie to suddenly, after all this time, show up out of nowhere with a mysterious urchin under his arm.

Ritchie had caught Big Joe's look and knew he had a hard bill of goods to sell. He knew what the answer would be: *No.* Even after he explained the whole situation to him the next morning at breakfast, Big Joe still refused to budge.

"We can't keep him here," was all he kept saying.

"Why not? I'm sure as hell not going to send him back to Indiana . . . and he has no place else to go."

"We can't do it." Big Joe slurped his coffee in irritation and smacked the cup down on its dish. "What do you think he is—some stray you found in the alley? There are procedures to follow, a whole legal can of worms. This is a *human being* we're talking about here—not a cat you keep on the back porch."

"So. I'll talk to Duffy." Duffy was a prosperous attorney in the neighborhood, a shrewd influential man who'd been a big cheese in city politics. Semiretired now, he still had a million connections, and the word was if you wanted something done, Duffy was the man to talk to. "Why don't I at least set up an appointment with him and see what he has to say?"

"It doesn't matter what Duffy says. It's what *I* say that counts."

At that moment Joey appeared at the edge of the kitchen in his little slippers, his stuffed yellow lizard wound around his arm.

"Good morning."

"Morning."

"How'd you sleep?"

"Fine."

"You hungry? I think we got some Raisin Bran."

Ritchie got up to get the cereal while Joey ambled over and took a seat at the table, opposite Big Joe. They looked at each other for a moment, each in pajamas and with unruly morning hair, and then Big Joe made a gruff sound in the back of his throat and hid himself behind a newspaper.

Ritchie called out from the fridge. "You say good morning to Big Uncle Joe yet?"

"Not yet."

"Say good morning."

"Good morning," the boy muttered, focusing on the wisps of hair that were sticking up above the paper.

Big Joe slowly lowered the paper and peeked at the boy again, his expression a mix of displeasure and astonishment. There's a little kid sitting at my breakfast table, he seemed to be thinking; I'm way too old for this.

"Say good morning to Joey," Ritchie barked at him.

"Good morning," Big Joe said and disappeared behind his *Trib* again.

For the next few days Ritchie kept working on him in the store, jabbing at Big Joe's conscience, softening him up with reminders of how the boy had been abused. He brought up the closet and the soap, asked Big Joe if he'd seen the marks on Joey's butt where the old witch had taken a stick to him. Big Joe said he had. Meanwhile, Joey settled in, eating his meals at the kitchen table and sleeping in the same bedroom Ritchie had shared with his brother many years before. It hadn't changed. It still had the same furniture, the same twin beds, the same patriotic wallpaper—George Washington crossing the Delaware, Paul Revere riding on his horse.

One day Hilda went out and bought toys. It was obvious she'd already grown fond of Joey, and so had Grammy Kohler, in her own oblivious way. At first she'd believed that the child was Ritchie, turning the clock back some fifteen-odd years, and finally Ritchie had had to bring the boy over and stand with him in front of her, side by side, in order to prove that they were not, in fact, the same person in two different stages of life.

The two women fussed over him, pampered him, brought him rainbow sherbet and cut his hair. Only Big Joe remained aloof. He'd come home from work and see the boy playing in his living room, firing tin race cars into the legs of the furniture or shooting rubber bands at plastic battle ships, and he'd make that noise in his throat and head upstairs for the bath tub, not yet reconciled to the idea that part of his mission in life—maybe his only mission—was to work like a dog until he dropped over so that little children could cavort through his house happy and carefree.

Still, Ritchie knew he was weakening. His glances grew less

hostile, his pleasantries less abrupt, and every so often Ritchie could see him lean back in his easy chair and watch the boy play from behind the obituary section of the *Trib*.

One night he asked Joey if he liked sports and Joey said they were okay, and then, before Ritchie knew what was happening, he'd gotten out of his chair and gone up to the attic where he kept his mementoes, returning moments later with two of his most prized possessions: his scrapbook and the moldy old football from his high school championship game. He sat down on the sofa and motioned for Joey to join him; then he opened the scrapbook and the two of them huddled together and looked at it, Big Joe slowly turning the wrinkled pages while Joey stared at the grainy photographs and the yellowed newspaper clippings with big excited eyes. They spent the better part of the evening this way—Big Joe had been closing at five—and it was clear to Ritchie not only that Big Joe's defenses were crumbling fast but that the boy's regard for him had grown substantially, as if he believed he was now living under the same roof with a genuine celebrity—someone on the order of the Incredible Hulk.

"I just talked to Duffy," Ritchie said to Big Joe the next afternoon in the store.

"Yeah?" Big Joe picked a little piece of gristle out of his teeth. "What did he say?"

"He said it wouldn't be easy, but it could be done. We'll have to file a petition, be interviewed, present our case at a hearing—all that kind of stuff."

Big Joe grunted.

"He said the best thing to do was shoot for legal guardianship. He's going to talk to his connections, explain the circumstances— no immediate family, an abusive unfit relative previously taking care of him, practically a stranger, elderly, possibly senile, no real affection for the boy. In the meantime he's going to get a restraining order forbidding the dingbat from having any contact with the child." Ritchie wedged his hands into his pants. "So it sounds pretty good. The only thing Duffy wasn't too happy about was how I threatened her that time—you know, when I made the telephone call?"

"What did you say to her—I can't remember."

"Nothing much. I just told her if she ever came near Joey again I'd run her over with my car."

"Your car's too light," Big Joe said. "Use mine."

One day, while Ritchie was walking home from the store—he'd been helping Big Joe fix things up in there, the place was a real mess—he spotted Joey at the back fence, talking to a slender young woman in a nurse's uniform. There was something familiar about the woman, particularly her corona of auburn hair, but it wasn't until he came right up and stood behind her that Ritchie realized it was Margie. She seemed like a completely different person— mature, composed, impressive in her white uniform and her matching white shoes. She must've dropped twenty-five pounds since the last time he'd seen her, but he couldn't help noticing, when she turned around to face him, that she still had that outstanding chest.

He grinned at her and said, "Don't you know he's not supposed to talk to strangers?" He meant it as a joke, but Margie didn't take it that way. She gave Ritchie a cool look and then turned her attention back to the boy.

"We're not strangers. We've already met."

"Is that right?" Ritchie said to Joey.

"Uh-huh." He had a stick in his hand and was rattling the fence with it. "She talks to me every day out here. Her name's Margie."

"I know," Ritchie said. He smiled at Margie again, but she refused to meet his eyes. He couldn't believe how she'd changed, how good she looked. He'd known her all his life but suddenly he felt awkward and tense, like he always felt when he was meeting someone for the first time. He shifted his weight from side to side and jammed his hands into his pockets.

"So tell me," he said to Joey. "What've you two been talking about?"

Joey shrugged. "Stuff."

Margie said, "He's been telling me all about himself. Mostly he's been telling me how he likes living here with Hilda and Grammy and Big Uncle Joe."

"Don't forget me," Ritchie said. "I live here too, you know."

A wind came up, swirling dirt and dead leaves down the alley.

Big woolly clouds were moving across the sky. Margie put her hands in her pockets and shivered. Then she glanced at her watch.

"Well, it's late. I gotta run."

Joey said, "Will I see you tomorrow?"

"Sure. I'll meet you right here by the fence." She leaned over and patted his head and then turned and walked back across the alley into her yard. Ritchie watched her until she disappeared into the house.

He picked up a flat stone and skimmed it down the alley. "You like her?"

"Uh-huh," Joey said. "I like her a lot."

That night, Ritchie waited until he saw a light across the way in Margie's bedroom and then he went over to the upstairs extension and picked up the phone. He didn't have to check her listing. He still knew the numbers by heart.

Margie answered on the first ring. "How was practice?"

"Huh?"

"Herbie?" There was a brief pause. "Who is this, please?"

"It's me—Ritchie." He was annoyed that she didn't recognize his voice.

"Oh." She seemed disappointed, a bit annoyed herself. "What do you want?"

It was a good question. Ritchie thought a moment. The phone felt sweaty in his hand. "I don't know. I thought maybe we could get together sometime."

"And do what?"

"See a flick. Get a burger or something. We could just, you know, talk."

There was another silence. A harsh, brittle crackling was coming through the wire, like it was a real bad connection. The phone still felt slippery and he put it in his other hand.

"Well?"

"I don't think so," Margie finally said.

"Why not?"

"I just don't think it's a good idea. Listen, I gotta go now. I'm expecting another call."

The next day, Ritchie made sure to walk back from the store at the same time. Margie wasn't there and so he waited in the yard with Joey for a while, tossing a little rubber football back and forth, until Margie finally appeared at the side of her house.

Joey dropped the ball and ran to the fence and waved at her. Margie waved back. Ritchie waved too, and Margie suddenly stopped waving.

"Who's Herbie?" Ritchie said when she came over. Joey had run back to get the football. He booted it toward the fence. Ritchie picked it up and held it delicately in his palm, like an egg.

Margie said, "Never mind."

"Throw me a pass, Kohler," Joey said. He ran into the yard and Ritchie lobbed the ball to him. He caught it and spiked it on the sidewalk and did a little dance.

"Look," Ritchie said. "All I want to do is get together and talk to you sometime."

Margie's eyes were set hard. "I told you, I don't think it's a good idea."

Joey kicked the ball back over and Ritchie threw him another pass. "What's the big deal? Why can't we talk?"

"How can you even ask that?" Margie said. She looked at him and shook her head. "How can you ask me why I don't want to talk to you? You aren't any different, are you, Ritchie Kohler? You're exactly the same."

"That isn't true," Ritchie said. "I've changed."

Joey brought the football over and handed it this time to Margie. "Throw me a far one." He spun around and ran toward the house and Margie hit him with a perfect bullet pass.

"I really want to talk to you," Ritchie said. "How about tonight?"

"I'm busy tonight."

"Tomorrow, then."

"I'm busy tomorrow." She turned and waved good-bye to Joey and said, "I'm busy for a real long time."

That night, Ritchie hid in the bushes in front of Margie's house. He waited until the sleek red Buick pulled up and tooted; then, when Margie came out and started down the walk toward the car, Ritchie darted out from the bushes and hopped into the front seat with her.

"Ritchie! What do you think you're doing?"

"Sorry, but I wanted to catch you before you went out." He reached across to introduce himself to the lankiest human he'd ever seen in his life.

"Ritchie Kohler," he said. "You're Herbie, right?"

Herbie nodded and stuck out his hand, which was as big and red as a lobster. "Pleased to meet you." He looked at Margie. "Am I missing something? I thought we had a date."

"We do. Mister Buttinski is just leaving." She attempted to ram Ritchie out the door with her hip, but he slammed it just in time.

"Look, I'm sorry to pop in like this but I just need a couple of minutes to talk to Margie. You don't mind, do you, Herb?"

Herbie shrugged. "I guess not."

"I do!" Margie said. "I mind tremendously." She had her hair fluffed out and was wearing lipstick and big gold hoops. Her lemony perfume filled the car. "Get out of here, Ritchie. Leave me alone."

"But we have a lot of stuff to talk about."

She reached past him and fired open the door and pushed him out onto the sidewalk. "No, we don't."

The next night, after Margie got back from the hospital where she worked as a student nurse, she went up to her bedroom to change out of her starched white uniform. She took it off and opened her closet to get a bathrobe, and Ritchie stepped out of the darkness from behind a rack of coats.

"Jesus!"

"Sorry." He removed one of her scarves that was draped around his head.

Margie was taking rapid breaths. "I don't believe it. What are you *doing* here?"

"Waiting for you."

"How'd you get in?"

"No problem. I knew your dad works late tonight, right? So, when I saw your mom go out a while ago I came over and let myself in." He showed Margie the spare key she had given him a long time ago.

Margie snatched it and threw it on the bed. "How long have you been hiding in there?"

"Coupla hours."

He came all the way out of the closet and sat down at the edge of her bed. Six or seven stuffed panda bears were lined up at the head of it and he picked one up and looked at it and put it down again. Margie was still over by the closet, glaring at him in a salmon-pink bra and matching panties. He'd seen Margie in her underwear before, but that was the old Margie; it was the new Margie he was looking at now and he felt something stirring inside him.

"Quit looking at me like that," Margie said.

"I'm not."

"Yes, you are."

"What do you think—I came over here to peep at you?"

Margie reached into the closet and put on a robe. "You're hiding in my bedroom, aren't you? What am I supposed to think?"

Ritchie grabbed the panda again and clutched it to his chest. "How many times do I have to tell you, Margie? All I want to do is talk."

"Why? You were never interested in talking to me before."

"I know. But things are different now."

Margie went over to the corner of the room and flopped down on a pink upholstered chair. She crossed her legs and pulled her sleeves up and said, "Okay. You're here. Now what do you want to talk about?"

"Everything," Ritchie said. He looked at the bulletin board on the wall behind the chair. It was covered with basketball photos, team shots and pictures clipped from the newspaper: Herbie dunking, Herbie rebounding, Herbie getting out on the break. He envied that display and wondered if Margie had a collection of the stuff *he* used to do, stored somewhere inside her head.

"I'm listening."

Ritchie's eyes darted and he fidgeted on the bed. It was easier to think now that she had some clothes on, but he still couldn't concentrate on exactly what he wanted to say. He had all these things he wanted to tell her, but he didn't know where to begin.

Suddenly he became aware of something in his pocket, a small flat object with a hard irregular edge. He felt it with his fingertips and then he reached into his pocket and brought it out.

"What's that?" Margie said.

"A present. Something Joey made."

Margie got up from the chair and came over to look at it. Ritchie held it up and showed it to her. It was a little piece of white cardboard from the top of an old shoe box, colored purple and cut out in the shape of a heart.

"He wanted me to give it to you," Ritchie said. "I almost forgot."

She reached down and Ritchie handed her the cardboard heart. She looked at it and smiled; then she sat down next to him on the edge of the bed and Ritchie started talking. The words poured out so fast he could barely keep up with them, and finally Margie got him to stop by thumping him on the arm.

"Hold it. Let's back up and start all over."

Ritchie blinked at her. "Okay. Where do you want me to start?"

Margie glanced at the heart again, which fit snugly into her palm. "Start with Joey," she said. "Tell me about you and the boy."

They talked for about an hour up in Margie's bedroom. Ritchie would've stayed longer—there was still a lot he hadn't explained—but then Herbie came over and Margie made him go.

"When can we do this again?" he asked her. She was frantically wriggling into her jeans.

"I don't know."

"Tomorrow?"

"Maybe." She zipped up her jeans and then reached on top of the dresser for a hairbrush. Meanwhile her old man kept hollering up the stairs.

"I'm coming!" Margie said.

Ritchie said, "I'll call you tomorrow." He watched her. She was standing in front of a mirror raking the brush through her hair. "Okay?"

"I suppose." She turned and stamped her foot. "Now will you please get out of here?"

Ritchie jumped off the bed and headed for the door.

"Not that way! Can't you climb out the window or something?"

"Huh? Who do you think I am—Errol Flynn?"

He sprang out of her room and bounded down the staircase. Henry Glotz and Herbie were standing at the foot of it, Herbie in his letter jacket and Henry in a hairy sweater that buttoned up the front.

"Say, Mister Glotz," Ritchie said. He turned to Herbie and biffed him on the shoulder. "How was practice?"

"Okay." Herbie glanced at Ritchie and then he looked at Mister Glotz. Then all three of them turned and looked up at Margie, who was standing at the top of the stairs smiling desperately and tucking a blouse into her jeans.

"Don't forget about tomorrow night," Ritchie yelled up at her. He bopped Herbie on the shoulder again and eeled past him out the door.

He went around to the side of her house and into the back yard, moving nimbly, vaulting over the gate. A full moon was out, hanging low in the sky like a big holy wafer. Ritchie felt like he could jump up and take a bite out of it, or pull it down and tuck it under his arm. He felt a little like he used to feel when he went to Confession—clean and grateful, with a shiny new soul. Sure, there were still some crummy places on it—smudges and dark dirty corners and a couple of holes—but he believed even those could be taken care of eventually. It was just like a store. You let things slide in there until everything goes to hell and all you want to do is get away from it or burn it to the ground, but then, when you got the ammonia and a mop out and started working, it was surprising how fast the place shaped up. It was like Big Joe always said: anything was possible if you were willing to work.

He danced through Margie's yard, feeling almost happy, almost full, but then those feelings abruptly vanished when he got to the alley and saw Joey running at the back of the house. Cha Cha was out there with him and the two of them were playing some type of game with a big oblong ball. Ritchie could see its shape clearly in the moonlight every time Joey bent his legs and hurled it in the air. It wasn't just any ball. It was Big Joe's most prized possession, that moldy old bladderball. He usually kept it in the attic with his trophies and his scrapbook, but ever since the night he brought it down and showed it to Joey, he'd been storing it temporarily in the den. Joey had had his eye on it for quite a while, and he must've sneaked in there and lugged it out into the yard when Hilda wasn't looking, probably when she went down to the basement to do the wash.

Appalled, Ritchie hurled the gate open and burst into the yard. He reached the back of the house just as Joey pitched the ball up again. The boy ran under it and tried to catch it, but he missed, and the ball hit with a wet splat and stuck in the damp muddy ground.

Ritchie bent over and scooped it into his hands. Cha Cha was running in circles, barking like crazy, and Ritchie told him to shut up. Joey was standing by the back of the house with his arms at his sides. Ritchie, meanwhile, examined the ball. It was the ball from Big Joe's high school championship game, for Christ's sake. The whole school had awarded it to him for his brawny valor, like the Congressional Medal of Honor. The date and the final score had been inscribed right on the side. You couldn't tell who won by looking at it now, though. The numbers were obscured—possibly obliterated—by a thick coating of mud, and the ball itself looked like a huge grotesque vegetable that had been dug up out of the ground.

"Goddammit! Didn't I tell you not to bring this out here?"

"Sorry," Joey said.

"Sorry? You'll be really sorry when the old man comes home." He went over and gently put the ball down on the sidewalk. "Wait here. I'm going in and see if I can find something to clean it up."

He went in the side door and down into the basement; the washing machine was going and Hilda had her head in the dryer, searching for fugitive socks.

"I need some rags," Ritchie said.

Hilda turned around and looked at him. "What for?"

"The kid's outside. In the yard. But that isn't the problem. He took Big Joe's ball out there with him."

"*The* ball?"

Ritchie nodded.

"Jesus," Hilda said.

"Rags," Ritchie said. "Hurry up. He'll be home any minute."

"Try the kitchen," Hilda said. "Under the sink."

He ran back up the stairs and yanked open the cabinet under the kitchen sink. Everything in the world was stored in there—tools, cleaning utensils, various detergents, rusty pots and pans. The rags were way in the back and Ritchie had to crawl halfway into the cabinet to get at them. He grabbed a handful—mostly Big Joe's old sleeveless undershirts—and started crawling back out when he heard Cha Cha barking in the yard again. Ritchie recognized that bark immediately. It was part bark and part growl, the special greeting the poodle reserved for the master of the house.

"Shit! We're in for it now." Ritchie extricated himself from the cabinet and dashed to the window just in time to see Big Joe's bulky shape materialize in the alley. He was shuffling slowly toward the gate, leaning forward and wobbling slightly like he always did when he came home drunk. The dog was barking at the fence and Joey was squatting on the sidewalk next to the ball, as though he were guarding it.

Ritchie felt like pounding on the window, but it was too late. All he could do was stand and watch Big Joe come in through the gate. He took a few steps toward the house and then paused and looked at Joey, who, in turn, quickly jumped to his feet, snatched up the ball, and ran to hide with it in the bushes at the back of the house.

Ritchie had a bad angle on the proceedings from where he stood and he had to race into the den to see what would happen next. When he looked into the yard he saw that Big Joe had moved in close to the bushes and was wiggling his fingers, motioning for Joey to come out of there and give him the ball. The youngster did so and backed up again. Now it was Big Joe who examined the treasured pigskin, turning it over in his hands. He seemed to be looking for something that ought to be there. He extended his arm and wiped mud off the ball with his coat sleeve. Then he studied its surface again. The notations it used to bear it bore no longer; from where Ritchie stood, the ball looked as naked as a squash.

Big Joe gestured at Joey again, beckoning the boy to come forward. Ritchie held his breath. It's ruined—that's what he was thinking. Just when it all seemed to be coming together, just when Big Joe was really beginning to like him, the kid had to commit a mortal sin.

The youngster crept out of the bushes and came up to get his licking. Ritchie shut his eyes. He expected that, at the very least, Big Joe would clout him a good one and then banish him from his sight, but instead, when Ritchie reopened his eyes, he saw something so astonishing he thought he was watching a dream. Big Joe had tucked the ball under his arm, and, crouching low in classic Bronco Nagurski style, suddenly began running through the yard.

Ritchie couldn't believe it. There he was, the old man, in his galoshes and heavy overcoat, high-stepping through the mud like a schoolboy; and not only that, he was waving for Joey to chase him, which the kid promptly did and Cha Cha too, the both of them scampering at Big Joe's frisky heels.

"Hilda!" Ritchie hollered into the basement. "Hurry up and take a look out the window. You will not believe your eyes."

16

Ritchie was gasping in his sleep again, drowning in smoke. He kept hearing music, a faint eddy of sound murmuring high above him, and he fought to reach it, but the smoke was too thick and the more he struggled, moving his whole body in a frantic wriggling motion, the more he sank like a stone.

Suddenly he felt something shake him, heard a voice, husky with sleep, close by his ear. "Hey—wake up. You're beating me to death."

He sat up in bed, rubbing the dream out of his eyes. Slowly the familiar objects in the room began to take shape in the darkness: the lamps, the closet, the dresser with its full complement of panda bears. The glowing face of the alarm clock on the table beside the bed told him it was one o'clock in the morning. Beside him, Margie's ripe body, six months pregnant, radiated warmth like a space heater.

"You all right?" she mumbled.

"Yeah. Go back to sleep."

She mumbled again and burrowed deeper into the blankets. She could sleep through anything, especially now. She fell asleep watching television, and at the movies. The second her head hit the pillow—zonk—she was out. Ritchie hunkered down next to her, hoping to absorb some of that languor, that immense tranquility, but it was no use; his heart kept pounding and he was afraid to shut his eyes.

He got up and went into the kitchen for a drink of water. The dream was still darting inside his head. It was different from the one he used to have, a long time ago, but some things were the same—the smoke, the helplessness, that panicky feeling when he heard the music coming from some nearby yet impossibly distant place. A hundred times he'd heard that music. A hundred times he'd been trapped inside that building and a hundred times it was burning to the ground.

He went into the living room and switched on all the lights. He felt the need to ground himself in the present again, to know exactly where he was. He went around touching everything in the apartment—the upper half of a duplex just around the corner from the store. He touched the tables and chairs, the cabinet where they kept a lot of their useless wedding presents—a set of cocktail wiener forks, the ornamental dinner gong. He touched the sturdy unvarnished case where Margie kept her nurse's books and the small vase sitting on top of it, filled with potpourri.

He had these things. As always when he was up late at night, he began taking a mental inventory of everything he had, all his possessions. He had wallpaper, coasters, matching silverware. He had a steady job in Big Joe's store. The place had changed very little during that time he'd been away. More diet stuff, fewer eggs; other than that it was just about the same. The faded gritty tiles, the dingy shelves crammed with canned goods, the heavy aroma of cheese and Polish sausage that had permeated the walls—he could summon all of that instantly, as if it were as much a part of him as his heart and lungs.

He had a family, a wife who was good to him and to the boy. Margie and Joey had hit it off right from the start, especially when she proved to be a much better athlete than Ritchie was. Even now, six months pregnant, she was always out in the alley with him, throwing a Spalding around. Once in a while, on her day off from the hospital, she'd take him out to Wrigley to catch a Cubs game, and sometimes they'd go to the park to work on his batting stroke. Big Joe would go too. He was delighted that he finally had a bona fide athlete in the family. The boy was quick, agile. He had a helluva pair of hands. Ritchie remembered how Big Joe's eyes lit up the first time he saw Joey connect—the kid was a hitter too! Another Stan the Man they had going here, Big Joe waxed enthusiastically, a Splendid Splinter, maybe even a hot new DiMag.

Every time Ritchie heard the old man talking like this he had to pull in the reins. Margie agreed: she didn't want to push the boy into anything. She respected him too much for that, respected also the memory of his real mother that the youngster kept alive. Her name came up fairly often. Sometimes Joey had to remind Margie that his momma used to spread strawberry jelly, not grape, on his peanut butter sandwiches—or sprinkle cinnamon on his toast. The next day, Margie would have a big jar of strawberry jelly right there on the table, and when she sprinkled on the cinnamon she always made sure to ask how much.

She was real excited about this new baby that was coming along. She was reading books, doing exercises, trying to settle on a name. Brendan. Theodore. She was sure it was going to be a boy. Ritchie was thinking Holly. Joey said, "What's wrong with twins?" He was excited about the new baby too and kept asking Margie a million questions, like what did it do in there all day and how did it get there in the first place? When Margie signed up for the classes, Joey said that if Ritchie couldn't handle being in the delivery room, *he'd* go in there instead. He had his own pair of rubber gloves and everything. He wanted to be a doctor, or an architect, or maybe play center field for the Cubs. He was getting tall and rangy, developing his own personal face, but he still looked a lot like his momma, especially when Ritchie did something stupid and he pursed his lips and rolled his eyes and looked at Ritchie just the way his momma used to look.

Lately they'd started scouting for a house. They'd need one pretty soon. The family was growing—they needed a lot more room. It was strange how one thing led to another. Margie getting pregnant, for instance. They certainly hadn't been planning on *that,* not for a while anyway, but they both got pretty loaded celebrating on the day the adoption papers officially came through, and one thing led to another and her diaphragm was in the medicine chest . . . so what were you gonna do? It was funny: he'd always wondered what it would be like to have his own kid, and then he went and got two on the same day.

He kept thinking about all these things until his heart stopped pounding and the dream slipped away into its hiding place. He'd gone into the kitchen and opened the back door, letting a breeze blow in through the screen. A slim quarter moon was out, and a few scattered stars. From his vantage point on the second floor he could see a long unbroken row of houses, solid silvery shapes in the street lights. Beyond them was the park where he used to pitch pennies, the sloping roof of the building where he went to school. Almost all his life he'd lived in this neighborhood, with people who drove big four-door American cars, who were on a first-name basis with their local hardware man and who stopped in at the corner ma-and-pa whenever they needed baloney and an extra gallon of milk. He liked living here. He liked going to work every morning. He liked paying the rent on time and having a little left over each month to sock in the bank. Thinking of the people sleeping under his roof filled him with satisfaction. So what was he doing up at one o'clock in the morning? Why couldn't he get rid of that dream?

Sometimes it came on so strong that he was tempted to get in the car and drive on out by the airport to make sure the place was still gone. Once, he actually did that, actually rushed out in the middle of the night with a feeling of dread, certain that he'd see it, that the building would be standing right where it stood before, like it had never burned at all. When he drove up he was relieved to see that huge empty lot with a wooden fence around it and the big No Trespassing signs—but only temporarily. The rumor was that Nicky had sold the land to some condo guys and had moved his whole operation out to the dunes, but Ritchie didn't believe it. He kept thinking they'd be back. He almost hoped they would come back— maybe then he could take care of that unfinished business that kept him awake at night.

Let it alone—that's what Big Joe always told him. He was probably right. Still, it was hard to get rid of those guilty feelings, and hard to consider that his enemy was still at large, moving around scot- free, unpunished, no doubt living high on the hog. "I can get away with anything"—that's what he'd said, and every time Ritchie thought about *that*, about the injustice of what had happened, the rage would start festering all over again and he'd want to hop a plane and go after him, to hunt him down wherever he was hiding so they could settle it once and for all.

He was still standing at the screen, looking out into the darkness, when the bedroom door opened behind him and Margie emerged. She stood at the edge of the kitchen for a moment in her nightgown, yawning, squinting into the light, and then she shuffled over to join him, moving in that funny penguinlike waddle she employed now that she'd headed down the home stretch. So far she hadn't had any problems. Her feet swelled at night but that was about it. The doctor said she was made for kids.

"What is it?" She had settled herself beside him, solid as a house. "Did you hear something?"

Ritchie didn't answer. For a long time they just stood there, looking silently into the trees.

"There's nothing out there," Margie finally said. "Forget about it. Come back to bed. It's like I've told you a million times—there's nothing you can do."

She was right, of course. He had a new life now. He had a job, a family, serious obligations. The future was what was important. Still, Ritchie couldn't help believing he was out there somewhere, hiding in the shadows, a spectral presence, a lupine figure moving just beyond his view.

"You sure you want to do this?" Big Joe said. They were in the Chrysler, heading west, out toward the airport, the early morning sun warm on their backs. "It ain't like just showing up for work."

"I know it." Ritchie turned and looked out the window again. It was late spring, and the morning was brisk and clear. They were traveling through a residential neighborhood, and occasionally Ritchie spotted someone standing on a porch in a robe or a windbreaker, reaching down to get the *Trib*. The lawns were starting to seem greener. Birds darted, rooting for crumbs on the sidewalks and pecking in the hedges for twigs.

"You think we got enough flowers?" Ritchie wondered.

Big Joe turned and glanced over his shoulder into the back seat, at the four large baskets that were packed in there side by side. Roses and tulips and a bunch of other stuff he'd never even heard of bloomed inside the Beast on Wheels. Almost a hundred bucks worth of posies they had back there.

"Christ, I hope so," Big Joe said.

Ritchie had gotten the flowers the previous night from the neighborhood florist. Margie had picked out the arrangements. This whole idea had been hers, in fact. He was still having that trouble sleeping, and finally Margie had said why don't you go out there and see her?

Ritchie said he didn't know about that. He hadn't been out there in a long time, not since the funeral. Joey had been out there— Margie had taken him a couple of times—but not him. Well over a year it'd been, and he still hadn't gone to see her. He was afraid to, he supposed.

"I think it's a good idea," Margie said. "I think you should go."

"I don't know." Ritchie thought it over. "You mean go out there all alone? Just by myself?"

"Take your father with you," Margie suggested.

He supposed it was a possibility—Big Joe went out there all the time. He'd know right where to go. Still, he wasn't too sure about it, even after Margie started throwing around all that technical noise she'd picked up in one of her classes, stuff about his psyche and catharsis and unresolved guilt.

"All right already," he'd finally said. "I'll give him a buzz."

When he'd called Big Joe he sure didn't bring up that psyche business; he doubted Big Joe even knew what a psyche was. All he'd said was he needed to go to the cemetery and he wanted Big Joe to go out there with him.

"When?"

"Tomorrow."

Big Joe had paused a moment on the other end of the line.

"Okay, but it'll have to be early. We got a lot of deliveries coming in."

When they got to the cemetery, Big Joe pulled in beneath the trellised archway and parked in a small lot just beyond an office building.

"Is this it?" Ritchie said. He didn't recognize the place. His heart was pounding and he was looking rapidly from side to side. "Where are they?" He meant the graves.

Big Joe said, "We got to walk over."

Ritchie shrank from the door. "Why don't we just drive?"

"No," Big Joe said. "It's better to walk."

He got out, handed Ritchie a couple of baskets of flowers, and set off for the graves. Ritchie tiptoed alongside his father, who hobbled forward on his ruined knees. They walked down a long tree-lined path, breathing that fresh morning air and looking at all the headstones. The more he walked, the better Ritchie felt. This wasn't so bad; it was kind of pleasant, in fact, like being in a huge church with elms instead of pillars and a wide blue sky overhead instead of beams.

It was still pretty early. Ritchie was surprised at how many others they encountered as they walked along, and he watched them to see if he might learn how to behave. It was interesting to see all the different ways people acted in a cemetery. Some prayed, some cried, and a few laughed, like they were already half loaded. Some just stood there, looking bewildered or embarrassed, with their hands at their sides. One elderly woman seemed to be having a bitter quarrel with the departed, rehashing old grievances and flinging insults down at the grave. Another was having a long, detailed conversation, bringing the deceased up to date on all the latest developments. Earl and Edna were going to Hawaii next October. Sidney's divorce was finally settled. The damn cat had hairballs again.

Big Joe and Ritchie walked about a mile, toting their flowers, until they came to a small slope bordered by sycamore trees. They veered off onto a smaller path, crossed a bridge over a clear, slow-moving stream, and walked up the slope toward a cluster of head-stones. Ritchie suddenly recognized the area. It was the place where Kohlers were buried. His mother was buried here. So was his grand-father, Big Hans, and a bunch of other relatives. It'd been a long time since he'd stood at this spot, and he was surprised that he remembered it so well. He thought that, after all these months, the place would be different—but then again, why would it ever change?

Assuming a proprietary attitude, Big Joe started pointing things out like a guide. "This is your grandmother's plot," he began. "And this one's for Hilda." He pointed to an empty space next to Ritchie's mother. "This one's mine," he said with satisfaction. "And these over here are for you and your brother—if he ever decides to come back."

Ritchie went over and frowned at his final resting place. It felt weird to be looking at his own burial plot—almost like he was seeing into the future—but then he took a more businesslike approach and began sizing up the grave site from various angles to see how he liked it. One thing he wasn't real crazy about was the idea of spending eternity this close to his asshole brother, but he supposed they'd just have to learn to get along.

"The one on the other side is for Margie, if she wants it," Big Joe hollered out.

"I'll ask her," Ritchie said.

Big Joe went up to Ritchie's mother's grave and put his baskets of flowers down. Then he stood back with his hands folded and looked at the stone. He didn't do any yakking. He was there to pay his respects. Once a month he'd been coming to this place. Once a month for twenty years.

Set back a few yards on the fringe of the Kohler plots was another headstone, and Ritchie went up to it and laid his flowers down. It was odd seeing that strange name among all the different Kohlers. He'd thought for sure that her crazy aunt would want to bring her back to Indiana, but she hadn't. It was almost like she knew Louise never wanted to go back there, that being buried here with a bunch of strangers was the closest to family she was ever going to get.

He stood there a moment, looking at that plain gray stone with her name and dates on it, a stone like all the others, and he wondered what to say. He knew there was a lot to say, but the words were all jumbled in his head, so all he told her was that he was fine and Joey was fine and he promised to take good care of him. For an instant, when he thought about how rough she'd had it, how what happens in this world to some people just wasn't right, a strong wave of feeling hit him and he almost started crying, but he didn't. Crying was easy. Living—that was the hard part.

So he said these things and then he heard Big Joe coming up behind him. "Okay?"

Ritchie nodded. It was time to leave. They had to get back and open up the store. They had bills to pay, baloney to sell. Delivery trucks were coming. Time was money. They had to get to work.